WHEN THE DAWN BREAKS

BOOKS BY B.R. SPANGLER

DARK SKIES APOCALYPSE

When the Sky Falls

When the Dawn Breaks

DETECTIVE CASEY WHITE SERIES

Where Lost Girls Go

The Innocent Girls

Saltwater Graves

The Crying House

The Memory Bones

The Lighthouse Girls

Taken Before Dawn

Their Resting Place

Two Little Souls

Our Sister's Grave

Her Last Hour

WHEN THE DAWN BREAKS

B.R. SPANGLER

SECOND SKY

Published by Second Sky in 2024

An imprint of Storyfire Ltd.
Carmelite House
50 Victoria Embankment
London EC4Y 0DZ

www.secondskybooks.com

ISBN: 978-1-83525-928-3
eBook ISBN: 978-1-83525-927-6

ONE

It hurt to think about her. It hurt to see her, that is, the last memory of her. And it hurt to wonder about a future without Sammi Stark. Everything hurt. That's all Declan Chambers had now. The hurt of her loss.

At times, there was sleep where the dreams found him. Some good like the ones where they were together and whole again. When he woke, though, the truth of her death returned, a heavy dread crushing his heart and soul. It was like a hammer to the head of a nail, striking over and over. Sammi was never coming back.

Declan slipped an arm into the top of his coveralls and prepared himself for Sammi's rite of cleaning and passing. He wondered if he would ever see Harold Belker again. It was doubtful. Everyone had said so. Harold had been exiled. He'd been physically removed, banished to live outside the commune.

But if given the chance, Declan decided that he would end Harold Belker. He decided that he would kill him for what happened. Anger festered and consumed him. Declan didn't care, though; he wore the rage like a well-worn coat.

A day after Sammi's tragic death, Harold was found alone in his dwelling. His parents came forward saying that their boy was blubbering about what had happened and saying that it was an accident. There weren't many who'd listen, though, nobody believing him. What Harold didn't know was that when questioned, Norm and Richie told the commune that Harold had pushed Sammi to her death.

Word quickly spread. It spread about what Harold had done. And it spread about losing Sammi Stark, Emily Stark's little sister, the daughter of Phil Stark, the machine's original architect. Word had also spread to other communes about the death of the fair, red-haired girl, condolences coming from communes in their region, and even a few from across their territory.

Declan's heart was weighted with an ache that slowed his step and slumped his shoulders. It also made him deaf to the people gathering, the ones reaching for his hands, their lips moving without words. He heard Emily's voice, though. Heard the sorrow when she insisted he stand with her and help prepare Sammi for the passing to the farming floor. It was ceremony; it was an honor.

Ms. Newl had been invited as well, and the old woman brought him into her arms, wetting his cheek with her tears while whispering how sorry she was that such an awful thing had happened. He nodded absently, but a twinge of nerves lifted his gaze and had him looking to where Sammi's body was to be prepared.

He stood between Emily and Ms. Newl in front of a cleaning table as Sammi's body was brought to them. Soft, hollow sounds were made as she was laid down on the metal slab. Her long locks of curly red hair hung over the steel edge like the fabric from the movie theater chairs where he'd found her. The mortician emptied her coverall pockets, giving Emily the small candle that Sammi had shared with Declan. He fixed his eyes on it, lips trembling while swallowing back the need to cry. His body shuddered, and he cursed the tears that wanted to come.

Ms. Newl commented that the pinned lock of Sammi's hair was missing from the front of her coveralls. Declan gripped his hand around the precious gift he kept hidden in his palm. The sharp edge of the pin cut into his skin, but he ignored the pain. Sammi had given it to him, and he'd never part with it. As Ms. Newl and Emily continued the ritual, he put the lock into his pocket and pressed it close to him.

Declan picked up the thin material of Sammi's coverall zipper and paused. Finding her dead eyes with his, he tried to understand how it could be that they'd gotten to this moment. Today was the day that they were supposed to have been joined; the day they were supposed to have made love for the first time. Instead, it was the day that she would pass to the farming floor, to feed the earthy loam and growth-beds, and freely give away the wealth of her body, the light of her soul. A sudden stubbornness turned inside him, and selfishness grew. But he didn't act on it.

He pulled on her front zipper, exposing her body from her chin to her navel while Emily removed the shoes from her feet. Ms. Newl brought them the cleaning cloth and bowl, taking great care not to spill the mix of water and decomp salts that would be used. When Sammi's body was freed from all civilized reminders and was as it had been on the first day of her life, they began.

Emily looked upon her younger sister's naked body, her weepy eyes moving over her broken leg, and then to what had killed Sammi. She gripped Ms. Newl, overcome by the sight. Declan took the cleaning cloth in his hand and began to remove the blood from around the wound. The place where the metal post had entered Sammi's body was a gnarled rip in her otherwise perfect skin.

The dried blood, scaly and brown, stained Sammi's fair skin like an affront to something pure. As he touched the cleaning cloth to her belly, the blood thinned until the stains were gone. He heard trickling water and watched as wispy trails of sallow red flowed along her pale legs to the end of the table. The water and blood would be carried to the commune's waste-recycler, where it would join the thousands of words he'd written during his short life, trapped forever in the gravelly ash and sandy filters. From his coverall pocket, he felt the outline of the writing stone she'd given him, and in that moment, he decided that he would never write another word.

When the wound was cleaned, Declan moved to brush Sammi's hair, while Emily cleaned her fingers and nails. He pulled the hairbrush through her long red curls, watching as Ms. Newl wiped away the remains of that awful day from Sammi's face. At times, he had to stop. At times, he thought he couldn't continue. But Ms. Newl consoled him and helped to keep him going. For the next hour, they cleaned every part of Sammi's body until all the filth from their gray world was gone.

When the rite of cleaning concluded, those attending said their final goodbyes, leaving Declan to be alone with Sammi. Before going to the theater, Sammi had shared with Emily that she'd chosen Declan; and as her chosen, it was his responsibility to see her through the passing.

At once, the emotion he'd been holding became too much. He took Sammi's body into his arms. Her skin was cold and lifeless, but he held her firmly as sorrow tumbled from his lips and spilled from his eyes onto her bare skin.

Declan cried until his body ached, and only when he felt the warm touch of the mortician's hand on his shoulder did he finally lay Sammi back onto the table. He kissed her, then: first her eyes, after gently closing them, and then her lips, for a final time. He told her that he loved her, and thanked her for choosing him, and then he reminded her that choosing meant forever.

Days after Sammi's cleaning and passing, the End of Gray Skies had already begun to reverse itself. But for that time, the world returned to something normal. The sun dwarfed the Earth, rising in the mornings and falling in the evenings. The clouds lifted back to the sky, crossing an endless blue sea as if the fog had never been. Children ran freely, untethered and fearless, shrieking and playing, staying out until the daylight faded into night. Declan tried to share in the miracle. He even forced himself outside, favoring the sunset over the sunrise. Yet, standing as the sun disappeared on the horizon, his mind and heart always returned to Sammi.

Sammi Sunshine, he thought to himself as he walked alone. He passed the theater a dozen or more times, doing so without the need for the morse lines. Still, he couldn't bring himself to lift his eyes from the painted markings. On occasion, he'd bring some food scraps with him and feed a few of the feral cats that trusted his company. Some days, he tried not to cry while the cats purred and ran figure eights between his legs. And some days, he even tried to smile. But most days, he just tried to live and imagine his life without her.

Then came a day of heavy rain, and the sun threw colorful rainbows over their commune's building. Afterward, a thick fog rolled in from the ocean and settled for the night, bringing back the salty stench for them to choke on. It was a sign, a small sign, and people had already begun to talk. Declan ignored much of what was said, uncertain of whether he wanted to care, or not.

He saw the rainstorm, though. Everyone did. The storm turned the sky black and spat green lightning streaks that cut through the farthest reaches of the looming darkness. The salty air expanded in violent throes, hammering thunder down on them and pushing acrid winds that nearly turned over every part of their commune. It was the beginning of the end, their sun disappearing.

The End of Gray Skies was over, and the heavy fog returned. Standing alongside his father, Declan listened to the commune's leaders as they tried to explain away the failure. The life he'd yearned for was already over, their words meaningless and senseless to regard. Outside their commune building, Declan stood alone, watching the thickness of the fog invade the skies. Clouds as tall as mountains lowered themselves to rest like loved ones coming together for a long sleep.

"Sammi Sunshine," he said aloud to anyone who could hear his voice. He said it again and again until every hint of the sunlight had disappeared from the face of the earth. The VAC-Machines had failed to turn their world back to its former self, but Declan found he didn't care, after all. It mattered nothing to him that the sunshine was gone. *His* sunshine had left him that day in the theater.

The day after Declan turned eighteen, he decided to leave the safety of his home. He left the familiar sounds, smells, and routines of the commune and ventured outside, in search of answers to the questions that occupied his mind. He wanted to know more about the VAC-Machines and the mysterious numbers on the thick index card found inside his mother's satchel. He wanted to know about his mother and sister, too, and what his father said about their death. But there was more— it was Sammi, she was everywhere. It drove him to leave the commune.

Emily and Ms. Newl objected. His father objected too. Declan ignored them and said his goodbyes, leaving them and the commune, stopping once to hug Ms. Newl and Emily, taking the fond memories of what the machine had shown him over the years. The classroom had never seemed so small and insignificant as it did during that final visit.

Declan followed the dotted morse line that led to the black sand beaches. Anticipation grew with the roar of crashing waves. His feet slipped in the loose sand, but he regained his footing and settled in with the decision to go to the VAC-Machine. He needed to be near it, to touch it. He needed to learn of its secrets, and the truth behind the End of Gray Skies.

More than once, he tempted the presence of the machine but couldn't muster enough courage to follow through. Maybe it was his grieving. Perhaps one of the stages he'd been told about. It was keeping him from approaching. When he was tired, he slept. When he was hungry, he ate. When he was thirsty, he drank. When the risk of Outsiders approached, he dug a shallow hole and lay flat on his belly, quiet and still, hidden from the footsteps that passed a few hands from him. While he was oblivious to most emotions, he wasn't immune to fear. Salt burned the abrasions on his fingers and stung the skin under his torn nails. Coarse sands reached every part of him, but the grainy wet discomfort was a simple annoyance compared to what the Outsiders might do if they captured him.

Then came the morning when it was time. Sammi's memory stayed fresh, anger eclipsing the warmest of them. As sands passed beneath his feet, the footsteps getting heavier, Declan wondered if the Outsiders had already found Harold. If they had, had they killed him? Although Harold was gone, Declan's gut told him he was still alive. For the first time since setting foot on the sandy beaches, Declan questioned whether he'd really left to seek answers at the VAC-Machine. He thought, instead, that maybe he'd left his home to find Harold. He faced the ocean with a sigh, afraid of what the truth might be, and of what he wanted to do.

On his coveralls, Declan wore the lock of Sammi's hair. He touched it from time to time, resuming the long walk, setting it as a reminder of why he'd decided to make the journey. Gripping her red hair, Declan spoke to Sammi when he reached the machine.

"I've found it, Sammi. I'm here."

The giant VAC-Machine was unlike anything he'd ever seen before. His breath was lost to him in wonderment at the size. There were no photographs, no descriptions, and no classroom history lessons that could have prepared him for what his eyes saw. Emily and Sammi had tried explaining it a few times, but it was far bigger than he imagined. When he moved next to it, the fog lifted from all around the machine. He could see a thousand hands in every direction.

To his left, the silvery beast stretched far, interrupting the land, spewing gray and white smoke. To his right, the machine reached deep into the ocean where waves rolled around it, ignoring it as it disappeared beneath the surface. Above him, the machine seemed to rise endlessly, and for a moment, he thought that he glimpsed a blue sky. The fog from which he emerged stayed just behind him as though a barrier were preventing it from touching the VAC-Machine.

The skin of the machine reflected the black sands in front of him, mirrored the skies and the ocean waves that swelled around it. It was magnificent. But when he saw the reflection of himself, he stopped, then shuffled back a step, shocked and suspicious.

Have I looked at myself since Sammi died? he wondered and reached for the image, disbelief weighing down his arm. The man staring back at him rubbed the scruffy growth on his face and ran fingers through an unkempt tangle of brown hair. He'd also grown thin and pale, almost ash-colored, and blended in with the fog. His eyes were empty, and his cheeks sunken. He was thin— too thin, a gaunt memory of who he'd been just weeks before.

Since Sammi's death, he'd lost time; or the sense of it,

anyway. How long had it been since he'd last eaten or slept? At once, fear and relief mixed like a wretched stew, and he dropped to his knees. If not for the seawater leaching through his coveralls, he might think that all of this was a dream and that he just might be dead.

But it wasn't a dream: the VAC-Machine suddenly heaved, swelling outward, then groaned. The sound was deafening; it shook the sands beneath his legs, the grains vibrating. There was an eerie silence then, followed by a metallic tremor. A dark and perfectly square shape cut into the machine's belly to reveal a door.

Declan moved back farther, and from the center of the black opening, he saw the figure of a beautiful woman emerge: tall and slim, and dressed in a white gown. The material shimmered and had a smooth sheen that revealed iridescent waves as the fabric moved over her body. With nothing to protect her feet, she seemed cautious to leave the machine, toes touching the wet sand. She paused once, looking behind her while remaining in the opening.

As Declan closed the distance to the machine, he realized that he knew this woman. His heart leaped into his throat. He knew her eyes, and her nose, and her mouth. Her hair was free of gray, though, and differed from the style in his memories, but the rest of her was the same—just younger and fresher. He knew her voice too.

"Hi, Declan. We've been waiting for you," the woman said and knelt next to him. The soft push of the sand against his legs assured him that this was, indeed, real. Declan looked into his mother's eyes while she took his hand into hers. A million questions danced in his head. Instead, he bit his lower lip and forced himself to take a breath. He wanted to throw his arms around her and feel her warmth. This had to be a dream, though. His mother was dead.

"Who?" was all he could think to ask her. "Who's been waiting?"

"All of us," she answered, turning toward the opening and motioning with her long, slender arm.

His mother's smell was intimately familiar, and the touch of her fingers on his face was warm. But at once, Declan felt a tingling sensation on his cheek. Soon, numbness blossomed and grew from where his mother had touched him. He looked in the direction she had motioned and found his sister standing outside the machine. When he brought his arm up to offer a hesitant wave, the world around him started to grow dim. More of his body disappeared from his consciousness, and he was no longer aware of his hands or his feet. Within moments, he'd lost his legs too. The sound of the ocean became distant and the image of his mother and sister began to turn gray.

Before the darkness took all of him like the fog had taken the world, Declan saw another figure come through the opening. It was a woman whose skin was as white as the garment she wore. Her hair was fiery red, with long tresses sweeping over her shoulders. The sight of her stole his breath. And while Declan stared at this woman, he unknowingly reached to touch Sammi's locket pinned to his chest.

Then he heard his mother's voice.

"He's ready now."

TWO

Peter Wilkes peered up at the executive guards and nodded. Their faces were like stone and remained unchanged. How many times since his promotion to four bands had he offered the simple gesture? How many times had it been ignored? After all, he was an executive, which should mean something. Shouldn't it? Peter shrugged, supposing the guards just didn't care.

Others cared once. Others, like Emily and Sammi and Ms. Newl. Peter stopped, a mourning ache in his heart. *Sammi, how terrible. How tragic.* He could still see her that first day when the clouds fell. She was small then, a tiny thing. But huge too. A real firecracker. In his mind, he saw Emily carrying her, both of them wrapped in plastic bags, the number of dead already piling up. They survived the mall, though. They survived the market and service tunnels and the move to the commune's building. They'd survived this world every day since. And now Sammi was dead. *Did Emily see me?* he wondered, having gone to the cleaning but staying near the back.

He gave a glum look to the balcony's ledge, a feeling of calm washing over him. In a moment, his final career advancement would take him to the top where he'd leap to his death. He imagined himself perched on it, his round frame trying to balance in the precarious moments before jumping. *Just how far down is it to the courtyard?* He quickly dismissed the question, knowing that it didn't matter, and knowing that he had to go through with it. There was no turning back, his options gone. It wasn't a decision that had come easily. It was calculated and purposeful, its intent meant to bring about the beginning of an end. That is, the end of what he'd helped hide all these years.

Peter paused, thinking of the lives he'd affected in the commune, the largest community in the region. *How many?* he wondered. *All of them? Alive and dead?* The number he saw in his head was daunting, each like a nail driven into his body. It was enough to make him slump forward, a whimpering cry pressing. *It'll be over soon enough and then they'll know. They'll all know.*

Before he could take another step, he heard the guards turn, his motions spurring their curiosity. Peter immediately realized what he'd done. Standing in front of the executive entrances was not permitted, even when you *were* an executive. Well aware of the rule he'd just broken, he drew in a resigned breath and moved on. Peter knew all the rules. He knew them because he'd written most of them, just as he had written his final one earlier that morning.

"What does it matter now, anyway?" he mumbled. "I'm a dead man."

He tugged at the collar of his coveralls, trying to make room for the folds of skin around his neck. He couldn't remember being skinny. Not until he saw Emily who hadn't changed once in the years since they'd married. He'd changed, though. Indulging when he shouldn't have. He'd changed inside and out. Choking back his breath, he shivered against a light sweat. It wasn't just the air; Peter shook out of fear. Death was following him to the ledge, and it was eager to make his acquaintance.

When he leaned over to see the courtyard, his stomach instantly shot into his throat. His breath stuttered, his belly threatening to heave. He'd never looked before. Not once. Peter shuddered, the height dizzying. But maybe that was a good thing. There was no chance of surviving a fall like that. He glanced over the ledge again, thoughts stirring while he tried to commit his mind to the jump.

Yet maybe there were options. Maybe he could exile himself? But the idea of fending for himself outside the safety of the commune made him laugh. Maybe once before when he was young and fit and had fought for him and Emily and Sammi. Peter clutched his chest, fingers disappearing into the doughiness. He chuckled, imagining a man his size running in the fog while the Outsiders chased him down, ripping into his skin like rabid dogs. Leaping from the executive floor was easier. It was quick and painless... he hoped.

Emily's face came to him again, his laugh abruptly ending. His smile turned upside down, focus on the ledge narrowing. After their child James was taken, he'd neglected her. He'd neglected them. He'd chosen the executive floor and the work over who they were. His work—his mistress—had called to him, lied to him. It told him half-truths about the good he would do in the name of the commune.

Emily had wanted to continue their lives together, even without their son, she'd insisted. He could have stayed with her. He *should* have stayed with her. Choosing was forever, and while *she'd* chosen *him*, Peter decided that life without their boy wasn't a life to have with her. Not anymore. He was wrong. Without a child to raise, leaving Emily was just the easier thing to do. *But easier for whom?*

Death's cousin was with him now, regret meeting him at the ledge. Peter slammed his eyelids shut and welcomed the darkness. He considered how there was more to blindness than just the absence of sight. He'd been blind to what he'd had with Emily, blind to the outcome of his ill-fated decision.

The four bands on his arm were just a promotion. He could see that now, but it was too late. It had been too late for a very long time. Peter wondered if maybe Emily had forgotten about him. In a way, he hoped she had, and that the pain he'd caused was only a memory of something that once was.

He could see the faces of those who had died because of his actions. But, of course, someone in his position knew they weren't just *dead*. It wasn't that simple. He'd come to learn that small fact and wished he hadn't. There were secrets at the machines and behind the doors of the executive offices, and he'd had his fill of them for one lifetime.

Peter gripped the ledge, his soft pudgy fingers scraping the coarse resin that was meant to protect against the fog. He looked briefly at the dimpling in his palms. *It never had to be like this.* He winced when trying to lift himself onto the small divide that separated life from death.

At once, he felt himself begin to struggle. Blood rushed into his face along with a stir of starry lights streaking across his eyes. He coughed and gasped, and finally dropped back to his feet. Turning away from the ledge, he began to cry. How pathetic had he become? He couldn't even lift himself anymore. From the corner of his eye, he saw that his actions had roused the guard's attention.

"Indigestion, is all," he explained, swiping the sweat from his head while waving. "I'll be fine in a minute."

The guard stared a moment, motionless, before turning back to stand at attention. Peter forced himself up and around and leaned over the ledge. The courtyard was nearly empty. A few children ran around, playing chase with one another, their parents gathered into small circles, trading stories or gossiping. He enjoyed watching the children run freely in the courtyard. The indoor public spaces child-tethering rule he'd authored that morning wouldn't have been enforced yet. The children were free today, but in a week that would change. A lot of things were going to change. More than one new rule was being passed, and his hands were on all of them.

His death would surely anger the other executives when they found out what he'd done. That gave him something to smile about, and Peter let out a deep, gratifying sigh. They would have exiled him for sure with that move. The weaponized flu they'd had him use would be too merciful, too quick. They'd want him to suffer at the hands of the Outsiders, or maybe starve on the black sands of the beaches, eating sand-fleas and drinking seawater until his insides burst.

An earthy scent reached him. He'd always loved the smell of the farming floor; it reminded him of the time before. Yet today, the farms struck a grim note: a reminder of Sammi's death and the ceremonies that came with it. With the redolence came images of him being alone during his cleaning and pass-ing. It was an unsettling notion, a truth he'd expect: nobody would be with him when he was passed to the farming floor.

I have nobody. At least Sammi had Declan. That's the boy's name? The one she chose. Declan was Sandra Chambers' son. Peter cupped his mouth, dizzied, his stomach threatening again.

He thought of Sandra and her daughter Hadley, and the executives that had attended their cleaning and passing. He was supposed to have gone too. He'd *tried* to go, making it part of the way. Biting his lower lip, he remembered how he'd stood at the stairs leading to the farming floor, just close enough to hear Declan grieving for his mother and sister. He'd stayed and listened until the completion of the rite and then the passing of their bodies. He'd stayed but was never seen.

Sandra Chambers knew too. That's why she took the index card. As proof. She knew what the upper-level executives were doing. *She wasn't supposed to know, though,* Peter reminded himself. *She was just a junior executive. Innocent. Finding out was my fault.* A rush of guilt hit him, knotting his gut as he leaned into the balcony ledge, overwhelmed.

It was just supposed to make her sick. I used the exact amount. Shaking his head, he regretted his naivety and the storm of lies he'd been so willing to trust. *They promised she'd be left alone if I did it. Why did I listen to them?* He leaned harder, the balcony pressing into his middle. *She was only supposed to get sick: sick enough to miss the meeting and the vote.* The damn vote, and the damn End of Gray Skies. Sandra's vote would have swung the decision to reveal the truth. *Only, it couldn't be revealed. Not like that. Not when we knew so little. And why was her daughter with her?*

His heart cramped, blood stopping. For a moment, he was certain he was going to keel over before he got the chance to jump. He imagined dying on the balcony, his heart exploding in his chest. His thoughts returned to Sandra's daughter, Hadley: another innocent victim in the mess he'd created. She was a bystander who drank from the same cup as her mother. Sandra's death and the death of her daughter were both his to bear, and the guilt was his to die with. And maybe that's what fueled the guilt faster, hotter. Death tapped his shoulder and told him it would douse those flames.

His cheeks burned with shame, his gut spilling over the ledge. How much more did he need to see and feel? Activity below drew his attention, stopping his climb. A balding man stumbled through the collection of children playing in the courtyard. The man shuffled his feet past the huddled parents, waving once, then falling. Recognition struck Peter, and it nearly brought him to his knees: the man was Richard Chambers, Sandra's husband, the father of Hadley and Declan. A pair of executive guards were already approaching Richard, eager to remove the intoxicated sight from the commune's courtyard.

I did that to him, Peter thought. *I broke that man.*

He shook off a tear as an unnatural calm came over him. He

huffed out the air in his lungs. He was ready. From his front coverall pocket, he pulled a small index card and turned it over so that the rows of numbers were facing him. He pushed his finger across the imprint of inky-black and typed glyphs, studying them.

"These numbers. They're what started it all!" he shouted and glared at the executive offices and the guards. They turned to face him while he ripped the card in half. The sound and feel of the shredding rushed through him like a climactic release. It ended what he'd started, his time was coming. Peter tore into each new half, eager to finish. He tore the halves again and again before throwing them from the balcony. The guards were approaching faster now, uncertainty and confusion replacing their usual blank expressions.

It was time.

The muscles in his arms quivered under the strain of his weight, shaking as he desperately pushed himself onto the ledge. His skin turned cold beneath the tears, which mixed with his sweat, needling his eyes. But it wasn't due to the thought of what he was about to do; it was because of the misery he'd caused Sandra's family, and because of the regret he felt at losing the love of his life.

He'd broken his bond with Emily, and for what? Who had he become? What was his contribution? Rules? Emily had contributed. As a teacher, she'd influenced and mentored her students. Her work was admirable: righteous and pure. He'd instead spent his time learning things he didn't want to know and writing rules to uphold them.

As he began to stand, he was no longer crying—he was laughing. Balancing with his arms outstretched, a rapid stampede of shoes struck the balcony floor, the guards hollering for him to get down. After all, standing on the balcony ledge was against commune rules. Peter had written that rule too.

His stomach leaped back into his throat when he peered

over his belly to the courtyard below. The pace of the guards quickened, and their words were heated and more urgent. Yet to Peter there was only the beat of his heart in his ears. And it was both rhythmic and calming. It was satisfying.

Though his eyes had aged, and his sight went blurry sometimes, Peter focused on the courtyard to where the remains of the index card had fallen. A few of the children had already picked up some of the pieces and taken them to their parents, surely with wonderment, with questions about what it was they'd found.

Peter leaned into the last step of his life. He said little, mumbling aloud a dribble of loosely connected words, confessing what he'd done to Sandra and her daughter and to the commune. And as he confessed, his mind emptied, and his body fell through empty space. A lot of time seemed to pass before he reached the courtyard. He kept his thoughts to a minimum, limiting his mind to seeing only Emily's beautiful face, and the son they lost. Once or twice, he mouthed the words, "I love you, Emily," and before the dense and unforgiving concrete floor finally met him and took his life, he had one final thought, one that he regretted having:

What if they bring me back?

THREE

FIFTEEN YEARS EARLIER

Isla Jenkins woke with a start, sitting up, a silky thin sheet slipping from her body. *Phil Stark,* she recalled. *He'd been on the beach with me. In the burning rain.* But this wasn't the beach. She expected to see Phil's narrow face looking at her, looking at the burns. *I was burning. I was dying!* Panicked, Isla ran her hands up and down her arms and then across her face and chest. Her skin was smooth and without a single blemish. She felt a great relief edged with confusion. *How?* She made a face, brow narrowing.

"This doesn't make sense?" she muttered, the relief suddenly replaced with fright. *The cancer. My lungs?* She dared a breath. A deeper breath then, the kind that'd reach the tumors and make her cough. Nothing came. Not even the itch that she'd never been able to lay to rest. Isla swung her legs over the bed, a carpet beneath her bare feet. She squeezed her toes, seeing them, feeling them. They were real and this wasn't a dream.

"The chemo port?" she questioned, and gently touched the area above her breast. It had been sore and tender since they got to the mall before the clouds fell. Jaw dropping, she was shocked; the port was gone. "How's this possible?"

"Nolan?" she asked, heart beating frantically, gaze darting around the strange place and seeing that she was alone. The walls were plain, the room round and without windows, a single door without a handle. The air was crisp with a chill, and without any taste of the foggy salt. Frowning, Isla realized that it was empty of all odors. She needed Nolan and dipped her chin, gaze falling to her feet, remembering the food court, remembering what happened to her fiancé. The tears came in a gushing wave, her body shuddering. "Oh God! Nolan."

A call. She raised her head. "What?" Uncertainty had her questioning herself. There'd been no voice.

But there was something that called her. It called her name. At once, she stopped crying and sat still, listening while suspicions grew. On the wall near the ceiling, there was a glossy black panel displaying softly lit triangles. *Did the voice come from there? Was there a voice?* A row of blue and green spun methodically, the look of the panel soothing, even calming. Beneath it was a slot with a small door. A sudden thought sprang into her mind, explaining that it was a food dispenser. She'd never know it by its look, though, but instantly knew exactly how to use it.

"What is going—" The panel lights flashed, interrupting. Isla clenched her teeth, grinding them with unease. A song was playing. It was soft, the direction of it coming from somewhere. She considered the idea that speakers were hidden in the ceiling, like the kind seen in department stores or the market. Covering her ears, the music didn't change. It wasn't muffled or stuffy sounding. Isla clutched her chest, squeezing. The music was in her head.

She jolted up, standing and ready to run. But before she moved, the colorful glyphs danced and fluttered, the sequence tranquil. It had both order and direction and was similar to the work she'd carried out in her previous life. Isla lowered herself, breathing deeply with understanding.

What would Nolan do? she wondered.

He'd tell you that you're safe, the panel answered.

Fingers splayed, bracing the bedsheet, the answer was in her head. Wasn't it?

"I wish you were here, Nolan." She whispered the familiar sentiment, thinking it'd ground her, believing his death was her fault and that her mind must be breaking. "I should never have fired that gun. Never!"

Silence descended, the panel turning black. Isla swiped her eyes, eyelids scratchy. Nolan was gone and she was in a place that was playing tricks. As the painful memories eased, she couldn't dismiss how utterly relaxed and alive she felt. *Ironic*, she thought, as she considered what she'd done on the beach. If not for Phil Stark, she most certainly would have been dead.

Isla sucked in a breath and held it when a tingle crept into her legs and arms. Her gaze darted around. The room stayed empty, but the vibrations went deeper, until all of her body was tingling. There was no pain. No discomfort. In fact, she thought it felt good and didn't want it to stop. The sensation was all over her and in her brain, a euphoria that enveloped every muscle. The lights on the panel were in motion again. They were doing this, but she didn't mind.

"I understand," she told them. "This *is* my home now."

She lifted her chin, a thought from the back of her mind questioning what she'd just said. There was a sense of attachment with the lights. If it *was* just her mind playing tricks, she didn't mind. She pushed away the questions and got to her feet, sensing there was direction to follow. The order and sequence of the lights would tell her what to do next.

Isla realized then that she had no clothes. A shallow laugh, she wrinkled her brow, surprised that she'd been sleeping in the nude. She'd never slept in the nude before. She blushed—but it was a good blush, a welcome one. The feel of her bare skin didn't bother her.

"The dispenser," she heard, understanding it delivered more than food.

"Yes," she returned and stood in front of it, clothes appearing. They were soft like the bedsheet, the white fabric comfortable and with an iridescence she'd never seen before. Without hesitation, she put them on, the fit snug. The colorful triangles flashed a new sequence, telling her that it was time to go to her lab and start working. That's what she was. A scientist. An engineer too. The panel knew it and knew she needed to work. "Okay."

Hesitating, for how could she know *anything*? But she *did* know, the lights told her. Distantly inside her mind, there were warnings for her to be afraid, telling her this wasn't right. The lights grew brighter, the triangles spinning faster. She went to the door, the panel sliding into the wall with a whoosh while her thoughts raced, competing with what she knew to be right. The fear wasn't because she didn't know *where* she was, though, or why she was there. It was because she didn't know *why*.

FOUR
PRESENT

"He's ready now."

His mother's voice was stronger, automatic, and seemingly void of compassion. Declan's chest heaved slightly, an urge to scream for help gaining with desperation. He couldn't move. Couldn't speak. And though much of his senses were gone, he stayed awake, somewhat. Thoughts of help became fleeting, as uncertainty and doubt eroded the idea like the waves breaking along the shoreline.

I must be dead, he thought, and imagined his body far away, half-buried in the surf and black sands, with salt-gnats burrowing under his skin while sand-fleas invited themselves in for a tasty morsel. He wondered if maybe he'd been captured by the Outsiders and had died horribly. Horrifically even. They'd torn him apart, breaking every limb and ripping his head from his neck.

What he was seeing now was the afterlife where those who'd passed before came to greet him. That's what this had to be. Right? It was a simple idea, really. He'd experienced the moment of his death. While the effects were intense, the visions weren't real. They were the last of his brain's electrical impulses, fired all at once; a torrent of random energy volleyed to his starving neurons. The images were just a random sequence of what he wanted to see, what he needed to see. His mother wasn't really there. And he didn't see his sister waving from the machine. None of it was true. And that included seeing Sammi. She wasn't there either. With this last thought, he felt a deep sadness. Pain. But with death, could there still exist a feeling so intense? Did it matter? If Sammi was gone, then he had to be dead; he wanted to be dead.

His mother's voice came again, the world around him disappearing and shifting to another place like it was a dream. Declan felt the sensation of being lifted and moved, and he tried to raise his hands and open his eyes. He didn't feel the press from hands beneath him. In fact, he didn't feel anyone touching him at all. He was being carried into the machine; he was as sure of it as he was afraid. Distant voices spoke back and forth, but he couldn't make out what was being said.

At once, he wanted to cry. He wanted to call out to Sammi and his family, to plead with them, to beg that they bring him back from whatever strange state of suspension they'd put him. The world went black then. No more voices. No sensations. Nothing.

Declan opened his eyes, spurred by the tickle of long hair above his chin and nose. It was Sammi's laughter that roused him, his gaze hazy, dreamy. Sammi was dead, though. This was a dream. A good dream. The kind he'd hoped for those nights after finding her in the theater. He let himself play the part in this dream, putting on a grin when she snickered excitedly. She shook her head, soft ends of her hair brushing across his face. When he found her green eyes and saw they were gleaming and large and inviting, the sleep faded and he jumped. This wasn't a dream at all. Sammi was real.

"It's about time you woke up!" she exclaimed. Leaning in and planting her lips on his, she kissed him deeply. For a moment, he was lost in her, but as the twilight of sleep waned, the reality of what was happening began to settle in.

"Sammi?" he dared to ask. He realized that he was trembling, scared. She noticed, the sultry smile fading. He shook his head, saying, "I saw you die."

She didn't answer. Not yet, anyway. Instead, she looked at him like she had in that moment when they were sitting on the theater's stage. Light freckles dotted her nose and cheeks and were as he'd always known them, memorized from when he'd first grown smitten. Gently, he ran the pad of his thumb over her belly where the theater's seat post had been. Not a single mark. Not even a blemish. Sammi touched his face and chest, her fingers running along his bare shoulders as if he'd died and she was cleaning him as he'd done with her. He didn't feel the urge to run. This was Sammi and she was real.

He glanced beyond her face to the bed they were on. But it wasn't anything like the old cots in their dwellings. It was thick and foamy and new, and nothing in their world was new anymore. A silvery blanket was jumbled around their legs, the material shimmering like the strange coveralls he'd seen Sammi wearing on the beach. Images of his mother and sister slammed into him then: his mother touching his face and his senses disappearing.

"Shhh," Sammi answered, pressing a finger to his lips. She moved closer and pressed her body into his, her curvy form melting into his. She paused once, fixing her eyes on his, the warm touch of her skin welcome. And as she feathered his eyes and mouth with her lips, her breathing deepened. "Just be here. Be with me."

"Where is here?" he asked sharply, alarmed by the memory

of his mother and sister. He pulled the blanket up, as though it would protect him. For a moment, confusion and emotion swept through him and stole his words. Uncertainty stayed with him, leaving him to wonder if his dream had become a nightmare. He squeezed the sleep from his bleary eyes, asking, "Sammi? Where are we?"

"We're together," she told him, her voice as it had been on the theater stage. He told himself how impossible it was, yet the touch of her fingers, her beautiful eyes, and even her smell told him that she was real, that they were real and together. And when his mind was finally satisfied, Declan held her. She repeated her words, whispering, "Be with me."

Reaching under the covers and taking hold of him, she made certain he knew what her intentions were. A flurry of anxiety and excitement tumbled inside him like awkward lovers, causing him to pause. Declan drew his head back and searched her eyes. In them, he saw that she was a little nervous too; he hesitated and frowned, asking without words if she was sure. She nodded eagerly and pulled him to her, kissing him like she'd never kissed him before. He returned the kiss, engaging Sammi, whom he thought he'd lost forever.

"I choose you, Declan Chambers," she told him, her words soft and breathy. Sammi pushed away the blanket to expose their naked bodies. "We're together, and we're home. That's all we need to know right now."

She lifted herself on top of him, moving her hands with his, touching as their breathing grew heavy and fast. He soon forgot the questions he'd asked, and a moment later, he was above her, resting on his elbows, his chest pressing against her breasts.

When she wrapped her legs around him, he said, "As your chosen, I accept you, Sammi. I love you."

She told him that she loved him too, and helped guide him closer, preparing to make love for the first time, and to make it last until they collapsed into one another's arms.

Declan eased himself from that place where dreams are sometimes real and where dreams are sometimes fantasy. Waiting for his bleary eyes to adjust, the questions were returning like the light in this strange place with Sammi sleeping beside him. Not wanting to wake her just yet, he looked around. Like the shapely curve of Sammi's body beneath the silver blanket, the walls in the room held no corners. They were smooth and uninterrupted.

Their home. That's what Sammi had called it. He recognized some of the art and glanced briefly at a panel that was nestled flush in the walls. The screen was black, save for a row of squares and triangles and circles, colored like the crayons he'd drawn with when he was a child.

An image in the artwork caught his eye. It was a great desert with hovering gray skies that hung broken like cotton balls. Nestled between them was the cautious eye of a white sun, its size significant compared to the Earth's sun. Sands in the desert image moved subtly, which surely meant his mind was playing tricks, his mother's touch still affecting him. But then he noticed the silvery sheet moving with Sammi's breaths, the sands in an eerie harmony. *A coincidence,* he told himself. It had to be.

The only door wasn't much more than a rectangle outline that was flush like the display panel. Above it were six small lights that held a dim glow. He'd seen them blinking earlier before they'd made love. A question stirred. He'd seen them active while they made love too. The flashes were in an odd succession, alternating colors and frequency. He was certain of it. Artwork? The machine's technology? Was he inside the machine?

Sammi stirred and let out a delicate yawn while wrapping her arm around Declan's middle. Stretching, her slender legs brushing his, she tickled his feet with her toes. "That was a nice nap."

"It was," he answered, heart swelling with the intimacy. Selfishly, he fought the urge to ask questions that needed to be asked. She shouldn't be here.

"I love this place," she said, voice sleepy. "I can get used to this... can't you?" Lifting the covers, she took hold of him in her hand, and moved to meet his eyes. She caught him off-guard then, as she gave a playful squeeze with her fingers.

"Well... I can certainly get used to that," he answered, laughing, the immediate questions forgotten in an instant. "But I'm hungry... are you?" Sammi nodded a quick agreement, letting him go.

Her eyelids peeled back, the whites in her eyes huge. "Declan, there's a food dispenser. You've gotta see this!" Intrigued, he said nothing as she moved from beneath the covers. She left the bed, walking free of their coveralls, breasts rising and falling with each step.

"I can get used to that too," he joked, meaning it. Had she ever been so free? Did it matter? Sammi turned to face him, letting him see her, really see her. "Definitely get used to it."

At once, her death came back to him in a flash. There were images of her naked body lying on the steel table, blood running along her pale leg while washing her wound. And what about her dead eyes before he shut them for the final time? Taken by the memory, Declan sat up, swinging his feet over the edge of the bed.

"What's wrong?" she asked, annoyed. She grabbed the sheet and draped it around herself. When he didn't answer, she asked, "Declan?"

"Sammi?" He reached for her hand. She only looked at his hand, her earlier smile turned down with concern. A moment later, she moved close enough to take his fingers.

"Declan, what is it?"

"You were dead… and now you're here—" His voice went hoarse with emotion, the day of her cleaning fresh and raw. Without warning, he pulled her toward him, Sammi's bare skin warm under his touch. He brushed his fingers over her belly as if checking it again. The wound that had taken her life was gone. Like the walls around them, she was whole and unscathed. He pressed his lips to where the wound had been as Sammi leaned over, her hair falling onto his shoulders.

"Declan, I remember what happened," she whispered, kissing the top of his head. "Some of it, anyway. Like the theater and falling and how terribly it hurt. I remember you being there too. I remember how you were looking at me." Sammi ran her hand through his hair.

"Sammi, please help me understand how it is that you can be here," he begged, gently lifting his chin until he saw her eyes and the tears racing down her face. "Sammi?"

"I'm sorry you saw me die," she said, kneeling, arms around him. "I'm so sorry."

With those words, he couldn't fight it and cried with her. And as he held her, she hummed a rhyme he'd heard her sing so many times before. The hymn encouraged more tears. Sammi was alive, and he wasn't sure if he cared how it was possible. Not now, anyway.

FIVE

Emily sat up, startled by a hollow knock. Reluctant to leave the warm comfort of bed, she clutched the blankets and fell back, flipping the pillow to rest her face against the cooler side. Knuckles rapped on the door loud enough to stir aggravation. She mumbled a few choice curses, irritated. The knocking continued, the noise forcing her awake.

"What!" she grumbled, annoyed, throwing off the blankets.

Wrapped in the darkness and the room's cold air, a deep yawn caught her, the drowsiness leaving. Seated at the edge of the bed, she jabbed the air with her toes until finding a pair of slippers, threadbare but comfortable. Blindly waving to shoo away the knocks, she followed a man's voice calling her name.

It was just her last name that he'd called out, the late-night visit a formal one. She was awake now. There were only a few reasons for the formality, and none of them were good. "Ms. Stark," he repeated, leaving her to wonder if it might be a student.

The morning bell? She considered, guarding against bad news. *I slept through it?* Were the children waiting? She imagined young Rick Toomey, rummaging through his desk, a toothy grin pushing his cheeks as he waited for the day's lesson.

When it quieted, she waited for signs from her neighbors or noise from the courtyard. There was none, this *was* a late visit. Dread suddenly took her heart, understanding the visitor's purpose. Slippers dragging, she grabbed a shawl to stave off a chill. Her eyes adjusted to the light breaking beneath the door, a pair of gray shadows shuffling, pacing. The visitor was anxious. She stared for what felt like a long minute, a second pair joining the first. Both paced and stopped and then paced again. When she was close enough, she could make out two voices chattering. They were careful to keep the words between them, leaving little to hear except a low mumble and her name. Carefully clutching the door's handle, Emily kept the door shut and checked the lock.

"Yes, can I help you?" she said in a dry voice that cracked. Clearing the sleep from her throat, she added, "Who would be calling at such an hour?"

She glanced through the peephole and cleared the grit from her eyes. Two messengers stood on the other side, single bands on their coveralls, each of them wearing a baseball cap reserved for the role. She missed the days before the clouds fell. When the phones worked and text messages were a swipe and thumb-press away. Even email would be nice. They'd tried getting it back once. A long time ago at the mall. But without an outside to connect to, the attempts died silently. Someday maybe?

"Yes, ma'am, I'm sorry for the late call. We're delivering a message from the bureau and farming floor—"

"Ms. Stark, please," she insisted, hating when anyone called her ma'am. She wasn't a *ma'am*. Not yet. "The hour, it's late."

"Yes, ma'am... I mean, Ms. Stark. With sincere apologies," the taller of the two said, his voice familiar. "It was supposed to have been delivered yesterday."

"It takes two to deliver a message?"

"No... no, Ms. Stark," the shorter messenger answered. "I'm working with my brother, Jonathan; he's training me."

"We're the McNaer brothers," the taller messenger said, moving in front of the peephole and forcing a smile. "I know it's been a few years, maybe you remember us?"

"Brendan and Jonathan," Emily said, a fond memory coming to mind. They were survivors from the mall. Siblings a few years older than Sammi, they played with her and helped with the other children. How they'd grown. At once, Emily turned the handle to see her former students. While it'd been a year or more, she knew the McNaer brothers well. The two were nearly inseparable since those early days in the mall, and even today they remained as one.

She opened the door, to find two nearly grown men, not the lanky adolescents who'd left her classroom when they were old enough. Broad-shouldered and filling out their coveralls, they were handsome. And big. If not for the one black band around each of their arms, she might have thought they'd been selected to work as executive guards. She couldn't help but smile when she saw the boyish faces in their smiles. It was them.

"Ms. Stark," they said together.

"Well, look at you two!" she cried, fingers sweeping through her hair, aware of how she must look. "My, how you've grown!" Her face felt flushed, and she pulled the ends of her shawl together.

"Hi, Ms. Stark," Brendan said, dipping his head.

"It's so very good to see you both," she said, mirroring the courtesy. The late hour took her smile, though, and she asked, "A message?"

"Yes, Ms. Stark," Jonathan began.

"*We* are sorry, ma'am. Brendan left your message back at our workstation. It's timestamped and was supposed to be delivered yesterday."

"When we saw it was *missed*, we rushed it over," Jonathan said, finishing.

"Yesterday?" Emily asked, mind spinning. There were only a few reasons for a message to be timestamped. Sammi's cleaning was over so that wasn't it. Reluctant, she held out her hand to accept the message.

"Again, we're so sorry," Jonathan said, the folded parchment in his hand. On the face of it was a waxy seal: a mortician's seal. Pushing her fingers over the red stamp, she pressed the cold wax, tracing the half-circle markings used to identify death in their commune.

A blood seal, she heard in her head. That's what the executives had decided to call it. *How morbid.* Emily recalled how she'd objected to it when Peter first mentioned the name. It was a small detail when considering the magnitude of managing the commune, but they'd argued. There were deeper issues by then. It wasn't just the name. They'd reached the beginning of the end of their marriage. "It's bad luck to touch a blood seal," she mumbled, continuing to run her fingers over it.

"Bad luck?" Brendan asked. Their faces turned curious as they considered what she'd said.

"Something the kids said in class once," she answered. "They were scaring one another, is all. You know, telling ghost stories."

"I'm sorry for getting this to you late... Ms. Stark," Brendan nodded respectfully.

Emily couldn't break her stare, her focus locked on the blood-red seal. She glanced once at the McNaer boys and gave them a short nod, appreciating that they'd gone out of their way to deliver the message. And without another word, they were gone.

A cup of tea between her palms, Emily drank the bitterness and instantly put on a face. It was only lukewarm and not nearly as hot as she'd like. She looked toward the far wall at the small array of batteries, the yellowing indicator light dim. The charge was nearly exhausted which explained the tea. Following the wires to the stationary bike, she shook her head, thinking begrudgingly, *I'll have to ride soon.*

Riding would wait, her hand resting on the mortician's waxy seal, the message untouched, unread. There was one reason a message would expire. There was one reason the mortician's messages *always* expired: once a cleaning and passing to the farming floor was scheduled, there was no delaying the ceremony, regardless of attendance. Whose name was inside? Who died?

"Maybe it's a mistake?" she muttered, sipping the tea. Nobody's name came to mind, though. Another sip. Nobody was old enough except... except, Ms. Newl. "Oh gosh, Jane!"

Concern stole her words as she gulped her tea, her insides warming a little. Pinching the seal, it snapped in half, the crisp sound filling her ears. Emily unfolded the parchment, slowing when the chalky lettering began to show. She looked for the letters spelling the name Jane, but it wasn't Jane Newl. The charcoal letters spelled the name, Peter Wilkes.

"Peter," she cried sorrowfully, voice heavy. Denying it, she wanted to jump from the table and go to his dwelling. He couldn't be dead. Not Peter. Not after everything they'd survived. Her mind flashed images of the market and the service tunnels. The rats that chased them and the mall when explosions rattled them like a baby's toy. "You can't be dead! It's impossible."

She flipped the parchment over thinking it was a cruel joke, the McNaer boys holding a slight against her for a failing grade. But they were students years ago and being selected as a messenger wasn't taken lightly. They'd never risk losing the position. A chill raced through her like a fever, every part of her trembled. Emotions mixed like a poisonous stew and caused her to feel every ounce of hurt that could be felt.

She shook her head, understanding why she'd been named, why she'd been requested to attend his cleaning and passing. They'd registered with the bureau, her choosing him as had become the practice in this new world. Sammi was there. A few of her students too. The ritual reminded her of the weddings from before the clouds fell, the small ceremony and party after they'd put their names together in the commune's registry.

"Choosing is forever," she muttered, and dropped the parchment onto the table. Clutching her heart, she found the familiar hurt of when he left after their baby boy was taken. He'd blamed her for the loss almost as much as she'd blamed him. Tears running, the hurt that had come with the end of their love was still strong. And deep down, she'd kept a reservation that one day they'd find forgiveness and be together again. But that was gone now, and Emily wondered if she'd ever find the courage to love again.

SIX

Sammi stood in the dark and stared deep into a painting. Though the room was dim, the colors in the picture were alive. This was one of her favorites. It was the one with the great desert and the white sun piercing through a looming gray sky. Declan had been looking at it, too, and she wondered if he saw the same, felt the same. He hadn't mentioned anything but, then again, making love might have kept him preoccupied. She chuckled softly.

A hollow thump jarred her from the painting. Sammi spun around to the door where the soft thump came again, this time louder. Declan didn't stir, his sleep deep, the silver sheet rising and falling. She rushed to answer before another knock woke him. She glanced at the lights and expected instructions from them, maybe a different set of orders for the day's work ahead, but they were quiet. Distantly, nagging questions piqued her for a moment. *Why do I listen to the lights? How is that possible?* The questions went unanswered. Forgotten.

The door opened, two visitors eclipsing the hallway light, the shadows soft enough for her to see it was Declan's mother and sister. Sandra stood tall and square, features without expression. And her daughter Hadley stood sheepishly awkward, hiding a couple steps behind her mother. Sammi thought it funny how people behaved around one another. She'd seen Hadley plenty of times in Emily's classroom and the girl was never so shy.

"Do you want me to wake Declan?" Sammi asked.

"No, no," Sandra Chambers answered, her silhouette shaking. Declan's mother took hold of her hand, the touch colder than it should have been. There was something else too. Sandra's voice. It wasn't right. When Sammi moved so the corridor light would show their faces, Declan's mother shifted to keep herself hidden. "How is he?"

"Did you do it yet?" Hadley blurted, stepping around her mother and tapping Sammi's arm. "Did ya?"

"Hadley!" Sandra scolded. She shrugged her shoulders apologetically. "Sammi, don't you listen to her. That's your business... yours and Declan's."

"Yes, it's official," Sammi decided to tell them, sensing both had the need to know. After all, gossip was one of the few luxuries they had to chew on. And who else was she going to openly tell, anyway? Hadley bounced up and down, chuckling. Sandra lifted Sammi's hands, kissing them tenderly.

"Welcome to the family," Declan's mother began and then stopped as emotion caught her words. "You two will be so happy. Make the most of it. Make the most of the time..." she stopped then and pulled Sammi into her arms. Soon, Hadley's arms were wrapped around her too.

When they were done, Sammi eased back, the corridor light shining on their faces. A sharp horror struck her, and she nearly stumbled backward. They'd aged since bringing Declan inside. A dozen years? Forty? Wrinkly creases cut into the corners of their eyes and mouths. Their hair was stippled and dry, straggly gray, the original color gone. Small tan blemishes pocked the tops of their hands and arms. Their bodies had become frail too, like their voices.

"What's happening?" Sammi asked, tearing up. "What's going on?"

Hadley looked at the corridor floor, embarrassed as though she were hiding an adolescent blemish. This was a lot more than a blemish. Sandra sighed and shook her face, shrugging. She surprised Sammi then, grabbing her hands forcefully. At once, the corridor lights blinked rapidly, catching Hadley's attention first, her focus dimming, expression emptying. Sandra squinted and moved close enough for Sammi to smell her. God, she even smelled old.

Sandra shielded her eyes, instructing, "Tell Declan nothing. Tell him nothing of what you've seen."

"But what's happening to you?" Sammi asked, the lights singing to her, their voices saying words her mind wanted to hear. "What's happening to us?"

"It's part of who we are now, understand?!" Sandra insisted. When Sammi shook her head, Sandra continued, "You'll understand when it's your time too."

Before Sammi could say another word, Declan's mother snapped her hands from Sammi's and turned her eyes to the lights. Like Hadley, the shine in her graying eyes vanished and her face emptied. Declan's mother followed her daughter into the corridor.

"Who was that?" Declan asked, stirring behind her. Sammi braced the doorway, terror coursing through her. What happened to Sandra and Hadley? *Is that going to happen to me?* She glanced at the backs of her hands to find a wrinkle or a browning age spot, anything like she'd seen on them. Sammi checked her mouth and eyes next but found nothing there. "Sammi? You okay?"

"Nobody. It's okay. Go back to sleep," she answered, turning to face him, the door closing behind her. Declan rolled over onto his side, and within a minute, his breathing grew heavy again.

Sammi returned to the picture to see it changing for her. The Earth was larger this time. It was big enough to make out the oceans and see its moon. She dared another touch like earlier and the surface threw a spark, the energy tingling. All around her, the room filled with the picture's details, rotating and revealing new sights. She was lost in the images and questions about her father, the man she could barely remember.

She spoke to him as if he could hear her. "Dad, this wasn't just you. Who made this machine?"

Isla Jenkins sat up, breath spilling. A silky thin sheet slipped from her body as an image of Phil Stark popped into her head.

"The beach," she cried, running fingers through her hair and across her face, the touch without any flaws. "He was on the beach with me. And the rain. It was burning."

She stood up, a chill racing over her bare skin when reaching for white coveralls nearby. Isla anxiously slipped her legs inside and covered her front. This wasn't the beach and there was no sign of Phil. "I was burning, though." Disbelief. A chuckle. "Shit, I was dying."

"I saw what happened to my skin! Felt it!" Sudden panic shot into her throat. The alarm was gone a second later; she was fine. She sighed cautiously, questioning, "I'm fine. But how?"

The wheezing and pain expected with each breath was gone. *The cancer. My lungs?* Fear returning, or was it shock? Isla dared another breath, testing the waters by going deeper than she'd been able to. When was the last time she'd been able to do that? Her lungs were clear, the absence of pain making her eyes teary.

"The chemo port?" she asked, searching the empty room,

the lights on the wall flashing instructions. She shoved her hand inside the front of her coveralls, the skin above her breast free of medical intervention. "But the lights."

She was alive and this wasn't a dream. Isla zipped up her front, unable to free her stare from the lights. In them, she saw the answers, her questions rested. Somehow, she could hear them in her mind too. And before they revealed anything more, they needed her to work.

Isla stood at the opening of a massive laboratory, jaw dropping, her eyes wide in wonderment. Had she ever seen such a place? There'd been the universities where she was a research scientist, her career cut short by the cancer. She reached for the chemo port that was supposed to be there but wasn't, her flesh clean. The cancer had wrung her out like a wet towel and nearly killed her. While she'd survived, barely, it killed her career. But this place. What was it?

The lights above the door eased her memories. She peered at the floor, the corner of her eye catching the shine. How did they work? That was another mystery to solve, and the harder she tried concentrating, the harder it was to grasp. Instead, the lights instructed her, telling her this was the place she needed to be. They also said that this was where her best work was waiting. After all, there was nobody better at the science.

The mysteries would wait. The lab was like a playground and Isla leaned into a lab table and brushed her hand across the surface, a lively giddiness filling her. She deserved this. She deserved the freedom to play after all the bullshit of chemotherapy and hospital stays. *If only Nolan could see this place,* she thought. Then it would be real.

Insides racing with an excited light-heartedness, it made her feel utterly silly. It was like her birthday with a table full of gifts waiting to be ripped open. She glanced at the untouched lab equipment, curiosity spurring at what the samples in the beakers were. There were more in the test tubes too; the liquids at differing amounts and colors. There'd been work already. Whose work?

An agitator table gently rocked, the concentrated whirring filled her ears, save for the constant hum of the building, the machine Phil Stark took her to. A frown. Where was he? There were others working here, but she hadn't seen him. Not once. Reading the labels on one of the flasks, she questioned the lab work.

"The other technician didn't finish their work. That's fine," she mumbled confidently, slipping a lab coat around her shoulders. "I'll pick up with whatever you were working on."

A volley of colorful lights beamed from above the door. It was instructions, directing her to a large steel door at the back of the lab. In its center, a small oval window, ringed in black. To her, it looked like a watchful eye guarding the lab. Unlike the rest of the lab, the door was unfamiliar to her. Pressing her lips together, searching her thoughts, she found no recollection, no memory of it. Unsettled, Isla answered the lights and went to face it.

For a moment, she thought the door's single eye had winked, giving her a fright. The image squeezed her heart, but she shrugged off the nonsense, recalling how late nights in a lab could play tricks with your mind. It was just a stupid door, nothing more.

Motion! Isla stopped. There was movement on the other side of the window. It was a set of dark shadows waving. A deep breath, she quickly saw a pattern and counted, seeing that it was mechanical. *A machine?*

Curiosity got the better of her and she dared to touch the strange door, pressing her palms against the steel. The metal was cold and empty of any motion or vibrations. The door was taller than expected, the top of her head barely reaching the portal window. She pressed her ear against the metal and heard the muffled sounds of movement. Annoyed by her blindness, she dragged a chair into place and got onto it.

Inside, a long mechanical arm swung from one side of the room to the other. It was quick and exact, humming a mechanical song as it passed in front of the portal window without a care that there was an audience. Instincts had her ducking, and she chuckled at the impulse, the arm passing without hesitation.

What she saw next changed every thought she'd had about her lab.

The room behind the door was larger than her lab and squared with the same silver steel on all sides. From the floor to the ceiling, there were hundreds, maybe thousands of shelves—all were filled with vials that numbered hundreds of rows deep. In each of them, a dark red solution filled more than half. Blood was her best guess. And it was her only guess.

But whose blood? And why so many? Isla dropped down from the chair, working the numbers in her head, the count of rows on one of the shelves along with the size of the room. It was an estimated count, and it was large enough to catch her breath. She spun back toward the lab, an understanding of the work going on in this place. With nearly a hundred thousand blood samples, it explained why the lab was as big as it was. *But why?*

The whirring grew, spurring Isla to look again. Another pair of arms were in motion, one of them with fingerless rubber tips gripping a vial. The tips closed gently and lifted it off the shelf. The same was happening farther back, mechanized hands moving them up and down, back and forth. Some of the vials were moved to other shelves, while others disappeared into the farthest shadows. Still others had their pink and lavender rubber stops pierced by a needle that extended from the mechanical hand, a sample drawn, the vials gently returned.

A sharp light bounced off the window, breaking her study of the activities. The lights were talking to her again, and at once she returned to the lab table, dragging the chair behind her. She was there to work, and her work was critical. At least that's what she'd been told. The mystery playing out in the back of her mind had steadied like a low chatter.

How were the lights saying anything? The lights flashed, the sentiment a reproachful one, she sensed. Isla dipped her chin and waited, afraid, expecting retribution. But the room remained quiet.

Carefully, she raised her head, the sequence flashing was like a shout. Squinting, she shielded herself from it, an ache tumbling deep inside her head. The pain faded and the lights softened; soothing, like a parent's comforting after a scolding. The sequence told her the next task. Without hesitation or question, she nodded, the urgency understood.

Returning to the lab table, the desk familiar as if it was hers, she picked through the contents, her hand falling on a lab journal. Thinking of the lab tech who had come before her, the work to continue, she mumbled, "Hopefully you left me some notes."

The pages were bound by heavy thread, thick and protected by a cover. She flipped it open, the edges stiff and sharp. Without thinking twice, she found a pen in the drawer and set to write a date and time, the clock on the wall indicating it was the morning. Thoughts drifted to the blood samples, the mechanized fingers, the activities observed. When her focus returned to the page, she saw that she'd written the descriptions down, a knot building in her fingers. She finished the journal entry, admiring the effort, trivial as it was compared to her past work.

"It's new to me, though," she said, fanning the journal's pages, the book new. With the page completed, she pinched the top-right corner and tore it away, flicking the piece onto the floor. *Why did I do that?* The motion was like a muscle memory, but she didn't remember ever having done it before.

Littering trash wasn't a best practice in any lab, and she quickly picked up the torn piece, pocketing it. Beneath the lab table, there were more journals, dozens shelved neatly side by side. And from the creases in the binders, they'd already been written in, most of them filled.

Isla bounced the tip of her finger from journal to journal, counting. Delight filled her belly, the journals a couple years old, some of them more than half a decade. She nabbed one of the volumes like it was a new science fiction from a favorite author. Straightening, she found relief in the darkness of the lights. They were quiet, which meant she was free to go to her room and read. Isla closed her lab journal, placing it alongside the journals she'd just found. They were identical, and if not for the creases, the fact the covers were older, she wouldn't have been able to tell them apart.

Before leaving, she took a look, restlessness playing a coy game. Isla flipped open the old journal where there was a name written in cursive handwriting. The penmanship displayed swings that were far and tall, and arches that dipped low. The writing was familiar.

Clearing her throat, she read the name aloud. "Isla Jenkins."

The lab filled with the echo of the journal slamming shut. Shaking her head, she searched the lab for someone, anyone. *What kind of joke is this?* The lights were quiet. Too quiet, which only added to the frustration. Voice shaking, "What kind of sick shit is going on here?"

With her fingers nestled between the pages, she opened the old journal again. A tear fell onto the page and bloomed silently. The penmanship was the same and she dipped her finger in the tear, the ink spreading like flower petals. Her soft cries ceased instantly when seeing the corner of the page. Fingers trembling, she touched the rough edge, the corner torn away. It wasn't just the first page either, the corners had been torn from *all* the pages.

Isla quickly fanned the pages, the air turning her cheeks cold. When she reached the first blank page, she stopped. The upper corner was still whole, an understanding striking like a slap.

"I've done this before?" she questioned softly. Lifting the freshly torn piece, Isla placed it in the corner of the old journal. The pages had aged, looking yellow next to the new piece, which was a near-perfect fit. Isla shoved the back of her hand to her mouth.

"This can't be!" she gasped. The practice of tearing the corners helped her find the next blank page. It meant, the torn corners were completed days. "How many days?"

A bitter taste filled her mouth, the hairs on the back of her neck standing. Her heart beat wildly, even painfully. Her head became heavy, and her ears filled with a ringing that made her deaf to the world. When the room turned on its side, she was sure her heart was going to stop.

It was happening again. It was happening like before when the caustic rains killed her fiancé. He melted in front of her, the images as fresh as the torn paper pinched between her fingers. She'd found a fix, though, and had quieted the chaos reigning inside her brain. The rains didn't just take the love of her life that day. They relieved her of the pain when she walked into the fog, Emily and Peter yelling for her to stop.

Isla turned once to the lights, finding them quiet, silent, and she wondered if she'd ever heard anything from them at all. The chaos was back inside her mind, and she needed to dull its voice. She searched her thoughts for Nolan, hoping his face would help her. The images were fleeting, though, leaving as soon as they came. Instead, she could only see his death. She could only see Ms. Newl pointing the gun and doing for Nolan what she couldn't bring herself to do. Falling to her knees and gasping, she covered her face with her hands and cried into them.

Her lab was suddenly too small. Its walls and ceiling were closing in on her, trapping her in a never-ending cycle of nightmarish repentance. She was losing her mind again. It was the simplest explanation; the easiest explanation. She was still mourning Nolan's loss and her guilt was never going to let her forget what had happened to him.

"I'm sorry. Nolan, I'm so sorry." Her words echoed as she curled herself into a ball on the metal floor. She shut the light from her eyes, welcoming the touch of the cold against her body, exhaustion taking hold. She had to stop trying to understand what was real and what wasn't.

Maybe I'm still on the beach and only dreaming of Phil Stark being with me? Maybe I'm really dead. That would be best. Being dead. The smothering heat began to recede and the thumping in her head had faded to a dull ache. The lab was a gray blur like the clouds that fell onto the mall. She didn't want to understand why; not anymore. Isla only wanted to disappear, even if it was for just a short while.

EIGHT
PRESENT

Emily stiffened, legs ignoring direction when she entered the farming floor. It was where Peter's cleaning and passing would take place. And if she was going to attend, it meant pushing through the reluctance. A dim light shined from the opened door, the crack foreboding. It was where the rite was scheduled, and it filled her with angst. She barely touched it, the hinges announcing her arrival. Before entering, she had to stop and arrest the temptation to cry.

They'd been apart long enough that the strength of the grief came as a surprise. Most of it was for their boy, for the family they were and would never be again. There were some things in life that you never got over—no matter how much you lied to yourself. As she entered and walked deep into the room, carrying thoughts of the short life they'd had together, Emily considered that maybe she *was* supposed to feel this way.

Shaking out her hands—they'd gone clammy—nerves rumbled and stole the spit in her mouth. *Choosing was forever.* That's what they'd come up with when she helped him author the first rules of their commune. It was a tenet for the community to live by, the ideas simple. But even the simplest of things can be made complicated. They'd found that out when trying to lead by example, turning the tragedy of the fog, their plight and survival at the mall, into something wonderful. Emily wondered if love born out of disaster could actually survive. She scoffed at the idea, knowing it could. She knew because it happened for them. Only, it couldn't survive the loss of their son. Both were gone now.

The mortician stood at the center of the room with his back to her, Emily hoping his eyes were warm and welcoming. She needed them to be. As if listening, he turned subtly, his narrow face nodding. There was a kindness in it, the same she'd seen at Sammi's passing. Following his lead, she took his outstretched hand in hers to proceed. Scanning the room, an awful realization came to her: they were alone.

Nobody had come to Peter's passing. How was that? Where was Ms. Newl? Peter had had his differences with her about the schooling, about how to establish it. But surely Jane would have seen past all that and come today. The door opened and relieved her worry, Ms. Newl's face appearing. Jane's bluish hair was pinned high, a splash of makeup on her cheeks and eyes. She walked with a cane and set it aside, saying nothing as she came to stand next to her.

Emily mouthed a "Thank you" while a narrow door opened in the wall. The end of a table appeared with two pale feet hanging off its edge. Emily covered her mouth, breath suddenly leaving in a gasp. Peter's left foot was a mess of broken skin and bones poking through. The rest of his body was riddled with more fractures, bones jutting through his coveralls, and ringed with blood that had long since dried. She fought the urge to turn away. She fought the need to run.

She couldn't perform the cleaning—not with his body like that. There'd been no news of his death, the executive floor doing well to quiet what happened. She'd thought it might have been from the flu or an infection, an illness that had once been taken for granted. But this wasn't that. Peter was broken. He was barely recognizable. Even with his coveralls still on, she could see that he'd died horribly.

Emily was aware of Ms. Newl's fingers pinching her elbow, urging her into motion. Did Jane know what happened? Emily glanced into the old woman's face and saw the same horrified disgust she felt inside. She didn't know. Nobody knew, except the executive guards tasked to bring Peter to the mortician.

"How... how did he die?" she asked, words hanging on a breath. The mortician kept his rigid posture, straight like a board, but rested a hand on her back. She thought his touch felt gentle and oddly calming.

"He jumped, ma'am," the mortician answered without emotion. "Two days ago, he jumped from the executive floor. Shall we continue?"

Her arms and legs were seized by the news. Head shaking, a fierce frown pinching her face, she said, "That can't be. He'd never do such a thing."

"I'm sorry, ma'am," was all the mortician said, continuing.

Emily gulped the dryness from her mouth, a tear turning cold on her face. She fetched the cleaning bowl and decomp salts, Ms. Newl helping. A cry took her hostage, Ms. Newl's arm around her shoulder and walking her through the motions. In her mind, she saw the courtyard, and saw Peter on the tiled floors. When she raised his arm to remove the coveralls, the amount of blood spurred a terrible thought. Before dying, he'd bled. He'd bled significantly.

The dead don't bleed? Emily stopped and considered Peter's final moment, his surviving briefly after the fall. She looked into his face, asking, "Why?"

The mortician thanked Emily for attending, her hand swallowed by his, disappearing as he shook it gently and showed her and Ms. Newl the door. Standing tall, he announced to the empty room that the rite of cleaning and passing for Peter Wilkes had concluded. The mortician added another "Thank you"—his voice softer, and more directed at Emily. Her eyes swept around the empty room, landing on the small door that opened to receive Peter's body.

From the small opening, the farm's earthy smell entered the room, pungent enough to make her blink and back away. With a gentle touch, the mortician guided her to where they slid the table forward, Peter's naked body readied to be processed. When she hesitated, the bite from the open door growing stronger, the mortician spoke a calming word or two and dipped his chin, assuring her that it'd be fine.

Peter was gone a moment later while she hid her mourning in the academic thoughts of how the processing worked: how it fed the plants and enriched the soil. Gloved fingers appeared on the other side of the opening, the sight startling her. She hadn't seen that at Sammi's cleaning. They waved the body on eagerly: fingers opened and snapped shut, hungry for his body like the hands of a cafeteria worker handling finished lunch trays. Once Peter's body was within their reach, hands took a firm hold of him, pulling on his feet. His broken bones shifting, Emily flinching when the sound clapped the air. She shut her eyes when his naked body slid across the metal table, the door closing.

"Thank you again for attending," the mortician said, breaking Emily's stare. While his expression remained warm, his eyes regarded her with the somberness his role carried in the commune. "I am sorry for your loss."

"Thank you," she answered, words mechanical. She fanned the air, the room suddenly small and suffocating. Ms. Newl must have sensed it and took her arm, looping the crook of her elbow in hers to lead her out the door. When the air changed, Emily wiped her brow saying, "God, I hope that's the last time I see that place."

"Well, I'm not getting any younger," Ms. Newl dared to say. The corner of her mouth turned up as she asked, "Too soon?"

"Yeah, too soon, Jane," Emily barked. She forced a smile, appreciating it. Breathing deeply, the salt pinched her lungs, the afternoon bell ringing. Her classroom would be dismissed soon. "I should go check on my class."

"Let me," Jane said, insisting, cool air replacing her touch. "You take the rest of the day. Heck, take the week, Emily. Okay?"

"You sure?" Before she could object, Jane planted a kiss on the side of her face, hand brushing her arm. "I appreciate it."

Emily stayed behind, watching Ms. Newl leaving. The woman walked with her cane, using it every other step, its need changing from day to day. A young woman with a child tethered to her side approached cautiously, Emily turning to see if the woman's attention was meant for someone else. It wasn't. When she turned back, the woman gave her a wave, her face familiar. "Mary Berger?" she asked, recognizing her from class. "How long has it been?"

"Hi, Ms. Stark," Mary said, knuckles white as she held the tether strap tight. The woman's face was fuller, round and maybe a bit puffy. Emily saw more of the schoolgirl she remembered in the daughter's face, the resemblance uncanny. "I'm sorry to rush, but I'm late and wanted to catch you here. I... I mean, catch *someone* here."

"I'm sorry?" Emily asked, confused. There was rigid concern in the face of her old student. Not just concern. She was frightened, the fear coming off her like it was heat. "Mary? What is it?"

Mary shut her eyelids tight and then opened them wide, starting again. "Well, you see, I didn't exactly know who I'd find here today," she began, leaning over to touch her daughter's hair. She shook her head, adding, "But, Ms. Stark, I had no idea it'd be you. I'm so sorry for your loss."

Emily nodded, appreciating the sentiment. Shaking her head, she asked, "You said you didn't know who you'd find here?" An ugly notion took her with a sickening strike. She searched the child's face for any resemblance to Peter. The girl held the tether strap tightly, her pudgy fingers pink and white while rocking. When her focus returned, Mary's face had grown pale, her lower lip trembling. *Peter would never do such a thing. Would he?* Afraid to ask, Emily forced the question. "Mary, did you know Peter?"

"No. I didn't know him," Mary answered, her gaze rising to the executive floor, the balcony where Peter had last stood.

At once, Emily understood the connection and a knot of regret formed in her belly. "You saw it?" Emily hoped the child hadn't been there, that she hadn't seen anything. When the mortician mentioned how he died, she'd hoped that nobody saw Peter leap to his death. But the hope wasn't realistic, not with a courtyard that was almost always busy. "You were in the court-yard that day... weren't you?"

"I'd never seen anyone die before," Mary began to say, her eyes wandering again. "He just fell... out of nowhere. And... and he was alive."

"I am sorry for what that must have been like." Emily closed her eyes and listened as Mary explained what she saw, and tried to remain the teacher, holding Mary's arm, caring for her as if she were eleven again and someone had pulled her hair. She felt the warm touch of little hands wrap around her leg and heard the girl asking her mother why the lady was crying. Mary's hands came next, embracing Emily as she sobbed. *It'll be the last time, Peter. I swear it.*

"He didn't live long," Mary said, seeking Emily's eyes, anxious to tell her more, to finish what she'd started to say, and then be on her way. "We went to him, to help, but he only lived for a few minutes."

There was only one question Emily could think to ask. "Did... did he say anything to you?"

Mary pushed her eyes up and shook her head. "No. Well, hardly anything we could understand. Seeing you here, I know it was your name he was saying. I saw it on his lips."

"My name?" Emily repeated.

"Uh-huh. Then he mumbled about bringing something back." Before Emily could say another word, Mary reached into her coveralls and produced a small pouch made from old fabric.

Mary hung it from her fingers. Emily looked at it and then back to Mary, who motioned for her to take it as if it were criminal to have it a minute longer. Emily reached up and accepted the small pouch. "Was this his?"

"Uh-huh," she answered and gazed at the executive floor again. "Before he jumped, something else fell: small pieces of an index card."

"An index card? It was torn up?"

"Best I could tell, your man tore it before throwing it over the ledge." Mary motioned to the courtyard floor, adding, "There weren't a lot, but there were enough for the kids to run around the courtyard, grabbing at them, making a game of it, the way kids do."

"How did you know it was from Peter?" Emily asked, opening the pouch just enough to see parts of a torn card.

Mary held out her hand, a single piece of bloodied index card between her fingers. "He was still holding one of the pieces."

"What is it?" Emily accepted the final piece like it was part of a jigsaw puzzle, the final image unknown.

Mary shook her head, answering, "No idea... and, I don't think I want to hold onto it. You should take it."

"Take it," Emily heard herself repeating while she added the last piece to the pouch. "Mary, what about—"

"It was good to see you again," Mary interrupted and forced a smile, voice breaking as her old student looked around them cautiously. Watching Mary's eyes wander again, a strong urge to turn around took hold. Emily refused it, playing along with Mary's concerns. "And I am so very sorry for your loss."

"It was good to see you too," she answered. Dipping her head to face Mary's daughter, she continued brightly, "And I'm expecting that in a few years, we'll see plenty of each other!"

As Mary walked away, Emily glanced at the pouch. *What were you up to, Peter?*

With a cup of tea, Emily sat down at the small table where she dropped the pouch at the center. She held the cup and let the day fall out of her, eyelids heavy. They were red-rimmed and sore, sleeves damp from having wiped them dry so many times.

"Too much crying," she said out loud. "First Sammi. And now Peter."

What's the mystery? she questioned, inviting the questions, tired of mourning. Eager, she tugged on the fabric around the neck of the pouch, pulling until it came loose. She tipped the small bag on its side, the pieces of the ripped index card spilling into a small heap, the questions of its purpose deepening.

Lifting a larger piece to her nose, she realized what was missing. "No salt." The card was newer—but that couldn't be! "Nothing is new anymore."

Emily sized up the pieces and spread them apart, shuffling a few to where the torn parts matched up. She felt the spur of interest, a puzzle taking shape. At some point, she'd leaned up onto the end of her chair, a toe pinned to the floor, her leg shaking. It was a habit formed years before, while grading schoolwork, trying to understand what answers her students were after. She stared at the puzzle pieces for what seemed a long time, the mystery on the table seeming to mock her, leaving her perplexed and baffled.

Using the blue lines and the single red one, the index card was nearly whole again, and an image of Peter's body came to her, fractured like the index card. Broken. Emily set the last piece aside. It was the one Peter had held onto. The one he bled onto as well. There was a faint image of his fingerprint, the swirly ovals and rings that could have been used to identify that he'd had the index card. What did these pieces have to do with him? Had he died for them? Had he died *because of* them?

There were numbers printed on the index card, a new puzzle presented to capture her attention. "Nobody wrote these by hand," she exclaimed, taking a sip of her tea and pressing her finger against one of them. "A computer? Like from an old printer?"

Jerry would know? she wondered. Thinking back to the mall and the electronics store, his help in getting some of the computers working again. There were still a few of them around, but they were leftovers from a time before, the parts impossible to replace once they died. "Could be they're working on the executive floor?"

In a hushed voice, Emily read the numbers aloud with the hope of stirring a memory, but they remained unfamiliar. The digits didn't match any of the sequences she recalled from school or the lessons she taught today. Not PI or Fibonacci. No famous addresses or dates or even phone numbers. To understand what they were, she'd need someone from the executive floor.

"Richard Chambers. Maybe he'd know." His wife had been a junior executive and reported to Peter. She might have shown Richard a card like this. If anyone could help tell Emily what these numbers meant, it would be Declan's father.

A pair of shadows shuffled past her door, the afternoon bell ringing out. Before sweeping the table clean of the puzzle, Emily jotted the numbers down, a stone and parchment in hand. It was safer this way. Easily washed if questioned. Once the numbers were copied, she put the pieces back in the small pouch and tucked it into her coveralls. There had to be more to Peter's death than despair that led him to leap from the executive floor. In her heart, she felt that there was more, and now she had a clue.

NINE

"How can this be?" Declan asked, spoon clanking against the bowl while he dug in for another mouthful. He stopped and clapped the back of his hand to his head. "My brain! What the—"

"Slow down! You got a brain freeze." Sammi chuckled, stealing a spoonful of his ice cream. When he realized, she offered her bowl. "Try some of this."

"It's too good," he said sloppily, chocolate dripping down his chin. "How is it even possible?"

"I dunno," she answered, eyeing the lights, waiting for instructions. "Food just comes out of the dispenser."

"Just comes out?" He lifted his head, grinning. "We could use this back in our building."

"We could," she returned, lowering her voice, uncertain if it was okay to mention home, what used to be her home. The lights didn't change, though, the moment free to do with as she wished. They could make love again. How many times was that? Maybe a game. Or maybe eat whatever they could think of from the world before. Pizza perhaps?

"I forgot how amazing this is! How does the machine make

it?" he asked, tipping a full spoon, melted ice cream dripping. It wasn't the first time he'd questioned the machine, and she sensed him becoming anxious and more curious as the days passed, their time in the room growing long. He wanted to know more about what was happening beyond the room, his questions going unanswered. Declan sat back, the earlier smile gone. "Are you going to work again?"

"Probably," she answered, glancing at the lights.

"And what is with those?" he asked, following her gaze. Before she could answer, he asked, "When can I leave? When can I see my family again?"

There was edginess in his voice. Impatience too. Worst yet, when he was like this, she felt the cold, felt him becoming distant. She set their bowls down and took his face between her hands, shaking her head. "I don't know. Not yet, anyway." She cautiously looked to the lights, but they had nothing to say. *Why can't he hear them like I do?* "You don't have to leave. You can just stay inside here." She leaned up to his ear and whispered, "Maybe later we can share more than the ice cream?"

"I'd love that, but—" She eased back onto her feet, sitting up. "Sammi. I just need to know more, and I need to see my family."

"Declan—" she began, interrupted when the lights flickered.

"You'd better get going," he said. His voice had gone cold again. "I know you can't be late."

"You heard them?" For a moment, she thought he'd finally heard them. When she turned back and saw his face, she corrected herself, "You didn't, though. Did you?"

"Uh-uh. But I recognize some of the sequences. Time for you to go, right?" he asked. She collapsed into his arms, offering no warning, and kissed him hard.

"I can't even guess how bored of this place you must be. It'll work out, though. Okay?"

"Sammi, I want you," he answered, leveling his eyes with hers. "But I need answers too."

"But the waiting has been fun, right?" she asked with a hopeful laugh. A brighter flash. A faster sequence. She couldn't wait for him to answer and hopped out of the bed. Before leaving, Sammi remembered the gift. Now was a good time too. It was perfect. She ran to the empty wall and pressed her palm firmly, the inside of it clicking, a table and chair emerging.

"You mean that's been in the wall the whole time?" he asked, brow raised.

"But wait, there's more," she said, trying to sound like the old television commercials. From a drawer, she fished out a ream of paper, the corners precise, the edges clean. She struck a winner with it, his smile drawn downward, awestruck. Next to the stack of paper, she produced a half dozen pens and pencils. Excitedly, she blurted, "I thought you might want to do some writing."

"Sammi," he began, but his words choked. He got up to cross the room and ran his fingers over the blank pages and picked up a single sheet, bringing it to his nose to breathe in the smell, a huge smile forming. He cleared his throat and placed his hand on hers. "Sammi, when you died, I participated in your cleaning and passing. In my pocket, I had the writing stone you'd given me. Do you remember that?"

"The classroom." Nodding her head, she pulled his hands together and pressed them to her heart. "I remember giving it to you."

"When you were cleaned and ready for passing, I made a promise that I'd never write again."

Sammi flinched, his words like a slap. She squeezed his hands and shook her head. "Declan, you don't get to keep that promise. I'm here, and I'm alive, and..." she started, but then lost her words in the guilt of his decision. "You don't get to keep that promise! Okay?"

"I know," he answered, trying to sound understanding. "What I am saying is that I'm going to write. I'm trying to tell you, thank you."

"You," Sammi said, eyes stinging. She slapped his chest and handed him another gift. "I got index cards too. You can write notes on them like character names and plot points. Stuff like that." Declan's hand snapped the index cards from her grip. He turned them over as though recognizing them. "Well, you're welcome very much," she said timidly.

"Sorry, I didn't mean to startle you," he said quickly, glancing at the desk and then to her. "I'm just really excited, is all. Thanks for getting these for me."

"That's all right." There was something more, though. She sensed he was holding back. The lights were urging her to leave. Sammi slipped her hands free of his, saying, "I hope you get some writing done."

"Sammi?" he asked, before she was out the door. "Where are my coveralls? The ones from home?" His question stung her. But it wasn't the question that stung—it was that he still considered their old building home. She wanted to correct him. To tell him that this was their home now.

"Why would you want those old things?" she asked, the idea of wearing them seemed ridiculous.

"It's the writing stone you gave me," he answered, his words hurried and direct. "I'd like to use it a little."

"I'm sorry, I have to go to work," she said, voice shaky as the lights flashed faster. Pointing to the bed, she added, "Check the drawers. They should be there." The lights played back faster, Declan glaring at them. Sammi's chest thumped, her heart racing to match the sequence. Her reaction felt forced, artificial, and a strange sense came over her: fear.

TEN

Declan said nothing as Sammi stammered at the door, words spilling hurriedly while the lights spoke to her. She raised her arm and pointed at the bed, then beneath it, before spinning around to answer the lights. For a moment, he thought he was going to puke. He thought he was going to scream and smash the lights, her reaction to them unnatural. What the hell was going on in this place?

He held his tongue and locked his arms and legs when she quickly spun back and waved her hand as if everything was fine. To her, everything was normal. But this was far from either and he pinched the table, knuckles turning white with fright. He raised his other hand to wave goodbye, uncertain that he could stay.

Sammi paused once at the door, lights beaming gray to white, blinking twice before the door opened. Air rushed in, lifting her hair and reaching deep enough to touch his face. Declan heard activity. It was distant and it gripped his ears. And it was enough that he wanted out of the room.

He rushed forward, craning his neck, trying to see down the

corridor. A row of people marched along an intersecting corridor. None seemed interested in looking at him, their heads were straight, firm, and their eyes glued to the lights on the walls. The sight of them made him wary. It left him feeling unsettled and worried.

The door shut abruptly, Declan shifting out of the way, its lips clapping loud enough to make him jump. He glanced over his shoulder, the lights dim. They were dark enough to make him wonder if he was seeing things. Maybe it was just paranoia—that was what he wanted to think, anyway.

Well, that's going to change, he decided and searched the drawers beneath the bed. In the second to last drawer, his fingers wrapped around the familiar feel of his old clothes. They stood out against the others; a blemish next to them. Was that all he was? Was that all that their commune was: a blemish? He couldn't help but compare this place—this seemingly perfect one—to his home.

He found Sammi's writing stone, and, with it, he found her lock of hair, the locket she'd worn up until the day she died. Guilt pressed him for having left it packed away in a drawer. The ugly twinge making him think he should have given it to her. But Sammi was different in this place, wasn't she? On the day of her cleaning and passing, he'd promised to forever hold onto her locket. Without thinking, he kissed it and held it tight. It was only sentimental, but with it, he felt a little more whole.

When he reached the last pocket of his old coveralls, the square outline of what he'd really been looking for was there. Carefully, he pulled from the pocket the index card his mother had brought from the executive floor. He took it to the table and placed it next to the stack of blank index cards Sammi gave him. They were all flat and smooth and with blue lines crested by a red one. The smell of salt was missing too, the index cards coming from the same place.

"It had to be from here?" he said, speaking to himself. And the numbers on it? Those were meant for the machine too. He thought of the executive floor and how the burly executive guards pushed his father around looking for the satchel. They wanted the index card, the numbers on it. But why?

He clenched his jaw, anxious about the path his mind was taking. What was the connection to the executive floor? "End of Gray Skies?" It had to be. They were the only ones with knowledge of the machines. "Or so they said."

His mother's face came to him, and he closed his eyes, trying to recall anything he'd ever seen before her death. Declan glanced around at the room, ideas spinning like a whirlpool. He'd seen his mother dead. His sister too. And Sammi, of course. Or had he? It was the only logical thought. They'd never been dead at all. The mortician brought them to the machine, and it was here where they recovered. How many others? And who were the people in the corridor?

Declan dropped, shoulders slumped, the questions overwhelming. The weight of them had him doubting what was real and what wasn't. Touching the locket, Sammi was real. He felt her in a way he'd never had before. They could stay in this room. Together like she said. Couldn't they?

Noise from the corridor bled through the door and Declan forgot about the worries. The questions that came with End of Gray Skies returned. What happened? And how could Sammi and his family be here? He searched his mother's index card, reading back the five rows of numbers. And searched the lights after each. They said nothing. Showed nothing. No reaction or response.

"Five rows," he questioned, thumping the printed numbers. "There are five VAC-Machines. One for each ocean." Was that it? Each row belonging to a particular VAC-Machine? Declan returned to the door and waved the index card at the lights. He waited again, staring at them, letting *them* see him.

"Tell me something," he demanded, but in the glass there was only his reflection, his face warped by the curvature of the bulbs. Seeing how Sammi responded to them, he regarded their power, a reverence for them. Turning away slowly like they were an angry dog, he mumbled, "Might be for the better you don't see me."

But they did have hold of Sammi, and his mother and sister too. Declan flicked the index card, snapping the air. His mother had the answers. She'd know what the numbers meant. He picked up Sammi's locket, thoughts heavy. Who was he to challenge what they had now?

Lowering his head, he had everything he'd ever wanted. He had Sammi, and paper and pens and pencils and food. Everything he'd need to be a writer. Declan took a deep breath and pressed the tip of a pencil to the paper. Writing didn't make him free, and it didn't answer the questions that brought him here.

The questions were his burden: shackling reminders that needed to be answered. He could never write until then. Resigned, he buried the index card in his pocket and went to the door. Bracing the wall, he ran through the decision to leave. What he'd seen on the beach was real. His mother and sister were there. He'd certainly felt his mother's touch. Hadn't he? Doubt nagged and countered the logic of what could and could not be. But Sammi was alive. That meant it was possible. It also meant, he was going to find his mother. And with her help, they were going to find out the meaning of the numbers, and why the End of Gray Skies had failed.

Standing at the room's entrance, same as he had so many times already, Declan waited for the illumination to brighten around the door. But the door stayed closed. Shifting, he shuffled forward and back waiting for a sensor to see him. Nothing happened.

He tried recalling if Sammi had touched anything or if she'd waved a hand to activate the door. When nothing happened,

Declan pushed against the seams, feeling for an opening, or maybe a lip to dig his fingertips into. But the door was flush to the wall, and, if not for having seen Sammi come and go, he'd never know that it was a door.

"I'm locked in," he exclaimed, cold sweat running down the back of his neck. His brow turned slick and cold, the feeling of being trapped growing. "I can't be trapped here."

Moving back to his desk, he considered breaking one of the table legs and using it to pry the door open. Picking up a pen, he saw Sammi's locket, the lock of hair, and stopped to take it, squeezing it.

Sammi, he thought.

"It can't be that, can it?" he asked, peering cautiously at the lights like he'd just cheated his way out of the game. "Or maybe it *is* that simple."

Declan stepped to the door and waved his hand, tightening his grip on Sammi's locket. At once, the door's edges glowed until the light became hot white, flashing twice and opening with a whoosh sound.

Startled, Declan jumped back, his eyes bugging wide. He waited to see if anything would happen, any alarms or executive guards. But there was nothing. From his hand, he revealed Sammi's locket, and then smiled and pushed it into his pocket. Somehow, the machine *knew* Sammi. How far would Sammi's lock of hair get him? Could it open all the doors?

Declan sucked in a breath, nerves climbing when the strange smells and odd sounds reached him. Men and women walked by, staring aimlessly, parading past without so much as a glance in his direction. He expected someone to give a cursory glance, or maybe a nod, but they looked past him as though he didn't exist. Following their procession, Declan slowly poked his head out the door, feet remaining planted inside. What he saw then turned his body rigid with fear as black as coal. He dug his fingers into the doorframe. His insides twisted with a stir of nausea, the creamy ice cream creeping into the back of his throat.

"What is this place?" he muttered, forcing a step, and leaving the safety of Sammi's room. Over and over, he reminded himself that he was here to get answers. Wherever... or whatever *here* was.

ELEVEN

It didn't take long for Emily to find Declan's father. It was the voices. Heated. An argument rising from the courtyard. She recognized Richard Chambers' tall figure stumbling near the middle of the crowded building. Her stomach tightened when his slurred words echoed, broken and incoherent. Reluctantly, she hurried into the open area. Declan's father was drinking already, the time early, his fight with another man escalating over a bag of potato juice. Stretching high on his toes, clothes untidy, he leaned heavily against the market seller's table, the yells reaching a fevered pitch.

The merchant was Jason Toomey, a past student who was the spitting image of his younger brother, Rick. From the unkempt and sometimes greasy hair to the narrow point in his chin and thin nose, she'd always recognize a Toomey. Cautious, Emily approached the table, passing those waiting in line. Jason glanced over, acknowledging her with a short nod, and continued to argue. Declan's father paid her no mind, yanking on the bag, fingers tightening like a vise.

"I promise to bring the vouchers tomorrow!" Richard spat. A desperate plea washed over his hard expression. "Please."

"Look, my pops said I can't. You still owe for last week!" Jason answered, jerking the bag hard enough to pull Richard. Declan's father fell forward, coverall shirt lifting to show he was mere skin and bone, landing on the market table, clumsily rolling while comments came from the line behind them. When the table legs screeched, Emily searched the upper levels to see if the commotion had drawn any attention, the executive guards standing watch. A pair monitoring the merchants gave them a cursory look but lost interest. Red-faced, Jason Toomey clutched the bag and spoke through his teeth, "Bug off before you get me shut down!"

Richard opened his mouth to speak, stopping when Emily shoved her hand beneath his arm. Muscles straining, the angle awkward, she got him back to his feet and standing on his own. *So skinny*, she thought, worried by his frailness, wondering when he'd eaten last. This wasn't the man she'd known. He'd become a shadow of himself. And even that was fading.

There was the smell too. Days of it. Impossible to avoid. It seeped from his pores, along with the slight stink of vomit and urine. Wrinkling her nose, she fought the urge to gag and directed her attention to Jason. "Mr. Toomey," she started to say, holding Richard's arm when he tried leaving. "I'm going to get that, okay?"

"Well, yes, Ms. Stark. I suppose that'd be fine," her former student answered. Jason glared at Declan's father, who'd started waving an objection. Like the shadow of his old self, there was a glimmer of pride in his bleary eyes. It was there a moment, brief but soon gone, and Richard licked his lips when payment was completed.

"You don't have to do that," Richard belted, eyes fixed on the prize. His words were firmer while trying to sound sober. "Really... really, I don't want you to."

"Let's go, Richard." Emily helped steady him and turned them away from the table. This wasn't the first time she'd seen what could happen with this stuff. It wasn't at all like the beer or wine she'd swiped from the garage with her friends when they were too young to know what was good and what was not. As a teacher, she'd seen how bad it could get. It was the withdrawals, the convulsions. That's what was going to happen to Declan's father if he didn't get a drink soon. It wasn't that he wanted it, but it was what he *needed* to survive.

"You didn't have to do that," he repeated, struggling with the words.

"But I wanted to," she answered quickly. Caution entered his expression, a peculiar smile joining. "I wanted to, so that we could talk. But you'll have to pay me back. That's okay, isn't it?"

"Uh-huh, pay you back." He relaxed, lips curled to a musing smile. "I always pay my way."

"I won't need it—"

He gave her a lazy wink as she spoke, his eye stuck halfway. When she nodded, he jerked his arm free of hers and spun around. "Always pay my debt. Ain't that right, Toomey, ya cocksucker!"

"Richard!" The outburst came like a slap in the face, the abruptness and speed alarming. The guards were looking now, and she wrapped her hands tight onto his arm, turning him back around. Peering over her shoulder, Jason Toomey ignored the insult, a middle finger appearing briefly. Emily walked faster.

"Where we going?" Richard asked, shoes scraping while keeping up.

"My place," she answered. When he cocked his head, brow lifting, she quickly added, "We have to talk."

"I can do that," he said, studying the bag, the potato juice sloshing.

"I stopped by your place, but another family was there," she said, asking questions to keep his mind occupied.

He looked at where he lived with Declan, mumbling, "That

floor is for families only." His focus returned to the bag. "I don't have a family anymore."

"Families?" she replied, realizing with Declan gone, Richard was alone. In a little over a year, the man had gone from a family of four to no family at all.

"Commune rules. I got no right taking a dwelling meant for a family," he answered with a shakiness that warned of what was coming. She handed him the bag. At once, his eyelids peeled back and he cracked the neck, guzzling deep and long.

"Not too much," Emily warned. There were rules about drinking outside the privacy of your dwelling. She took hold of the bag, Richard objecting with another swig, juice running to his chin.

"Here ya go." Handing it back, he swiped the tip of his face, catching the last drops and slurping them from his hand. She didn't mean to stare, her insides shrinking when he saw her looking. Shame filled his eyes. "I need it, is all. Since Sandra and Hadley. I need it or I get sick."

"Richard, I didn't come to you about your drinking," she said, returning the bag to him. "I'm here because I need your help."

"My help?" he said with a laugh. Mumbling again, he spoke into the bag, "Nobody needs my help."

"You might know some things that could help me."

"What kind of things would I know?" he asked, eyes pegged to the side while he kept his head forward.

But before Emily could answer, Richard dipped his head and grunted. He dropped to his knees, the bag falling, the remainder of its contents spilling across the ground. And before Emily could do anything about it, Richard Chambers tumbled onto his back, body arching upward, a seizure stealing his dignity.

A day. It had been nearly twenty-four hours since Emily brought Richard Chambers to her dwelling. A man's heavy breathing and loud snoring sounded strange in her home. Foreign. While it was odd, she was relieved that the fits were brief and had now stopped. Sitting at the table, a cup of tea between her cupped hands, she patiently waited for him. An arm's length away, there were questions sitting in a tidy bundle, one of them bloodied by Peter's death.

She sat up when a long stretch of nothing came, Richard's breathing stopped. It was followed by a gasping cataclysm, the snores continuing. Each time after, she feared that his heart would give out. Emily closed her eyes, hearing his cries that had come during the deepest part of the night. That's when he'd woken up screaming, calling out the names of a dead woman and child. Would he remember it? Would he remember telling her that he wanted to die, insisting she help him end it all? And if she was being honest about it, there was one point during the night when she thought that it might be the most humane thing to do.

Soon, the man in her arms fell away, body weakened, his cries fading to a whimper. Emily welcomed the respite. Needed it. For now, the painless silence of his unconsciousness was the best place for him. Sitting back, sipping the tea, the towel around his middle slipped. She wondered if he would be offended when he found she'd bathed him and given him a shave. *Could be, he won't even notice.* Glancing toward the kitchenette, finding the waste recycler bin, tufts of his old coveralls hung over the lip. Emily brought the cup up to her lips and looked over the brim to check on her guest. The towel continued to fall, sliding enough to leave his bottom exposed. She caught herself staring, a warm flush on her face.

"It's been a while since you've seen anything like that," she chuckled, and went to cover him. Richard stirred, eyelids opened wide, staring up. Breath caught, she froze, the towel still in her hands. Unsure of what to say, she blurted, "Morning."

"Where? Huh?" He bolted to a seated position, gazing down at himself. "I'm... why am I naked?"

"About that," she cringed, red-faced. Emily grabbed Peter's old coveralls, saying, "I got these for you."

"What... what about mine?"

She shook her head, glancing at the trash bin. "I tossed them." Urging him to dress, she added, "These are newer. And clean."

"Uh-huh," he answered, standing, the clothes still in her hands.

"Tea?" she asked, suddenly nervous. Richard ran his hands over his face and rubbed his cheeks, realizing he was shaved. "I hope you don't mind. I wanted to help."

"Thanks." A nod. A small gesture. But in it she saw gratitude, an appreciation. He slipped the coveralls on, the sleeves and legs a bit too short, Declan's father being taller than Peter. "They're a little tight."

"I can get another—" she began, hanging a thumb over her shoulder.

"These are fine," he replied, groggy but lucid. "Tea. Sounds good."

"Tea it is," she said, wishing she'd ridden the bike to charge the batteries. "Warning, it's not that hot."

"I'm sure it's fine. It's better than what I've been drinking too."

"You're right about that," she chuckled. Embarrassed, she shrank back and shook her head. "I am so sorry about that."

To her relief, Declan's father was laughing, a pair of dimples appearing. "It's quite all right." He turned serious then. "I had the shakes, didn't I? The bad ones."

"It wasn't so bad," she lied, hoping to ease his discomfort. She realized then where Declan had gotten his good looks. Was that why she was feeling nervous? *This is silly*, she thought, pushing the sentiment away. He sat across from her, cup of tea in hand and gaze falling to the small pouch between them.

"It's good," he said, lifting the cup, gaze remaining on the pouch. "I appreciate what you did at the market. I'll get out of your hair in a few minutes."

"No need to rush," she told him, questions building.

The corner of his mouth dipped, hesitating. "Well. I need to get more... you know, soon."

From beneath the table, she put a bag of potato juice on the table, placing a cup alongside it. His brow lifted, eyes round and more alert. Carefully, she poured some into the small cup. Richard flinched when she spilled a few drops. "Sorry."

But Richard didn't hear her. By then, he was fixated, licking his lips. He drank down what was handed to him. "More," he demanded.

"I'm sorry, but no," Emily told him. He scowled, the good looks replaced by anger. "I need your help, and I think I might be able to help you too."

"Help me?" he scoffed.

"Give the monster a sip," she told him, pouring a little more. He drank eagerly. "But just enough to ease the fits."

"You're talking about weaning?" he asked, staring hard at the bag. "My hands are already shaking."

"I have something for that," Emily offered. He followed her with his eyes when she opened a cabinet. From inside, she fished out a bag of candy, the sugar in it too much. The older it got, the sweeter it tasted, and sugar was what he needed.

When she handed it to him, he frowned and asked, "Seriously? Candy?"

"It's the sugar; it'll help. But don't eat a lot, otherwise you'll throw it up."

With a nod, he pulled out a piece, staring at it a moment before biting down. After a minute of chewing, he began to blink fast. "Gosh, that's sweet." Richard leaned forward and propped his elbows. "How can I help you?"

"It's inside," she said, wagging a finger at the pouch. He picked it up and began opening the top. Emily braced as though ghosts were going to escape. And in a way, it was Peter's ghost haunting what was inside. "Pour it out."

"Okay," he said, dragging out the word, tipping the bag until pieces of the index card fell. She didn't have to ask. Richard knew the task and started assembling the puzzle. She helped, recognizing the edges, his eyes moving from piece to piece. In them, she saw his interest blooming. The sugar was helping too, though he might not have noticed it. As he worked the pieces, his hands had already steadied. When the puzzle was done, he said softly, "What do we have here?"

"An index card with numbers."

"That it is," he commented, nudging one of the pieces. "Where did you get this one?"

"This one?" Emily sat back, chair creaking. There was more than one? Of course there would be. "Then you've seen one like it?"

"Sandra, my wife. Her index card had rows of numbers on it too. She said it had something to do with the VACs."

"The VAC-Machines?" Emily regarded this, realizing the count. "Five machines. Five rows of numbers."

"That's right." He started to say more but then stopped, concern silencing him.

"What?" she insisted.

"Sandra said it had to do with the End of Gray Skies too."

"Do you still have it?"

Richard didn't reply but picked up the piece stained with Peter's blood and flipped it over, studying it. "Declan took it with him. He said that he wanted to find the answers."

"You let him go with it?" Emily said, voice rising with fright for her student. Richard reeled back. "I didn't mean to—"

"No, you're right to have said that." He chomped a piece of candy, chewing fast. He surprised her then. "I shouldn't have let him go. That's why I'm going after him."

"Going after him?" Emily shook her head. "Declan could be anywhere by now."

"Perhaps. But there's one place he would have gone to first," Richard said, finishing another piece.

"The machine," she answered, thinking of her father. If he were here, he'd know what the numbers meant. For all she knew, he might have been the one to come up with them in the first place.

Holding the bloodied piece, Richard asked, "Where did you say this came from?"

"It was Peter Wilkes, a senior executive," Emily said. Richard sat back, dropping the piece at the mention of Peter's name. "He jumped from the executive floor."

"Good!" Richard spoke without emotion. "He deserves to be dead."

The words jabbed her heart, emotion clawing into her reply. "Why... why would you say something like that?"

Richard's lips thinned until they were gone, a long pause settling between them. "Because I'm certain Peter Wilkes is the one who killed my wife and little girl."

"What?!"

Richard leaned forward. "And who was this Peter Wilkes to you?"

"My chosen," she answered. "Before he jumped, he tore the index card and threw the pieces over the ledge."

"I didn't know that he was with you," Richard said, sounding apologetic. He squinted and shook his head, stammering. "Or maybe I did and didn't remember. Sandra, she was the one who knew everyone. Listen, I'm sorry I said that."

"But you did say it!" Emily glared. "What did you mean by that?"

Anger returned. It shined from his eyes with a fierceness that had Emily backing away. "When my wife was dying, she told me that Peter Wilkes did this to them." Instinctively, she brought her arms up. She didn't know this man well enough and the look on his face had her on her guard. Red-faced, his eyes drifted to the bottle. "I think if he wasn't protected, I would have killed him. But... but I didn't do a thing."

"Peter would never..." Emily said, stopping to wipe her eyes. "I can't believe that."

"Doesn't matter now. He's dead. They're dead too." Richard dropped the bag of candy onto the table and took the potato juice. He poured a stiff drink, swallowing it in a single gulp. Emily couldn't muster an objection. Not with what was just shared. "Declan. He's all I've got now. I'm going to bring him home."

"Then I'm going with you," Emily announced and poured herself a drink. She gagged and choked and was sure it'd come back up in a hot gush. She grimaced and shook but held it down. There were too many questions that needed to be answered. "If the index cards have something to do with your family and Peter and the End of Gray Skies, then I need to find the truth."

TWELVE

FIVE YEARS EARLIER

Isla shook herself awake, eyelids flicking open, her gaze locked on a ceiling that wasn't familiar. It wasn't just that, though. The surface was smooth. Too smooth. Surreal. She stirred and lifted her arms beneath a thin sheet covering, her clothes missing. The aches were gone too. The ones deep in her bones and inside her chest. They'd become as much a part of her as a limb, an ever-present reminder of her slow demise.

The beach. She sat up, feeling brighter than she had since the cancer was first revealed. *The burning rain. I was with Mr. Stark.*

Goosebumps raced across her bare skin when she swung her legs over the edge of the bed. She ran her hands up and down her body and across her head and face, searching for the injuries that should have been there but weren't. *This isn't possible.*

When she reached for the chemo port above her chest, the lights on the wall flickered, the sting in her eyes registering the flashes as words. She shook her head, confused, but listened and heard them. They told her to get dressed, told her to put on the coveralls. She did as asked, confusion playing like this was a strange dream.

I'm not awake. I'm on the beach, dying.

Death was inevitable. Without Nolan, why live? The run into the rain was meant to end the agony. She was dying already, what difference did it make if she ended it sooner? Fingers splayed, Isla dared to pinch the flesh above her breast. The medical port was gone, her skin whole. Not just whole. She was without pain.

"This isn't a dream," she said, chancing the words.

"Work," the lights replied. Or did they? She shut her eyes, the flashes bleeding through in warm pink colors, insisting she go to the door.

"I will," she answered, the urge to learn more about this place resting. *But not forgotten*, she told herself, the insistence quickly fading as the lights grew brighter. "I'll leave now."

Her hand was tiring, fatigue finding her fingers with a cramp, the number of words written terrific. Isla dropped the pen and wrung out her hands while glancing back at what was added to the lab journal. Like the words, a long day was behind her, and twenty new earth samples were analyzed. Rocking on her heels, heart lifting with the end of the day near, Isla stopped and grimaced. The lights were busy again, blinking and telling her to keep working.

Deep down she wanted to be back in her room, beneath the covers with her legs tucked close to her chest. In the warm bubble of her body heat, she'd be alone with Nolan, the memories of him, his smell, his touch, all of him. But the lights made that impossible. She was a scientist, the lights speaking with an impossibly loud voice that frustrated her. How did they work? How was it she couldn't ignore them? They were like a kind of hypnosis, the suggestions they delivered as real to her as her own thoughts.

Turning to her terminal, the screen reflected a warped image of her face and the lab behind her. Isla glimpsed her image and tried to see the impact of the chemotherapy, and what the cancer had done to her face. By all rights, she should look terrible, rotting from the inside out. Hair thin, skin taut and a sickly color. Only, the image was deceiving. She looked as though she hadn't been sick a day in her entire life. And she certainly looked nothing like she had at the mall when she'd left the service tunnel and walked into the caustic rain.

Moving closer to the screen, she gently pulled the skin around her eyes and forehead. There wasn't a single wrinkle or blemish. There wasn't a single sign that she'd been sick. Running her hand through her hair, it was lush and thick, the color rich. Did this place do something to her?

She dared to open the front of her top, lowering it until the cleavage appeared on the screen. Where was the chemo port? There was no scar or any signs it had ever existed. Clutching her chest, she mouthed, "Did this place cure my cancer?"

Eyeing the lab journals, it was her writing on those pages, the written words that said more than had ever been intended. She'd confirmed in the pages that ten years had passed since the clouds fell. It had also been ten years since Nolan's death too. But to her, his face and voice, even his smell, were as though they'd been together just yesterday.

Isla waved at the screen, the glassy panel coming alive. A bright white flash made the pixels dance before settling to a cool black background with rows of green text. From the bottom of the terminal, an animated keypad appeared, the illumination hovering beneath her fingertips. The eagerness to finish the day was winning her attention. She ran a finger along the lab journal and began entering the day's data.

A penance, she thought distantly, the word rising out at the back of her thoughts. From the corners of her eyes, she glimpsed the lights. *This is some kind of penance for having stepped into the caustic rain to end my life.*

Today was one of those days where work had been a chore, the minutes dragging, her feet too. The repetition of it was a mind-numbing hell. The sooner it was finished, the sooner she'd be back to her room. A page typed, Isla transcribed the day's activities while thoughts drifted to the trip with Nolan. What would have happened to them if they'd never stopped at the mall? *Probably would have died, anyway.* And as she finished, she wondered if that would have been better.

Flipping the page, she tore its corner, the paper ripping to finish the day and prepare the journal for tomorrow. When she turned back to face the screen, she found that she'd inadvertently typed Nolan's name, and had added comments about the mall and the carousel. She'd also typed a happy birthday, remembering that today was Nolan's birthday. *I'd never forget your birthday. Never.*

"Happy birthday, Nolan. I love you," she said, speaking to the empty lab. Scrolling to the top to check her work, the happy birthday hadn't been her only slip, the date was a year off. Stare rising to the ceiling, her jaw fell open. Isla realized that she'd mistakenly entered the work under the prior year, overwriting the older entry.

"What the actual shit," she muttered and thumped the desk. All hope of returning to her room early was dashed. Resigned to fix it, she talked to herself, a growing habit, "Isla, don't cry over spilled milk."

Stepping back and stretching, she inched onto her toes until the knots in her back were gone. Daring a look beneath the desk, she would have avoided the journals altogether if not for the mistake. Like the lights, there was a mystery in them. Every page was written with her handwriting. And every page had the corner torn. Isla remembered none of it, though. Where did the ten years go?

"For another time," she said, nervously chuckling at the pun and yanking the lab journal from the previous year. Opening the cover, air brushed across her face. She dropped the journal next to the current one and fanned the pages until reaching the date. On it, she saw Nolan's name, the sight unexpected. Bewildered, she ran her fingers across the inky-black, confirming it was her handwriting. But in this journal entry, there was something different: a single letter, *E*. "Uh-uh. I never wrote this."

It wasn't just his birthday either. She'd also added the date of his death. Shaking her head, she cowered back with arms crossed, on her guard. Worry building, the moment lasted long enough to glance at the lights. They stayed dark as she grabbed another journal, repeating the check.

She flipped the pages in chunks until reaching the midway point with the same month and day, Nolan's birthday. The paper was already aging, dust irritating her nose. On it, Nolan's name was written like the others, her handwriting immaculate. There was a single letter too, different than the others, a *T*.

For the next ten minutes, Isla fished through every lab journal from the last nine years. Knees aching against the hard floor, the journals splayed in a semi-circle, the arch wide. They were opened to Nolan's birthday, and on those pages, she'd written his name along with the two dates that meant the most to her. For the previous nine years, she'd also given herself a clue. When the letters were pieced together, a single word was offered.

"Reanimate." What did that even mean? Breathing heavy, a paper cut stinging, she stood up, the lab rocking with a dizziness that rifled through her head. There were tears too. These weren't the manic tears of a person losing her mind, though. No, they were for the proof of having been here, having worked in this lab the last nine years without remembering a single day. "But why stagger the letters? What does reanimate mean?"

Suspicions blazing, ideas bouncing inside her head like a ball. She glimpsed the shine from the lights, the message intended for someone else. *Why stagger the letters, reanimate? Was it to hide the clue?*

Touching the side of her head, fixing her stare on the journals, "Maybe it's why I don't remember them." Focus returning to the lights, she spoke directly to them, asking, "What are you doing to me?"

"Work," the lights returned, the warning coming in a flash of brightness that struck the back of her skull like an icepick jabbed through her eyeball.

Hands raised to shield herself, Isla turned away, spelling out the letters, "R-E-A-N-I-M-A-T-E." She was facing the large steel door, its lone eye staring back at her, winking as one of the mechanical arms swung by. Were the answers inside there?

"That's where I have to go," she said in a tone guarded with fright. "The blood vials. Whose blood is it?"

Her heart fell hard and zapped the strength in her legs. If she'd written Nolan's name the last ten years, how many times had she regarded the vials filled with blood? How many times had these same revelations been questioned? Leaning against the desk, she also wondered whether she'd already been inside the vault and if she'd already found the answers.

The caustic rain, she thought wildly. "This repetition, it's because I gave up and went outside?"

THIRTEEN

PRESENT

Something was different; Sammi could feel it. Deep down inside the middle of her, it was a sense of something new that hadn't been there before. It was a good different, though. Wasn't it? A faint and maybe even silly grin was pasted on her face, thinking of an impossible and even marvelous thing happening. Sammi tried dismissing how she felt, questioning if it was a figment of her imagination. When an unexpected heat rushed through her, fast and fevered, it caused goosebumps and made her lightheaded. She regarded the machine; was it talking to her again? Cautiously, her gaze rose until meeting the lights.

The strobes shined and sang a flashy tune, a colorful sequence. Only, the message wasn't for her. Dread suddenly roosted inside her like a cancer. What if *what* she was feeling was the same thing that happened to Declan's family? Maybe she was aging like his mother and sister? She searched her hands, the skin still young and pure, the sight telling her it wasn't the same.

For a moment, Sammi thought warmly of Auntie Jane, and could hear her sweet voice talking about feeling butterflies. A flutter tugged inside her strong enough to tell her the butterflies were real. "It can't be." She covered her middle, dashing thoughts of what couldn't be. "Not yet. Not so soon."

"Falling," she muttered, clenching her hand where the injury had stolen her life and where the faintest possibility of life was beginning. The memory rifled through her, the waking nightmare making her shudder. "Harold pushed me from the balcony and... and I died, didn't I?"

Uncertainty washed over her, the machine unexpectedly feeling alien to her. Sammi nervously glanced around the room, but nobody seemed to notice that she'd stopped working. She knelt on the floor and watched feet shuffling back and forth, soil samples and rocks and other earthy things pounding atop the tables and conveyors. It was a mindless grind of sorting, identifying, and indexing. The theater returned to her with the opening in the roof, the blue sky beyond the gray fog. There was Declan too, his handsome face in silhouette, the sun blazing... but then, there was nothing.

"Nothing. Because I was dead." Sammi wrapped her arms around her front, fearful of the blank spot in her mind, the void as empty and soulless as those in this place. "What happened to me?" Concentrating until it hurt, she searched for the lost memories, unable to see beyond that last one.

"Maybe I was only unconscious." The lights suddenly came alive, streaming a message. Brighter than usual, louder, scolding like she was a child. Her eyes watered from a searing pain. Muttering past the demands of her body, she said, "I was brought here, and the machine fixed me."

"There was a cat too!" she yelled, and then grabbed her mouth, stifling the sudden outburst. Again, she looked around, waiting for someone to notice or question. They remained uninterested. "It was one of the feral cats that stayed with me," she continued, her voice now a whisper. A warm, fluttery wave bloomed inside her, bright like a child's face when listening to a story.

"The theater seat post!" she exclaimed, gripping her belly harder. She could feel that memory and sucked in a breath, holding it until the stabbing pain passed. Clutching the injury, fingers trembling, she asked, "Is that what I'm feeling?"

That pain had passed, and she remembered squinting to see Declan's face, forcing herself to keep her eyelids open so that she wouldn't miss any of the sun's return. She did so, no matter how bright it got. *I'd eat the sunlight*, she recalled having said once.

Warmth rose on her neck, prickling her skin as though she'd done something wrong. The lights attempted to direct her, but the flashes only added confusion. Sammi looked away, feeling ill. The dryness in her mouth was replaced by a sickly wet. Queasy heat took hold, stomach reeling, she folded over, and her insides splashed across the floor. Sammi heaved again, arching her back as she sucked in air.

When was the last time I've gotten sick? She thought back to Emily's classroom and the time she'd spilled her lunch, the soup violently disagreeing with her. The other kids had been cruel too. Of course, they'd always been cruel. "*Sammi Sunshine got sick*," a few of them had teased, having added another verse or two, the words thankfully forgotten. It was Declan who'd come to her side that day, shutting the others up. He'd knelt down next to her to pull her hair out of the way when she vomited. She remembered being afraid to look up at him, worried that he'd think differently of her. But he'd only wiped her chin and offered to walk her back home. Sammi clapped a hand over her mouth and wished Declan was with her now. She needed him.

Sammi waited for the lights to say something. And for what? Curious, she pretended to vomit again, heaving even louder and slapping the table, metal clanking like a gunshot.

The work continued. It was as if they'd no idea that she was missing.

Her belly flipped again, but it wasn't from being sick. No, it was the unlikely miracle returning to say it was real and that it was growing inside. Sammi froze, understanding the wonder that was a part of her and Declan. It was doing for her what she couldn't do for herself: their miracle was opening her eyes to this place. This wasn't a salvation at all. She didn't know what it was but understood why Declan had begun to ask questions. From above her, she caught a glimpse of flashing lights, the shine bouncing off everything in the room. It was getting easier to ignore them now and she recognized why.

"It's you," Sammi said, hugging her middle while standing to give the room a hard look. It would be the last time she'd ever be in here. She glimpsed a reflection of herself in the steel tabletop and took hold of her coveralls. "It's missing?" Without thought, she cut a curl from her hair and used a loose bit of wire to fasten it to her coveralls. At once, she felt like herself again. She felt good; she felt whole. "That's better."

A deafening sound pierced her ears, a brilliant white flooding her eyes. Instantly, her knees buckled and she fell against the table. Only once before had a sensation been so unmistakable, so painful. And it had been her last when she'd been pushed from the old theater's balcony and landed on her back.

Is this the beginning of death? she questioned distantly, gasping, trying to breathe past the assault. Beneath the unforgiving tones and incessant lights, there was torment, a fiery path traveling from her brain and down her neck and into her spine. It bore into her heart relentlessly, her flesh buzzing as though suddenly energized, the hairs on every part of her body standing on end. She shook hard enough to rock the table and had to pinch her thighs together when her bladder nearly let go.

Another minute more and she was certain she'd burst into flames.

What's happening? she cried inside, her face and voice frozen. Yet there was a vague awareness that this wasn't new, that this had happened before, inside the machine. Throbbing and alive, the burn behind her eyes eased somewhat, becoming tolerable. The explosion of brightness faded to a pair of soft, glowing spotlights that pulsed to the thrum in her ears. She knew the rhythm—the sequence, anyway—like a childhood memory of a nursery rhyme. It was a message. She was being programmed by the lights like she had that first time. "How can I know that?"

The pain began to dull, easing enough for her to stand straight and shake it off. She shut her eyelids tight, the bright colors bleeding through them, its voice turning mute. "It doesn't hurt anymore." Strength returning, she'd said that once before when her body lost the battle for life. Only now, it had a different meaning. "The lights don't hurt."

Opening her eyes, the commands came in rapid succession. The messages needled some, poking into her consciousness, repeating, stronger each time. Sammi shook her head until she became dizzy. She surprised herself then and turned away from them. Giddy, a laugh slipping, she was able to ignore them at will. There was a fading urge to look back, but the need to obey was gone. The earlier flutter returned, strengthening the sense of something new. Glancing across the workroom, the small conveyors carrying rocks and mineral samples, the lights glared, their brightness splashing rainbow shades off the iridescent coveralls. Peering over her shoulder for a brief moment, she said, "No more."

The fluttering grew stronger, its presence undeniable. And as a new heartbeat grew, the urge to listen to the lights was gone. "I'm listening to something else now." Sammi reminded herself that it had to be too soon and then leaned against the table, lifted her coveralls to reveal the injury that killed her. Her skin was smooth and without blemish, no sign of what happened in the theater. "If the machine could bring me back whole, then maybe the impossible is possible." And with that, a pleasing calm settled into her, and she felt the first kick of her unborn child.

FOURTEEN

Stranded. To Declan, it was like their eyes were lost, the life in them gone. *They're like a doll's eyes.* The thought creeped him out, but it was the best way to describe that numbingly cold stare. Did they actually see him? Did they see anything? Mindless bodies brushed past while he clutched Sammi's locket, using it like a key. The bright red tuft gave him a freedom to roam the corridor, the length of it daunting. The earlier terrors had eased some. Not a lot. But it was enough to stop the nervous sweat from dripping down his back.

Declan sidestepped to the left, a woman coming directly at him. *Stony eyes*, he called her, steering clear, unable to look away. She moved abruptly when the wall lights flashed, a knobby shoulder jarring his. "Whoa, sorry," he said mannerly, the bump knocking him sideways. She didn't budge or flinch and paraded forward with a dozen more behind her. "What is going on here?"

The corridor was busy, the traffic heavy, rows marching endlessly. All of them wore the same white coveralls he'd seen his mother and Sammi wearing. Hadley wore the coveralls too and nobody had black bands on their arms or any kind of insignia. The iridescence glinting in the machine's strange light, the place wasn't too dissimilar from his own courtyard, particularly on days when the market was open. Only there, at home, people spoke and smiled and there was a sense of camaraderie. There was none of that here.

Marching bodies churned forward—step after step, passing him in a mindless shuffle. Amongst the masses, he saw no children, no tether straps or parents in chase. There were no old people or even pre-adolescents, the youngest of them around his age. He stopped and jumped out of the way, a larger group rushing through. The crippled and maimed were missing too. This was an army. A strong army. What would a machine need with an army?

For the moment, he could only stand with his back to the corridor wall. Everyone was going someplace, needing to be somewhere. It was direction, the lights driving them. At once, it was overwhelming and left him feeling uncomfortable, homesick even. The fright from earlier returned with overwhelming force. "Sammi, where are you? I want to go home."

A man and woman stopped in front of him, their faces familiar, similar too, like they were brother and sister. The woman inched close enough for Declan to smell her. Only, there was no smell. Her skin was clear and smooth like a baby's, her hair perfectly in place.

If he didn't know any better, the two could have been the Stewart twins, the brother and sister who'd been in the accident last year while cleaning one of the waste recyclers. That was impossible, though. Both had died horribly. The brother knocked unconscious and falling in. The sister tried to save him, and both had drowned in the turbulent wash. His father shared the details of it with him and his mom. Hadley wanted to know what happened, but she was too young for such news. Little did she know, she'd become the news herself when the flu took her a month later.

"Can I help you?" Declan asked, unsettled by the long stare. But of course, they weren't staring at him. It was the lights above his head. He stepped aside, the pair gazing. Had they blinked? He didn't think so. A moment later, the lights flashed and the two were on their way. "I gotta get out of here."

Was Sammi becoming like them? She was affected by the lights, following directions too. She didn't know he was watching earlier that morning when she'd stood beneath the lights, her clothes gone, her body bathed in color. The sight scared him. In their lifetime, he'd never seen her obey anyone before—not like that. A dreadful thought occurred to him then. Was Sammi able to leave the machine?

This place was not what it seemed. It wasn't the oasis Sammi thought it was. And while she was blinded by what the lights told her, he couldn't share in the blindness; he knew this was a facade, the truth hidden deep inside the machine. It was deceiving them, taking their sight and twisting it so they saw what it wanted them to see.

Declan jumped, startled by the sudden shift in the colorful sequence. The bodies closest pivoted and changed direction, reacting immediately to the change in instruction. Declan didn't understand what the lights were saying. He didn't understand what Sammi was seeing, what everyone was seeing. "This is Sammi now," he mumbled, and then dropped his chin and continued forward.

The corridor opened into a round area that was a hundred times the size of their building's courtyard. His jaw dropped, a gasp ripping across his throat, "Oh man!"

He spoke loud enough to be heard. Nobody was listening, though. Bodies passed in rows of four and more, a few brushing lightly, one jostling him with a slight bump. The VAC-Machine was big. He'd seen it when his mother approached him on the shore of the black sand beach. But to look at this room, its depth and height, he was left shocked, even bemused. *How could something seem bigger inside than on the outside?*

But this isn't the heart. Is it? he wondered, the question of how the machine worked a concern. And then he remembered how deep into the ocean the machine went. A heart would be deeper. *It'd be somewhere safe.* This lobby, was that a good name for it? This lobby was just an exchange. There were more corridors. Many more. The openings lining the giant lobby. It meant that the one from Sammi's room was just a vein, a small one. "The lobby is a hub," he muttered, which was also like their courtyard—designed to empty traffic into and return it elsewhere.

There were thousands moving in every direction, seeming to know exactly where to step, no two ever bumping, bodies just missing one another. They never hesitated or waited as if every step was orchestrated like a perfect dance. He squinted until the iridescence connected and blurred into a stream, snaking all around him. There was a level of order to it that reminded him of the beehives Andie's videos showed them in class. Only, there was no queen here. Or was there?

Lights were here too. They were everywhere. And flickered nonstop as the iridescent waves rose and fell like a tide. A man of little weight and with a squished face turned course abruptly and bumped him hard enough to hurt. Declan spun around to say something, but the man was already lost, absorbed into a group draining into one of the corridors. When his other shoulder was hit, the same thing happened.

"Shit, I'm in the way," he realized. "They're following directions. A path."

The paths were predetermined. Declan glanced at the shiny black floor and expected to see the fixed drawings of a morse line like they used in the fog. Lifting a foot, there was nothing to see, but with the next bump, he was certain about the path. Ducking out of the way, he stepped left and right and then darted left some more. But this new position was worse than the first. A young woman barreled into him, her breasts bouncing against his chest.

"Sorry," he said, apologizing bashfully. He scurried quickly to the other side, finding a spot without any traffic.

It was the center of the lobby, and nobody was crossing where he stood. For the moment, he was safe while the bustle of traffic came and went. Looking up, the ceiling made of glass, Declan saw through the machine to the outside. He expected a rolling fog blanketing the view, but it was clear. High into the dusky blue sky, wispy clouds lumbered aimlessly. They were puffy and round and cottony-white and without threat. His knees went weak when the sunlight peered through, the bright edge of the sun winking as if to say, "You missed me this time, but come back tomorrow."

For a moment, the heat from the sun was on his face. It vanished suddenly and his body turned instantly cold when he saw his sister nearby. She wasn't more than thirty hands from him, her face empty, her skin pale like old meat. There were stony smudges cradling her eyes and her hair had become thin and was graying. Hadley was a ghost, a shadow that walked with the others.

"Hadley!" he yelled, unafraid of the machine hearing him. She turned without seeing him, continuing toward one of the larger corridors. "Hadley, wait!"

Too far, he thought, slipping past another man whose face was familiar like the Stewart twins. The balcony, he recalled. It was one of the men who'd been applying resin to the executive floor balcony. But he was dead? A fall. Declan dismissed the coincidence, running faster, chasing his sister. Only, this wasn't like the games of fast-tag they'd played as children. There was something wrong with her.

He pushed past the bodies around him, shoving one man nearly to the ground. His heart raced and thumped hard.

Flashes entered his eyeballs, striking. Shielding his eyes, there were bodies suddenly in front of him, arms out wide, hands pawing at him, holding him. At first, Declan didn't let himself believe it was intentional. Not until someone's fingers wrapped around his arm and another pair of hands clamped onto his shoulders, fingernails biting painfully into his skin.

"Hadley," he screamed, voice raw, the view to her clouded by bodies. They saw him now, and suddenly it seemed that a thousand or more were surrounding him and holding him. He climbed onto his toes, desperate to see his sister. Hadley was gone.

FIFTEEN

Isla had to stop and rest. Panting, she sat on her heels, toes bent painfully, and fell against the sheet metal. Cursing the sting, beads of sweat rolled into her eyes, her face plastered against the thin steel. The trek had only just started, yet she was already exhausted. Heart walloping fast, she gulped the air and wished she'd brought some water. She'd never been an active person, her days spent in classrooms and working in labs. And then there was the cancer which made her a prisoner to a chemo chair. God, how she hated it. Had she ever felt so cold? So sick?

Crawling through an air duct wasn't the kind of lab work she was meant to be doing either. She wanted to laugh at the crazy idea that got her this far. But of course, it wasn't crazy— not at first, anyway. And it wasn't on the spur of a moment either. It was months of planning, like it was some kind of jail-break. Her arms and legs twitched eerily and then began to tremble as if repulsed by the sudden activity of what she was doing.

It was months into the new year, the fifteenth time she'd been reanimated. She cringed at the idea, but that's what the clues told her to call it. *Reanimate.* Her lab journals were chock-full of notes planted by her. Blinking slowly, the thought of them made her head spin, sweat dripped from her brow. She ran a finger over her face and watched a drop plunk onto the sheet metal.

"By all rights, I should be dead." It wasn't just the cancer. It was the caustic rains that killed Nolan. From the lab journals, the going theory she'd worked up was that each year since that day on the beach when the rain cut through her, a new version of her was born. "Born," she laughed, the wording wrong. "Reanimated." It was the only fitting word for it.

Isla searched ahead, into the air duct's black depth. A mechanical churn echoed from inside the blood vault, the sound pinging along the metal. There was a clue waiting for her behind the mysterious door with the single window. From time to time, she'd hitch up onto her toes and look inside to see the mechanized orchestra of swinging arms and dancing blood vials. Not once had she ever seen a drop or slip. There was only order and perfection. But then one day, there was something new, something overlooked. It was small and tucked away in the shadows of the blood vault's corner. And that clue had led to an idea: a crazy idea.

It was a vent cover near the floor. When studying the walls and the ceiling and the floors, she imagined how the ductwork was routed, questioning if it was connected to her lab. With a chair on the lab table, climbing slowly until her body shook with fright, she listened to one of the ceiling vents. In it was the steady whirring of the robotic arms. When the sound matched the shadowy motions in the blood vault's window, she knew there was a way inside. It couldn't be the ceiling vent, though. That path had to drop to the blood vault floor, and that meant falling. What if she got stuck?

From the small portal window, following the rear corner, across the far wall, and into her lab, Isla found another vent cover under one of the lab tables. The cover was outfitted with simple spring clips and had easily popped off the wall. At one point she'd ducked out from under the table, glancing up at the lights which stayed dark and empty, uninterested in her pestering curiosity.

"One vial," she mouthed, peering into the vent shaft. "One sample." That's all she needed to analyze and get some answers.

An explosion echoed, blasting into her ears with a start. Isla jumped, realizing she must have started to fall asleep. The sheet metal was humid from her breath, and she drew a circle in the condensation, poking two dots for eyes and a squiggly line for a mouth. Grinning back at the face, the moisture dripped a crooked path and, when she moved to wipe it away, another explosion came, duller this time. Leaning forward, the metal buckled, showing her she was the source. She held in a laugh and thought of how Nolan would have teased that she'd scared herself.

Moving faster, turning twice, the first signs of soft light came into view, yellow blades cast across the shaft, shining bright enough to guide her. She crawled faster, knees knocking against metal ridges, bruising. She winced, but the familiar hum from the mechanical arms was louder now, urging her. Isla stopped ahead of the light, slowly waving a hand. She waited, listening for an alarm. Nothing came, the whooshing arms continuing the endless chore of work.

Lowering her face, she could see farther into the blood vault, and now she could smell it too. It had a sterile smell, utterly absent of... anything. Heart beating harder, faster, she rushed to remove the vent cover, fingers prying between the louvers. They bowed with a groan, a spring clip popping free. With one corner loose, she quickly went to work the others, fingers wriggling along the edge. The cover jarred open but caught her with its metal bite. She reeled back, staring at the cut on her hand.

"Careless, Isla." Her voice sounded tinny in the ventilation shaft, bouncing oddly. Her finger began to bleed, spattering onto the vent, a dull tick echoing with each drop. Shaking her head, she tore a piece of her coveralls and tied it around the cut, hoping it'd be enough. "I can't turn around now."

Breathing steadily, cool sweat beading above her lip, she turned her attention to the blood vault. The makeshift bandage was already sopping wet, the cut throbbing. It caused the cover to slip from her hand and tumble onto its corner, clanking heavy with a metal-on-metal crash.

"Fuck," she whispered, the noise clamoring in every direction, on and on. She shut her eyes until it stopped. Just how far did the vents go? How many rooms were connected? "Everyone had to hear that."

She listened for footsteps, the approach at an alarming rate. She waited for the holler of voices too. There was silence, the subtle push of the vent's air lifting her short hair. It was blowing strong enough to cool her nerves and encourage her to enter the vault. Sucking in a breath, Isla stretched her arms into the opening, and then carefully pulled her middle and legs through.

Blood oozed around the makeshift bandage, an image of the first-aid box hanging on the lab wall coming to mind. She could turn around? The bleeding was slower, the pulse more nagging, though. "I'll keep this trip short."

Eager to finally see what was in the vials, she ducked the robot arm, air whooshing past her head. It was riding from a narrow track in the ceiling, the elbow joints knobby, the rubber-tipped finger picking up a vial and then placing it down elsewhere. Isla nudged one of the vials, its crimson prize shimmering.

But there was more than just blood: each vial was marked. She thought of the computer next to her desk, the green and black characters displaying the lab's inventory. Everything, every single item ever used in the lab, was listed. Everything except the blood vault. Could the terminal decipher the numbers on the vial?

Spinning the vial around, Isla was shocked to read a name on the label. It was only the first initial, though, followed by a last name. Unable to contain her curiosity, Isla lifted it, tipping the blood. The glass was colder than she'd expected. The blood was dark and seemed less alive somehow compared to the bright red color seeping through her bandage.

"Who are you, M. Stephens?" Beneath the name, a barcode was printed. But it wasn't like the kind from before the clouds fell. And there was nothing like it in her lab.

Without warning, air brushed against her hair, forceful enough to startle. It was the robot arm, the rubber-tipped claw snapping, its jaw opening and closing near her ear. She could hear the motors, its internal gears whistling when in motion. It stopped and waited, the mechanicals quieting to a purr.

Frozen, she didn't know what to do. Her heartbeat thumped wildly enough she was sure her heart would leap out of her chest. The mechanical arm waited. But waited for what? When she made a turn to leave, it blocked her. The second mechanical arm swung into position, blocking both sides of her. Skin clammy, Isla bit down on her upper lip and shook her head.

They moved closer to her, rubber tips clapping again, the scent of their greasy lubricants filling her nose. Isla jumped and let out a shallow yelp when one of the arms swung in front of her face. It extended its rubber tips, and then snapped its jaws closed. When it opened its jaw again, the science she lived for replaced the fright. In the palm of the robotic hand was a long syringe that was used to extract the blood.

"Don't you stab me with that or I'll—" she began to warn, voice heated. The threat was a lie, her knees buckling, warm tears filling her eyes. She shook her head, trying to hold them back. A tear dropped onto her cheek when one of the arms swung around and nudged her hand. She peered down and the arm nearest to her nudged her hand again, an understanding telling her what the robot hands wanted.

Images of a farm came to her, a bed and breakfast she and Nolan had stayed at. His favorite breakfast was eggs and bacon, and there was nothing better than the freshest brown eggs the farm had to offer. "Fresh from the hen's bottom," he'd say; but, on that particular occasion, the hens didn't agree. Reaching beneath their feathered hold, he'd pulled out one or two eggs, kissing them with a hungry smile, which she thought was a bit gross. Most didn't mind, but that morning, one of them got it in her to peck his fingers until he let go of the eggs. It had even jumped at him and chased him clear of the nest.

"You want the vial back," Isla said, the farm incident putting a smile on her face. As if it heard her, the mechanical hand took the vial from her fingers. A pinch of embarrassment warmed her face, and she found herself apologizing to the machine. "I'm sorry... I should never have picked it up."

She felt silly for saying anything at all, the air rushing past again, the mechanical arms returning to their routine of lifting and moving, rotating and placing. Isla memorized the name and some of the label, repeating it to herself over and over while crawling through the vent. The answer wasn't in the blood vault. The answer was in the computer.

Isla stopped her return when motion bounced across the lab floor. It was the vent cover, when she dropped it. Someone did hear it. Vision narrowing, she focused on the opening, a shadow breaking across the light. She sucked in a breath and held it, lungs cramping immediately.

Someone was in the lab. She swallowed hard, throat closing while waiting to see if they'd leave. She just about died, heart stopping, a scream rising when a man's head appeared in the vent. The figure was in black, face silhouetted.

Blood draining, he motioned toward her and called out to her, not by name, but to ask, "What are you doing in there?"

SIXTEEN

"Hadley!" Declan screamed, guttural objections surrounding him. A low growl filled his right ear, a woman spitting while Declan struggled to free himself. There were too many now, their weight aching in his knees. His scream was answered with another rush, footsteps ascending, clopping loud enough to knife his heart with dread. When he tried jumping, the top of his sister's head appeared for a moment but then was gone.

Shouting, voice hoarse, sweat teemed across his head and ran down his face, the fight escalating. "The fuck off me," he shouted, jerking an arm from around his neck. Declan slipped free of the grasp, the light flashing like a convulsion, arms wrapping around his middle and his legs. "This can't be!" The lights were telling them to hold him. He was being held so that Hadley could get away.

Before they could regain a full hold, Declan bulled through the crowd. He kicked his knees high, painfully clocking a man's jaw, teeth breaking and skittering across the floor. *Move faster.* Fright fueled a run, the bodies coming at him two and three at a time. The crush of hands and shoulders bounced him back and forth, arms flailing, fingers diving through his hair. The crunch of another bone sickened him, but he didn't stop and threw a woman out of his way. Terror twisted through every muscle while he shoved and pushed himself to freedom.

"Hadley," he shouted. His sister was closer, thirty hands. Maybe less. But she still couldn't hear him, the heat of frustration building. Or was she made deaf and blind by the lights? Was she being told to ignore his pleas?

Declan followed her into the large corridor, the wave of attackers fading behind him. Their hands slipped from his side, and their fingers let go of his hair, a clump of it gone. A moment later, he was standing alone. Confused, Declan spun around to see a row of dead stares that was four wide and three deep. They waited in the lobby and wouldn't cross the threshold, the lights prohibiting it. When they began to disband, Declan shouted, "That's right. You'd better get moving."

He was closer to Hadley now. She was continuing, the corridor narrowing and the traffic heavier. It slowed her enough for him to catch up. Winded, breath whistling as he sucked and blew fast, he had to stop, the crowd jamming at the entrance of another corridor. A smaller one.

"This place is like a maze—" he began, voice breaking when eyeing the people around him. They were like Hadley. Faces wrinkled and old, their skin the color of ash. And their hair, it was colorless and drab, graying. He realized why the others didn't follow him. This corridor and the smaller one he was passing into, it was a funnel for people like his sister. "Hadley, what's happened to you?"

Hadley joined one of the lines entering the smaller corridor, Declan catching up, running until he was behind her. When he reached out, placing a hand on her shoulder, she turned around. But it wasn't her. His heart stopped, chest rising in an empty breath. It was his mother. "Mom?!" Her beautiful skin had become as pale as his sister's. Creases stretched around her eyes, etching deep grooves in this new leathery skin. She looked at him then, and for a moment, he thought she was going to say something. But she didn't see him. She didn't seem to see anything. She was like the others, the stare empty, her voice gone, expression gone too. Declan reached to touch her hair, feeling for the soft comfort he'd known as a child. But all he found was a brittle coarseness—an offense to life—dying.

"Mom, what's happening to you?"

Surprisingly, his mother spoke. "I'm ready now," she said slow and raspy. Her eyes grew wide, and, for the briefest moment, she saw him. His heart swelled instantly.

"Mom?" When her cold fingers touched his cheek, Declan took her hand. "I'm getting you and Hadley out of here!"

Her fingers slipped from his hand, an old man clutching his arm, holding him while his mother turned. Her eyes had already changed, returning to the doll's eyes that haunted their faces. Declan lurched forward, jumping to get his mother. A sudden rush of arms came at him like a raging current and drowned the attempt. Hands surrounded every part of him. Fingers probed him, digging and scratching. They were in his mouth and ears and ripping at his clothes, the sheer weight smothering as disbelief flooded his mind.

Above, the ceiling spewed reflections of the lights, lively and unforgiving, throwing a storm of flashing colors to his attackers, driving them. The machine wanted his mother and sister, and it somehow knew that he was trying to stop them. "Mom! Hadley!" he screamed, held prisoner, his mother disappearing into the crowd.

Knees buckling from the weight of restraint, Hadley was next to him then. She met his eyes with the same emptiness. That same awful stare. It crushed his heart.

"Hadley?" he pleaded, lips quivering, bracing her face between his hands, begging her to see him. Her skin was cold, the touch of it dry and flaky. "Please?"

The plea lasted less than a second, arms and hands grasping

clumsily, the machine driving bodies to intervene. They nearly took him to his knees while he muscled forward, yelling with the struggle to stay on his feet. Hadley was gone almost as soon as she'd arrived. It felt like less than a blink. Declan kept his eyes on where they were headed, bodies flooding the space between them, obscuring his view.

He had to break free if he was going to save them. *Fight!* The nightmare held him firm until he began swinging. The first wide arc connected immediately, a jolt of pain bolting up his arm when a mouthful of teeth cut into his knuckles. It was an older woman, her grip loosening at once when she lost her balance and pinwheeled backward. His other hand crashed into a man's ear, splitting the long lobe in half, blood spitting onto their pristine coveralls. The man let go, falling to his knees with a guttural grunt. Declan swung wildly then, fists circling and landing, feet kicking, and one by one, the bodies released him. By then, his mother and sister were far ahead of him.

Declan whirled around, dizzying himself in the process as he took off in a run. With a jump, he cleared the bodies, hurdling a couple, the corridor passing with each fleeting step. The running felt awkward—cumbersome and strange—after all, how often did he get a chance to run, their building was only so big? His heart beat hard, and his knees and feet were punished by the unfamiliar gait.

He shoved past the graying bodies and entered into another room, the floor rolling beneath him. The momentum threw him forward, stumbling onto his elbows and knees. Sweat dripping, his scalp itchy, nobody was moving; they'd all stopped. It was a conveyor belt, the moving floor passing them into the next room. Declan jumped up and tried to see beyond the line ahead. When that didn't work, he broke into a run again, the sprint making him suck wind. Gaining speed, a foul smell whooshing past him, he ran until the floor was gone entirely and he was swallowed by the darkness, falling.

He slammed against a grated floor, pain booming hollowly in his middle. His lungs emptied in a gush and stars shot past him, zigzagging with wispy tails. Gasping in a wheezing breath and planting his feet firmly, he climbed up, clutching metal, the round tubing moist. It was a short platform he'd fallen onto, a giant chasm open beyond it. Choking, he gagged, the air filled with salt and a putrid decay that tasted acidic. He spat, the powerful taste sticking in his throat.

His stomach flew into his throat when he looked over the platform. He clutched the railing until his hands hurt. Afraid, the drop from the platform was more than a thousand hands. Glancing up to where the conveyor was, he'd missed the connection to another conveyor, running past it. The ceiling was a dome-shaped cavern, the height making him wobbly. Gripping the metal, he forced himself to lean over and look below and maybe understand what this place was.

"That's gotta be where the heart is," he mumbled. "It's deep inside."

Declan searched for his mother and sister, scanning the faces riding the conveyors. The connecting conveyor belt turned inward toward the black walls, winding downward into a long spiral that stretched clear to the other side. The distance was vast, and if not for the line of white coveralls standing against the dark walls, he thought he would have lost sight of it.

Beyond it, there was another landing like the one he was on: a metal square jutting from the cavern wall. There was one for every moving conveyor that entered the cavern, all of them empty. *Maintenance*, he thought. *Like the workers in our building*. He realized there was no easy way off the platform and scraped the rocky wall. It was wet and stank of the same salt in the fog. But that wasn't the source of the foulness, the decay stuck in the back of his mouth. That came from somewhere else. He peered over the rail, looking down into what he couldn't see.

"They *are* mining something," his voice echoed, recalling a conversation between his mother and father. The VAC-Machines were said to have drilled deep into the earth, digging for compounds to use with the ocean's water. Staring at the round chasm, it was one giant hole. What kind of machine could drill something so big?

Below him, more conveyors moved across the open expanse, crisscrossing back and forth with a steady flow of white iridescence. There were a few conveyors, farther from the one he fell on, the bodies were naked, their coveralls gone. They stood motionless, the conveyors carrying them deeper into the cavern. Heart sinking, Declan spotted his mother and sister in one of the lines. Bodies naked, they moved obediently forward and stared ahead without expression.

"Mom! Hadley!" he screamed, waving his hands. They ignored the yells or chose not to hear. In his mind, he knew it was the machine doing it. It was making them the way they were. "Up here!"

At the end of their moving conveyor, there stood a robotic arm, chunky metal whipping through the air, swinging wide. Its articulating arm flowed smoothly, without hesitation, a large claw at the end with rubber-tipped fingers. Whirring, the arm swung from one conveyor to another, alternating back and forth, its claw opening in the face of each person.

"What's it do—" he began to ask, words stifled when a woman reached it. The arm swung into position and touched her. Declan brought his hand to his cheek, remembering how his mother had touched him there. Instantly, the woman's skin began to turn, a dark gray color sweeping from her temple and then downward like the spiraling conveyors around the cavern. When all the woman's color was lost, she collapsed in a heap, arms and legs in a jumble. Declan flinched when the floor beneath her opened suddenly, her flesh sliding into the cavern's black depths.

Guts turning, "Twenty," he counted. That's how many

people were in line before his mom and Hadley reached the end. Urgency struck immediately, the fear of heights forgotten. Declan ran from one side of the landing to the other, the metal ringing out as his shoes struck. The robot arm spinning. "Nineteen!"

He was drippy wet, sweat stinging his eyes, racing down his face while he desperately searched for a way off the platform. He swung a leg over the front railing, hoisting himself up, but hesitated and dropped back down undecided. *Seventeen!* There was another sound. A ca-thunk. Whir and ca-thunk. Over and over, each one stabbing him in the heart. "God, fifteen!"

Climb the wall, he thought. *It's the only way down.*

Holding his breath, he grabbed hold and perched himself on the railing, balancing precariously. The fall wasn't survivable. But he had to do it. Had to save his mother and sister. Declan's hand slipped against the wall, the motion nearly tipping him, his mouth jarred open in a silent gasp. "Mom! Hadley! Please!"

Declan dug his fingertips into a fissure, gripping the stony lip, and shifted his weight to his arms. They shook at once, trembling. The hold was secure enough to climb and he shuffled farther from the safety of the ledge. *Eleven!*

Another fissure secured his foot, his toes jammed in, tips of them surely bruised and cut. Sweat pestered his eyes, and he fought the urge to wipe them. When he dared a look below, an overwhelming nausea wet his mouth and closed his throat. A new crack, Declan shoved his hand into it. A jagged shard stabbed into his fingers, splitting one of them open and prying up a fingernail. He reeled back, hand bloodied, fingernail hanging loose. *Eight people!* "God, Mom wake up, please!"

His arms and legs were shaking, violently trembling beneath his coveralls. He wasn't going to make it. He tried to ignore his quivering muscles as he looked again at the closest conveyor. If he jumped, he'd fall off, he was sure of it. He might land on the conveyor, but he'd tumble over into the chasm below. *Six people.*

Just as he was about to move, his hold broke, the brittle stone clutched in his hands falling, tumbling. He fell onto the landing, the metal treads biting into his palms, ringing crisply off the cavern's far wall. Declan locked his focus past the metal grating, through the mesh of raised steel triangles to see his family. There were only three remaining in front of them.

Choking on his breath, and knowing that he couldn't save them, he counted, anyway. Two people. Had he ever felt so insignificant? So lacking and small. Every bit of strength ran out of him like his parchment words down the drains in their building. He pressed his teary and sweaty face into the metal, bloodied fingertips poking through the grated holes, and watched.

When it was his mother's turn, Declan squeezed the grate hard enough he thought it'd snap, shouting, "Mom! I'm sorry! So sorry!" A sorrowful heave stole his breath, the view stretched and pulled behind the tear-filled stare. His mother and sister stood quietly, never looking back to him, never looking to see who was calling.

Before it happened, Declan wanted to turn away, wanted to hide his eyes, but he didn't.

His mother advanced on the moving floor, stopping at the machine, and the articulating arm swung around, welcoming her with a whirring whisper. It extended a finger and touched her temple, her color fading. When the last of it was gone, his mother collapsed, lifeless.

Declan screamed, voice hoarse. He covered his ears, hating the sound. The sobs rocked his body, Hadley advancing. Again, he forced himself to watch, owing it to his sister, owing it to them both for having failed to save them. When her body fell from the conveyor, he finally shut his eyes.

Rolling onto his back, he closed his eyes, tears sliding down the sides of his face. He stayed there for a while, listening to the mechanical arm swinging back and forth, delivering its deadly touch. He listened to the crumbling of fallen arms and legs, and then to the sickening sound of flesh sliding off the conveyor belts toward the black depths. In his mind, he saw a tangle of bodies piling up at the bottom of the cavern, like a fleshy hillside of blank faces and empty doll eyes jutting out in every direction. He hoped to hear a scream, just once, but he never did.

The dead don't scream, he thought, and felt hysteria rising in him.

He pushed the madness down when, somewhere in the distance, he heard another mechanical sound. It was a churning, and a *thump thump thump*: a machine-driven grind that repeated without pause. As he focused, listening harder to the new sound, it became louder and clearer to him. And eventually, the sound overpowered the whooshing and whirring of the mechanical arm. Soon, it was all he heard. It started deep inside the black hole where the bodies went. From there, it crept up the muggy walls and reverberated over the moving conveyors. Declan swallowed hard, beginning to understand what the cavern was, what it was meant for; and what it *did*.

The VAC-Machine was eating.

SEVENTEEN

With her feet sinking in the ocean surf, Emily kicked the foamy water, Richard jumping nearby. It was cold and felt good. She wiggled her toes, a crisp chill rising, the salt on her breath strong enough to scratch the back of her throat. With the walk behind them, Richard agreed they stop and rest. Feet and hip aching, Emily stared into the fog to where she remembered the ocean was. It was still there, the waves muted, lapping gently. She missed the days when the winds were strong and the sea roared, the waves crashing.

Without the wind, the ocean was quiet and calm. There was still a current and a tide, but it was different than before. *A soft breeze*, she thought, wishing for it, especially on days like today when the fog was heavier and wet. Reaching, the fog rolled around her fingers, wispy tails weaving between them like a needle and thread. She sighed, feeling the airy pocket they'd found begin to collapse.

"Sit for a few, before it's gone," she told Richard who was also staring ahead, face blank. With his hands on his hips, he entered the ocean, a swell rising to his thighs. "We'll want to get moving again soon."

Squeezing her toes and clutching the gritty sand, the fog turned thick, the details of Richard's face and body fading behind the haze. She saw Declan in his father's face, the two sharing the same nose and chin. Only Declan's eyes were from his mother—soft, with extra-long and thick eyelashes. Foot raised, a clump of sand plopping, Emily froze when a sound returned from beyond them.

"Shh," Richard told her, carefully kneeling, a finger pressed to his mouth.

"Uh-huh," she said, ears perked, trying to listen. Thick fog closed around them in a damp hug, the landscape changing again. The walk from the commune had been uneventful, solitary and quiet. While the fog was heavy at times, they needed it for cover from the Outsiders. *The perfect travel weather*, she thought, amused, trying to ebb the mounting fright.

A touch, warm and gentle. Richard shifted closer, guarding, fingers closing on her shoulder. He continued gesturing silence and tipped his head to listen. More than once, he'd warned about the state of the weather, its changes and the Outsiders taking advantage to make a move on the unsuspecting. He'd also explained how they prowled and hunted in groups, using the fog. The threat menacing, foreboding.

"I think it's okay," he said, rising, a splash sounding. The water's surface rippled, relief on his face. "It's just some fish jumping."

"Fish," Emily barked, clutching her chest. She jumped up and kicked, seawater spraying. "You damn near had me scared to death."

With a grin, he ducked the watery assault with a shrug. "We can't take any chances out here." Shooing at a gnat, one of the few bugs to survive the fallen clouds, his grin turned into a smile, mischievous and daring. Without warning, he smacked the water, a curtain of it raining across her face and front.

"You!" she growled, hair and face and chest soaked. Salt

water dripped into her eyes and mouth, she spat, gobsmacked, saying, "I can't believe you did that."

"I... Seriously, I had no idea it'd be that big," he laughed. Brow rising, offering, "If you turn around, I'll wet the back too?"

"Uh-huh. I don't think so," she answered smartly, kicking back. He was fast, though, and dodged the attempt before falling headfirst into a wave. It was awkward and fun and warmed her instantly, the break a good one. He floated and rolled onto his back, spitting the seawater like a fountain. She sat at the ocean's edge, staying near him, and asked, "How you feeling?"

Blowing raspberries, water spraying in the gray light, he answered, "Not bad. Not bad at all." There was an appreciation on his face when he smiled at her. Gratitude for the help she'd been.

Arms and legs stretched, floating shallowly, his toes stuck up like mini headstones. *What a long way he's come.* The candy helped with the cravings, and keeping him busy helped more. Emily eased onto her elbows, feeling safe. It had been a couple days since they'd left the commune. That meant days without a drink. It wasn't magic, though, his moods becoming an ever-shifting thing like the fog. But things had steadily gotten better and that included his company.

Swiping at a gnat, it was the questions that drove her and she couldn't forget it. Not for a minute. There were more than few, the count increasing like the miles they'd traveled. For Emily, this had to be about Peter and the index card. She couldn't fathom his ever being involved with someone's death, let alone a wife and mother and daughter, a family ruined. That wasn't the Peter she knew.

Water splashed, the spray startling. It struck her from behind, an instant chill rifling up her spine. "Gotcha," Richard yelled playfully.

The chill swept through her, she reared up, swiping the

surface but was too late. He was already gone, disappearing into the fog, his feet sloshing and giving him away. When she was up, Richard was suddenly with her, arms around her middle, their noses nearly touching, laughter rising. His smile gave back years and made him look almost boyish.

He broke free and turned like it was a game of fast-tag. But Emily was quick, fingers draped across his arm, clutching his hand before he disappeared again. She spun, his arm wrapped around her, the move subtly romantic and making him pause. Without warning, she took his legs out from beneath him, the move remembered from one of the self-defense classes she took her freshman year of high school. Submerged, Richard's eyelids went wide, his mouth puckering, the move surprising him.

"Shit!" she grabbed his collar, jerking him out of the water. "Sorry, I didn't mean to—"

Gagging and coughing, "Got me." Emily helped him to his feet and realized she could see through her wet shirt. He glanced briefly, a stir of embarrassment making her cover up. He grinned, saying, "Best we get dry?"

"Yeah, dry," she answered, red-faced, thoughts wandering. There were *what-if* questions rising while she fancied the curve of his shoulders and the strong muscles she could glimpse through the front of his open coveralls. He took her hand then, surprising her, the gesture seeming more than just helping her return to the beach. In the fog, she suddenly saw Peter's broken body, his face a gnarled mess. Emily abruptly let go, saying, "Thanks, I got it."

"Sure," he answered quickly, confusion on his face. He said nothing else and turned and entered the fog.

"Appreciate the help," she followed, trying to sound encouraging. Disappointed at hurting him, she questioned, *Is it okay to have feelings for this man?*

Footsteps growing louder, she fixed her eyes on him when he rushed out of the gray. The fog tailed him, losing its grip, her heart stopping when she saw his face, saw that it was stricken with terror. The sight of him had her bracing and instinctively retreating. But there was only the ocean behind her. When he was close enough, she asked, "What?"

"There's someone out there," he said hurriedly, voice a gruff whisper. Fingers pinching her arm, Richard led them away from the ocean, moving along its edge. "Outsiders. Five voices, maybe more."

Emily couldn't breathe, knees buckling while they held still in the shallow water. Richard's touch turned soft, and he encouraged her to continue following. Leaving the water, sand coating her wet feet, the salty taste of congestion filled her mouth, lungs wheezing while she tried to keep pace with Richard. They ran blindly, stride clumsy. She tripped once, falling face first, sand coating the rest of her. He groaned against the strain of her weight and lurched forward until her legs were underneath her again. In a rasp, he commanded, "Here!"

They stopped behind a steep dune, an urge to pee suddenly overwhelming. Her insides felt heavy like her feet while she buried her legs in a thick bar of black sand. Richard gently squeezed her arm when the first voices reached her. Blood left her body instantly. "God!" she mouthed, terror-stricken.

The voices became louder, men chatting back and forth, the banter reminding her of what it was like before the clouds fell. But there was no safety, no law or courtesy or kindness in this world. Not now. The Outsiders closed the distance. Fright turned her insides to jelly, and she was sure every part of her was trembling. What would they do to her? To them? Would they kill them?

No, she thought morbidly, knowing the answer with a sickening dread. *They'd take turns until they were done.* And there was no knowing how long that might be. Terror and revulsion welled inside her, and suddenly she wasn't sure if she was going to vomit or if her bladder would give way.

Richard began shoveling handfuls of sand. Without a word, he showed her his plan: to dig and hide. With a thick enough pocket of fog, the Outsiders might pass right by them without ever knowing that they were there. Driving her fingers into the moist sand, scooping handful after handful, it stung her fingertips, ripping them raw. Breathing heavy, they emptied an area big enough to lie inside.

Huddled close, sand covering them loosely, the approaching voices were gone. Richard's warm breath touched her neck and she opened her mouth to speak. Richard placed a finger across her lips and lifted his chin slowly, motioning to the patch of fog behind them. It was eerily silent, though, leading her to think they'd moved on.

The first hit came out of the fog in a blink, startling Emily, but not Richard. He'd never even seen the attack. The back of his head opened against the fat end of a club, blood splashing the side of her face. It was slick and sickeningly warm, the impact driving his face into hers with a dizzying flash. Grabbing his collar, Emily wrapped her arms and legs around him, holding him as hard as she could. Blood spilled down his face, his eyelids blinking rapidly, dazed by the strike but conscious.

He was gone from her hold suddenly, turning to fight, his scalp bleeding profusely like gray paint covering his eyes, and turning his coveralls dark from his shoulders down to his chest.

"Get outta here!" he screamed, swinging wildly and punching the air like she'd seen in the courtyard. Laughter returned from the fog, a club whizzing by Richard's head. When she tried blocking it, her lungs collapsed, another club planting in the middle of her back. The force of the hit threw her face first into the sand, her insides squeezing until she thought she'd die right there. Richard's voice bellowed from the fog, ringing distantly, "Get off her!"

She peered up in time to see a club's round end hit Richard in the middle. He fell over without a fight, gasping like a fish out of water, four or more hands wrestling with him. The air was coming back to her, the adrenaline speeding the motion in her legs, "Richard—"

The gifts returning were gone a moment later, stars in her eyes zipping errantly when a thousand pounds of force crushed her from behind. She coughed a haggard breath, sipping the air, unable to satisfy the thirst. A voice called to her by name, his breath in her ear, teasing, "Ms. Stark!" He pressed the top of his knee into her lower back, pain rifling into her bottom, the breath she recovered spilling in a scream. He was on her next, pressing his middle into her, a hand wriggling beneath. "Do you know how long I've wanted to shut you up!"

"Get off—" she began.

"Maybe today, I'll teach *you* something!" The voice was menacing and raspy and impossibly familiar. It was Harold Belker. He'd somehow survived the exile, the punishment for having killed Sammi. Emily realized then what level of evil was in the boy she'd known for most of his life. There was no repentance. No remorse. Instead, having found a place with the Outsiders, Harold was going to kill her. Maybe he'd always been one of them; maybe he'd been an Outsider the entire time.

"Harold, please," she pleaded, the fear quickly turning to anger, strength returning. Emily tried pushing up, arms shaking violently, the weight heavy. Harold was strong and laughed, striking again. She cried out, cursing him and swinging her arms, clutching at handfuls of sand and air.

Please, she begged in her mind, seeking the strength to rise and fight. Pushing with everything she had. But Harold met the attempt with a heinous laugh. He told her to shut up, her face driven into the damp sands, shoving the grains into her eyes and nose and mouth, clumps finding her tongue and throat, suffocating her. She struggled to breathe, but that only made the attack worse, the coarseness peeling the skin from her face.

When the hand against her head relaxed, she lifted her head, gasping.

"What... what happened to you?" she begged to know.

"I found my home," he answered, and then continued to suffocate her. She was going to die. She was going to see her mother and sister again.

Her eyes remained above the edge of the surface which let her see the beach ahead as more Outsiders approached. Her lungs starved beneath Harold's hand, nose and mouth remaining covered. Footsteps surrounded them, sand shuffling while the salty taste of blood invaded her mouth.

Death was coming and she reared once more, trembling viciously until her arms and legs finally gave out. Harold pushed harder, shoving her down again—which was where she stayed. Unable to breathe, her pulse soon slowed, and she welcomed the increasing distance that grew between her and what was going on around her. The scene quieted; the approaching feet had all passed. She stared absently ahead, until their gray world invaded her eyes, stealing what little remained of her sight. Oddly, she felt grateful when her senses were gone, and everything around her went black.

EIGHTEEN

The machine's main hub bustled with the rhythmic footsteps of a thousand bodies. Phil Stark sneered, seeing them for what they were, *zombies*. They reminded him of the movies he loved when he was still young and dumb and didn't know such horrors could become real. Smile fading, he regarded their reality now.

"Bunch of zombies." A laugh. The humor thin and forced. Down deep in his brain, thoughts stirred about what'd happen if he didn't laugh. This *was* a horror movie. A real-life, living and breathing one. As if daring his situation, he grabbed a woman by the arm, jerking the coveralls hard enough to tear the stitching. She stopped and Phil stared into her eyes, the distance close enough to feel her breath. "You're a zombie. Do ya know that?"

Lights flashed a steady reply, a pair of zombies steering in his direction. Phil let go, the woman rejoining the parade, mindlessly traveling into a corridor.

"Here come the guards!" Phil circled the lobby, glancing over his shoulder to see them following. He jumped into the middle of the activity, bodies on all sides, blending somewhat with the same coveralls. Spinning, the zombie guards continued, the persistence surprising. Moving faster with a jump into another row, the lights on the wall reacted, flashing again, the zombie guards changing course. "Shit, must've really pissed them off this time."

Heart thumping and breathing faster, he nearly missed a broad woman, young and pretty. Fingers clutching, he squeezed her arm, shoving her behind him. She tumbled hard enough to take three others down who fell into four more. With a sharp clap, he yelled, "Like bowling pins!" A man not much older than he was bumped his shoulder hard enough to knock him off course, the momentum carrying him forward another jump. "Should I try for the spare?"

A quick run and he found himself halfway across the hub, standing at the exact center of the great room. Shoulders slumped, the rush of the game leaving as fast as it came, the zombie guards had given up and were gone. They couldn't do anything even if they tried. Gazing at the ceiling, untouched by the fast traffic passing all around him. This was one of the machine's little secrets—no zombies ever crossed the middle of the great room.

"That's how the traffic keeps moving. Keep the center clear. No crossing over. No intersection." He turned slowly around to watch them, their pace brisk, dizzying, entering and exiting the hub. "I could stand here all day. Wouldn't be the first time."

Gazing at the sky, the only place in all of the machine where he could see it. There were days he'd spent standing in exactly this spot. If he looked hard enough, he was sure he'd find the floor was worn, smoothed by hundreds of hours and the thousand little steps made while watching the clear sky. This was the other secret about the great hall. The window was real. It was glass and not one of those translucent panels that could be toggled on and off.

While the machine's position made it impossible to see the sun, Phil had watched plenty of stars when the night was dark enough. But today, there was nothing to see, the window blocked. He slouched, disappointed. The mining activities were at peak capacity, white plumes blanketing his only reprieve. In the ceiling's glass, Phil saw a memory. He felt it, too, and gingerly touched the scars on his face that were no longer there. It was the mall, the men beating on him, the tall windows with the fog rolling against the glass.

"Dad, what's happening to him?"

"Who's that?" Phil shouted, spinning around to find the source, lip quivering. And for a moment, he thought he saw his daughter Emily passing by him, dressed like the zombies, her eyes dead. "Emily?"

The lights on the wall caught his eyes. A warning. Subtle. Nearly unnoticeable. It was a mirage. If he tried hard enough, he'd see Sammi and his wife too. He'd see every person who'd been in his life. He shook his head fiercely, spit dripping like the memories haunting him. "They're only voices in your head."

Air flow compromised. The lights spoke. By now, he could decipher them without much effort. *Blood vault 73-83-76-65.*

"That's not possible," he answered, annoyed instantly. Mouth twisting, the message had to be an error. Nothing failed in the machine—not in a long time. *Blood vault 73-83-76-65.* He tried to recall that one but couldn't. Interest replaced the agitation, Phil answering the machine, "I don't think I've ever been to vault 73-83-76-65."

It wasn't far, the second to last corridor behind him, and then half a mile deep, possibly less. Rows of bodies were to his left, paying him no mind, Phil made a dance at one of the inter-sections, humming the Willy Wonka song which had been stuck in his head for at least a week. When he reached the lab, the song was gone. "Well, blood vault 73-83-76-65, let's see what's going on."

He stood at the entrance, assessing the lab to find anything out of sorts. The blood vault was exactly where it should be, faint shadows from behind the window. It was the tenth of twenty, the number of them and the number of their contents significant. Disappointed, he glanced at the lights, saying, "False alarm. Better get a tune-up." Turning, a foot out the door, a thump came from behind the wall. It was ductwork, the hollow sound unmistakable. "There's something in the ventilation?"

As if listening to his words, the lights blinked again: *Air flow compromised. Blood vault 73-83-76-65.*

"Yeah yeah. Glorified janitor," Phil grunted and approached the place where the vent shaft would be. In the years since his sentencing to serve to the machine, there'd never been a mouse or rat or anything in the vents. "'Cause none of the four-legged bastards survived what you had done to them."

Another thump, the lights repeating: *Air flow compromised. Blood vault 73-83-76-65.*

Aggravation returning, he retorted, "Uh-huh, I got it!" On the far wall, perpendicular to the blood vault's door, and beneath the longest of the lab tables, a vent cover had been removed. There were lab technicians working in all the vaults. They were programmed like the others. Single tasks. One at a time. Has he ever seen a lab tech wander? *Curiosity making him giddy,* he knelt and faced the opening. "Come out, come out, whoever you are."

The lab fell silent, the air still enough for him to question the vent cover. Running his fingers over the clips, was it possible that it fell off? After years of change in the air, with expansion and contraction, did the metal work its way loose, crashing onto the floor? "It was loud enough. Yeah, I bet that's what happened." Muttering to himself, Phil slid the vent cover over the opening to secure it.

"Wait," a thin voice pleaded.

"Jesus!" Shock rifled through him like a lightning bolt. When was the last time he'd heard someone speak to him. Phil stumbled backward, footing lost, the vent cover crashing. He snatched it quick before the machine questioned the commotion, metal vibrating. Silence descended into the lab while he held the vent cover close to him, using it like a shield. Sweat teemed on his face and the back of his neck. The whirring behind the blood vault doors continued, the work an endless chore, perfect for the mindless. Impatience followed the stillness, Phil realizing he'd been hearing things again. He knocked the side of his head with a thump. "It's probably getting close to recycling."

Motion. In the gray shadows beyond the vent's opening, there was motion. His heart skipped and he bit his lower lip until the salty taste of blood touched his tongue. Was this real? Desperate for the truth, Phil stuck his head in the opening and remained still until his eyes adjusted. Narrowing his focus, the figure of a woman appeared. A small woman. She sat against the vent, crumpled and frozen in place.

"Hey you," he called, voice raspy. "What are you doing in there?"

"You won't hurt me?" she replied reluctantly.

"Huh? Hurt you?" Reeling back, shock returning. The woman wasn't a zombie. She spoke. Shaking his head. "Um, no. Only if you don't hurt me first."

"Okay then." This time, her voice was soft but stern, reply echoing into his ears like a song.

"Who are you?" he asked, thinking the voice was familiar. But how many had he seen come back? How many had died at the mall, only to show up working here? None had ever spoken to him, though. Not like this.

"I work here," she returned, sheet metal making a *wub-wub* sound as she stepped that reminded him of distant thunder. "This is my lab."

"Your voice—" Phil closed his eyes, listening to the woman. When was the last time he heard someone speak? That is, actually speaking in conversation. Fifteen years? The last time would have been on the beach, the afternoon with the gray rainbows. It was with Emily and Sammi... wait. No! It wasn't his daughters that he spoke with last. His eyelids sprang open, widening when the woman neared the opening. "Isla?"

"Phil?" she asked. Without thinking, Phil offered a hand. She took hold, the touch of human flesh as real as her voice. "Phil Stark?"

"It is," he answered and realized he was half nodding and shaking his head at the same time. His stomach was in his throat, guts turned inside out. This was Isla from the mall, the woman who'd helped save Emily and Sammi before her fiancé was killed. She looked healthier. *But, of course she does*, he reminded himself, knowing why. Skin and hair a warm brown, healthy. And her eyes, they were alive. A brownish-green color that sparkled. They were nothing like the others in this place, especially since she was looking right at him. "You died."

She nodded, agreeing. "On the beach. When I ran into the rain."

"You remember?" Phil asked and began to wonder if she was stuck in the machine too, this prison.

"I remember you picking me up." A frown, expression hard. "Nothing after that, except working in here."

He caught himself staring at her chest, but not because it was a carnal thing, his last contact with anyone being so long ago. When they were in the mall, she was sick. *Lung cancer*, he thought, trying to remember. Out of practice in the art of conversation, he blurted, "You were dying, right? Cancer? It was terminal?"

"Yeah, you remember." Isla surprised him then, opening her top enough for him to see where there'd been a chemo port. Her skin was smooth and like bronze and without any blemish. "Reanimate?"

"Yeah," he answered, the idea as sickening today as it had been that first time. Was now the time to talk about it? Perhaps.

Perhaps not. He peered inside the air shaft, asking, "What were you doing in there?"

"The vent?" She looked at her hand and tended to a blood-soaked wrap. He hadn't noticed it until now and searched the nearest lab table behind him, picking off a bottle wash and a towel and handing them to her. She answered his question with a question. "Do you know what's in that room?"

"I do," he answered. "But do *you* know?" Without thinking, he took her hand to help clean the cut. "Has to do with what you said."

"What I said?" she questioned.

"Reanimate." He spun the towel around the cut, tightening it. "All the blood vaults."

"All? How many?" she asked, frown deepening. "And whose blood is it?"

"The samples," he began to answer, motioning for her to hold the towel. "The samples are us. That is, you and me and every other zombie in here."

"Zombie," she scoffed. "Seems harsh."

"You're aware. I'm aware." Phil motioned to the door, a group walking by. "Them, not so much."

"Why so many?" she asked, sounding overwhelmed and upset. There was a time when the sound in her voice would have upset him because he wanted to help her understand. Today, he found her expressions adorable, a gift after so many years of living with the expressionless zombies. It was the life in her eyes that he couldn't get enough of, as though he'd been starving to see her. Fingers snapping. "Phil!?"

"Yeah, sorry. We're the workforce," he answered, having no better way of telling her. Her expression emptied immediately. "But not everyone is aware like we are."

"Aware?" she questioned, sounding frustrated. "But what does that mean?"

He nudged at the wall, the lights. "You don't always listen, right?"

"Not like the others." She nodded cautiously, her eyes darting from the lights and then back to him. "So, the others here aren't the same?"

"Nope," Phil answered, shaking his head. "Might be because we were first—" A slap, his head rocked sideways. Cheek stinging, he narrowed his focus, unsure of what he'd said or done. The strike was hard enough to make his ears ring and he shook his head, her eyes glistening wet.

"Why didn't you leave me on that beach? I went out there to die."

"I... I couldn't let you do that." Phil skated around the truth, feeling it singe his soul like a burn. He motioned to the lab and then made a grander gesture. "This. All of it. It was my fault what happened to Nolan and you and everyone."

Her mouth puckered tight, lips gone, she yelled, "This fucking place should have come with an instruction manual."

"Come again?"

"I thought I'd died and woken up in limbo, or maybe Hell. Only, I didn't think Hell would be this quiet." She blinked slowly and sighed, Phil watching while he rubbed the sting from his face. Isla inhaled deep, chest rising and falling, her lungs sounding clear. "Freaking Catholic upbringing haunted me the last fifteen years."

"Sorry." He didn't know what else to say. Guilt was guilt. "This machine was supposed to save us. Save the planet."

"I remember that," she returned, voice rising, surprised by the recall. Facing the blood vault, she asked, "Why does the machine bring us back?"

"It's got to be something you can do." Phil looked over the lab and then back at her but wasn't entirely sure. "Something that only *you* can do."

"It's my work, like before I got cancer," Isla nodded,

seeming to understand, and added, "One of a few in the world..." she corrected herself, "or maybe the only one left in the world."

"Now you're thinking like the machines think."

He saw pity then. Isla touched his cheek softly. "Sorry. I shouldn't have hit you."

"I deserved it."

"Nobody deserves being hit," she said, continuing to rub the sting away. "For you, every year? All fifteen?"

"Uh-huh. None skipped. How about you?" Phil asked. Other than his years, the highest count he'd seen was ten years. It was a young man with a penchant for engineering—a gift really. The man had become aware almost immediately, and with his gift for working computers, the machine brought him back ten times. On the eleventh year, Phil couldn't find him, a chess game they had started—the board's pieces fashioned out of trash—remained unfinished. "The machine decides when and if you come back."

Isla said nothing and gazed at the shelf beneath a lab table. Phil followed to where there was a set of red books—lab journals. Picking up the oldest, he thumbed through the pages and found the odd scientific entries. But he also found some personal entries too. They were cryptic, puzzling, and unrelated to the work. He recognized how Isla became aware of the years, admiring the strategy of writing things down where the machine's computers couldn't wander: a book. Leafing through another lab journal, he found the notes made to pass to herself.

"My lab journals. That's how I figured it out," she exclaimed quietly. "I know they're just lab journals, but there arc things I write in them..."

"Things from each time before," he said, finishing her thought. "Like a clue or a message?" Her face brightened. Phil had left plenty of his own clues, a lifetime's worth it seemed. But they were all in his head, and he got to relive them every time they brought him back. He flicked a quick glance at the lights to make sure they were safe.

"Yes!" she almost yelled, sounding thrilled.

"All fifteen years?" he asked, shelving the lab journal and counting the others. When she nodded, he added, "It's hard, though, isn't it? Being alone."

"Sometimes," she answered, shyly covering her front. "Most times it feels like it's a penance."

"It does, exactly!" How often had he felt the same? He took her hands and turned them away from the light. "Isla, we're good at what we do, that's why it keeps bringing us back. But I'm planning to end the cycle. End it forever."

NINETEEN

Declan collapsed to the floor of Sammi's room, gasping and trying to catch his breath. His face and chest ached, the sobs deep and painful. Horrible images of his mother and sister swam in and out of his mind, the waking nightmare relentless. Only this wasn't a nightmare. It was real. He was there when their bodies turned gray like rotten meat and then tumbled into the machine's jaws. Their bones crunching climbed the walls next, entering his ears, the awful sounds stuck like tinnitus—incessant and never-ending.

"And they never screamed," he muttered gravely. "Not once. Not a sound."

He clutched Sammi's locket, finding it hard to be thankful that it let him pass through the machine undetected. A sigh, chest shuddering. *I am thankful.* It let him see his mother and sister. It let him see the truth. Declan glanced at the wall, the black beach sands somewhere beyond it. Squeezing his fingers, he wondered how far the locket could take him. Could he pass through all the corridors, including the ones leading to the outside? "That's where we belong. Home. I just need to convince her of it."

She doesn't know what this place is, he considered, having no idea how he'd ever talk Sammi into leaving. *She has no idea they're clones, that she's a clone, the machine feeding on them.* Over and over. *Sammi, a clone?*

This thought came with the nightmare of what he'd seen. Was Sammi next? He searched the lights, their color dark. Would they be calling for her soon?

He shook his head and cried and felt sick to his stomach as he tried to reason with what he saw and what he thought he knew. The door opened with a whoosh, the suddenness startling. Declan jumped to his feet and braced himself, expecting an attack. But the lights were still dim, and, in the doorway, he found his soulmate standing, waiting.

"Sammi!" he yelled, his heart gushing with relief. "This place... this place isn't what you think it is."

Sammi cautiously stepped into the room, the door closing behind her. For a long moment, Declan completely lost her in the darkness. When his eyes adjusted, he sensed something was wrong with her. He saw it in her body language, the way she approached him. He saw it again in her expression but realized how he must look to her.

If only she saw what I saw. Her face in shade, fears grew that what happened to Hadley and his mother was happening to Sammi. There was something different and his insides were trembling. He forced a step, and another, repeated until her face was near his. There were no lines or creases or paling gray skin. No straying hair or sagging bags beneath filmy eyes. None of it. Sammi looked more beautiful and more perfect than he had ever seen her. She looked radiant.

"I know," she finally said, drying a tear. "Declan, we need to go before the machine doesn't let us. Do you understand?"

"Yeah, of course. I was going to tell you the same exact thing. But you? What do you know? What happened?" Pinching his mouth, he stopped the flood of questions. And before she answered, she was in his arms, holding him. He needed to hold her and to tell her what he had seen. Voice breaking, he whispered, "It's my mother and sister. They're gone, Sammi. It was the machine, it killed them. I saw what the machine is, a monster."

"I'm so sorry, Declan," she said, crying with him. She squeezed his hands—skin warm and soft—and placed his palm on her belly. A kick. He yanked his hand away, legs suddenly weak. Declan felt himself wobble but stared hard at her middle. She nodded that it was okay, his hand returning, fingers splayed. There was movement. He was certain of it. "You felt it?"

"Sammi?" he asked, voice lifting, his eyes growing wide and wet. "Are you? Are we?"

"We are," she nodded, embracing him tight enough to hurt.

He gently pushed away, shaking his head. He knew nothing of doctoring but knew enough to ask, "Sammi, it can't be possible? Not yet?"

She didn't answer, not right away. Instead, she took his hand like before, and ran his fingers through her hair. Declan was confused by the motion and clouded by the emotions as she guided his hand to where the injury killed her, and finally said, "Declan, I'm not possible. Your mom and sister. They weren't possible either."

"This place," he began, conceding to what it was and wasn't. "This place made that happen."

"It did," she returned while gazing around the room. "It makes the impossible possible."

He touched her belly again, instincts rising, guarding. In his head, he heard the robot arm swinging from person to person. He heard the conveyor belt opening and the sound of flesh sliding from it. The crunching was next and it stabbed his heart cold. "Sammi, I think if you stay here, this place will take you like it took Hadley and my mom."

Sammi's gaze was fixed on the lights. "I don't know if it can anymore." She rubbed where their new life was beginning and smiled at him. "I can only hear you and our child."

"You don't hear the lights?" Declan asked, moving between her and the door, hopeful she was safe. When she nodded, he added, "Might be you're safe from the lights. Neither of us are safe from the rest of them."

She touched the bruises on his arms and face, the scratches around his neck. "They did that?"

"Uh-huh, when I tried to save my mom and Hadley." Emotions tugged him in a half dozen directions. "We've got to leave. We're not safe here. Not anymore."

"But how do we get out of here? We—that is, your mom and sister and me—we were allowed to leave before, but that was only to get you, to save you, to bring you inside."

"I'm not sure," he answered, shaking his head, clutching her fingers. She followed him to the door, a faint glow shining in the lights. "Can you still read what they're saying?"

"I don't hear them like before," Sammi began and looked away quickly like she was going to be sick. "I can hardly even look at them!"

"I think it knows," he told her, the urge to escape escalating. "The machine knows about us which was why it had you guys bring me inside."

"What are you saying?" Sammi asked. He could see sharp fear on her face. When she understood, she covered her belly like a protective mother. "The machine planned this?"

"It must have," he answered, half nodding and shaking his head at the same time. "It's the only reason the machine would have let it happen."

For a moment, Sammi looked as though she was going to cry. "This is our baby—" she said, bursting into tears.

Hugging her, uncertain of what to do, Declan said, "It's all the more reason to get us out of here, to get us back home." He scoured the room, scrambling, looking for anything that might help them. Declan ripped a sheet from the bed and waved it high into the air, throwing out the folds until it was flat. With his teeth, he gripped a corner and tore into the fabric. Within minutes, he had twelve long stretches of material. "It's a rope, take the end."

She shook her head quizzically. "What are you doing with it?"

"It's a tether," he told her. And at once she understood and braided three of the loose strands. "We'll need to stay tethered when we get to that big hall, the main hub." He braided the other loose strips of the bedsheet, tying the frayed ends as tight as possible, the fabric creaking against the pressure. When it was done and they were tied off and secured, Declan led Sammi to the door.

"I'm not sure I'm ready for this," she confessed, voice shaking. "I'm terrified, Declan."

"I am too," he said, lifting his voice to sound assuring. From the look on her face, it didn't help. "Sammi, we don't have a choice."

"I know," she replied, leaving the room. He looked back once, seeing her stare into it, the door whooshing closed while he thought, with hope, it'd be the last time they ever saw that room.

There was a sea of bodies marching through the corridor, staring ahead with blank looks, likely ignorant of their own presence. Declan muscled into the line, forcing them to join, Sammi racing to keep up during the first steps. The pace was fast, the footsteps heavy and with purpose. Sweat stood out on his face, his knuckles white on the tether strap, Sammi close behind.

When they turned to enter another corridor, Declan reached behind and took Sammi's hand, her fingers weaving with his, assuring her that he had her. The tether strap swung in a droopy smile between them but stayed tight in the binds they tied. His mind raced with uncertainty as he tried to figure out where exactly it was that they could go in this mammoth labyrinth. He squeezed Sammi's hand, realizing for the first time that he held his whole family.

"I'll never let go," he mumbled, speaking more to himself than the bodies parading around them. "Forward. Just move forward."

The great lobby came into view, a hundred hands ahead, Sammi asking, "Where to after that?"

"I have no idea."

TWENTY

In the gray daylight, a faint shadow crossed Emily. She was alive and breathing, staring up at a tall man who was waiting and watching to make sure she was okay. Emily carefully brushed away the sand from her chin, wincing at the briny sting. She felt a little sick to her stomach too. Straightening, the pain in her lower back was far worse. It was where she'd been struck, the club hitting a bone in her spine. *Wiggle your toes.* She did, and slowly closed her eyes, relieved. When she opened them, he was there, standing near the tall man. He was staring too. The sight of him striking fear almost as painful as the club's strike had.

Harold sneered wickedly at her, a part of his face hidden when he stepped behind the other man. He poked his head around again, that terrible smile curling. It left her thinking that he enjoyed watching her in pain. Next to her, Richard was nursing injuries. A knot on the back of his head from the fat end of a club and a jagged cut above his eye. She nudged an elbow against his thigh, getting his attention. When he saw her staring, shame and embarrassment instantly filled his face.

He was blaming himself. But this wasn't his fault. Nobody

won against the Outsiders. She decided to tell him so the first chance she had. His hands shook when he poured water onto a torn cloth, offering to clean her face. Reaching, Emily steadied the tremble, guiding, while he wiped the blood and dirt from her face.

"Thank you," she managed to say, taking the cloth from his hands, using the moment to clutch his hand. "And thank you for trying to stop them too."

He rocked his head, half nodding, somewhat agreeing, and her heart ached for the self-reproach he was putting himself through. A laugh. Richard glared at Harold, shifting to get up, threatening to finish what was started.

"Now, now," the tall man said, intervening. "I'm sorry my scouts attacked. That was never the intention." He had a long face, and equally long hair that reached his shoulders. It was brown and poker straight and moved gently like the ocean swells as the man turned to face them. "And I promise you, a punishment will be delivered. Swift and firm."

"Better make it so," Richard warned, and backed away to continue helping Emily. She flinched at the sound of cloth tearing as he fashioned a bandage from his coveralls.

"Just exactly who is *us?*" Emily asked, revolted at the sight of Harold's face, at the idea of what he was going to do. She winced again, the swell on her lip throbbing. "*Who* are you?"

How far had Harold fallen? He killed Sammi and then joined the Outsiders, raping and pillaging anyone who had made the unfortunate mistake of crossing their paths.

The attack was still hazy, but it was the tall man who'd come to her rescue. That wasn't at all like the Outsiders she knew of. Harold was on top of her, and just as he was about to take her life, she felt the air rush across her like a rare wind coming off the ocean. A moment later, the tall man was helping her to sit up, offering fresh water and brushing away some of what Harold had done to her.

The tall man's stare was gentle. From his sunken eyes, eclipsed by a thick brow, she saw compassion. Yet, she knew to be nervous in his company, in the company of Outsiders. After all, they'd taken her boy.

While he hadn't said so, she could tell he was the group's leader. As Emily continued to clean herself off, the fog lifted enough to see the commotion instead of just hearing it. Men and women and children joined her and Richard, everyone busy with a chore, something to do in establishing a camp as if this location were predetermined. Ten or more were seated nearby, along with women and children, tents stood up with small fires, the smell of meat cooking.

"You call us the Outsiders," the tall man finally answered, cringing. At once, Emily could see that he disliked the name. He made like he was going to spit, as if ridding his mouth of the word, but didn't. "We're not the violent people that your stories describe."

"I'm not so sure about that," Richard said, shaking his head. He motioned at Harold to prove his point. "We were attacked."

"Stark had that coming!" Harold snapped. "Been teasing me with those—" His words were cut off by a quick backhand from the group's leader. The suddenness and the sound of flesh-on-flesh startled Emily, Richard flinching too.

Harold's nose bloomed, splashing blood across his cheeks as he tumbled onto his rear. Emily smiled which felt good. She hid it, though, as best she could, pressing her lips firm. Harold squirmed along the sand, tending to his bloodied nose, his complaints sounding like a squeal.

"What this one did was unfortunate," the group's leader answered. "We're still trying to work with him. That's not who *we* are today." He leaned forward, eyes deepening with sadness. "But there was a time when more of us were like him."

"Who you are today?" Richard questioned, a guarded distrust in his voice.

"Dark times, the four horsemen a reality," the leader began. "I wish the stories weren't true, but they are. Once we overcame the constant threat of starvation, survival granted us a community."

"How many are you?" Richard asked, his guard lowered. He looked around the ground and what could be seen. "More than this?"

"Many more," the leader replied, a smile hinting achievement. "We are many."

"Then why stay hidden from us?" Emily asked. "Why not find a home with our commune?"

The leader wiped the blood from the back of his hand, his focus shifting to Richard and then returning. Emily felt uncomfortable in the bubble of silence as he regarded the question, thinking she'd said something wrong.

"I fear that it is *your* commune that can't be trusted," he said in a steady tone. Nudging his chin toward the fog, he continued, "The machine, it doesn't exist without your commune. And your commune, it doesn't exist without the machine. They are one."

"What do you mean?" Richard asked in stunned disbelief.

"In time," the leader answered. "But first I need to tend to my people."

Richard mumbled, agitated. Emily said nothing but questioned what the leader professed. There was a level of sincerity in his voice which told her that he knew more. A lot more about the machine than they did. But what did he know about their commune?

"Sir?" she asked, a question pressing, burning even. From the pocket of her coveralls, she brought out the picture of her son, a drawing of him made weeks before he disappeared. Richard looked on with surprise, and she realized he didn't know about it. The leader took hold, glanced at it a second, a question forming. "It's my son. Would... does...? Does he look familiar?"

"Your son," he began, and sighed with an understanding that told her he knew of the stories, the worst of the worst. Her heart fell when he returned the picture and shook his head. "I'm sorry."

"Thank you." It was all she could think to say, the old scars opening, a shudder rocking her. Her insides squeezed tight, the ache of loss pressing. Richard put his hand on her back, his eyes filled with sympathy. He understood the loss of a child, the devastation, her body trembling. There was no getting over it.

"What's your name?" Richard asked the leader. The change in topic was a good cue to take, the small talk helping Emily to think about anything but the child she'd lost. Richard extended his hand, saying, "Given the circumstances and all, a formal introduction seems appropriate. I'm Richard Chambers, I was studying to be an engineer in the old world."

Emily followed, hand leading. "I'm Emily Stark," she began. In the calloused hand, she felt the weight of leadership, the hardship and strife of leadership. The man held it firmly, a moment longer than expected. Did he know about her father? Rather than talk of who she was, she added, "I'm the schoolteacher in our commune."

"Geoffrey Schmidt. I was a mail carrier in the old life. For ten years, I went from door to door to deliver the mail." His brow rose, his stare fixed as if waiting for a reaction. "I believe it took the clouds to fall for us to truly recognize who we were intended to become. Might I ask a favor?"

"A favor?" Emily replied, curious, uncertain what she could do for the man who'd saved her. Saved them. "Yes, of course."

He cupped her hand in his, a softness entering his eyes. "When you return to teach in your commune, would you speak well of us?"

"Certainly," she answered. She caught herself, hearing the

enthusiasm. These were the Outsiders, after all. The same they'd feared all this time. Only, Emily didn't feel afraid. Not of their leader Geoffrey Schmidt. "I mean, there's so much to tell everyone—"

"Good," he said, letting go, his attention gone. With a sharp snap of his fingers, he motioned to the group. Heads turned and the low chattering hushed. At once, everyone began working, even the children and a few elderly. As if on cue, Harold wiped the blood from his face and entered the center of activity. There he dropped to his knees, resigned to the work before him, and began to dig a small pit in the sand. He burrowed down, hollowing out a small space where he propped branches and lumber for a larger fire.

Feeling the unease arresting in her, Emily got up to help where she could. She couldn't stand seeing others work while she watched.

"May I?" she asked a young girl who had lopsided ponytails and crooked bangs. Emily knelt at the blanket's corners, offering to tie down straps.

"Uh-huh," the girl answered, smiling excitedly. Emily realized then who the real outsiders were. It was her and Richard. But this child was not scared. She was excited to have them there. The girl wove the cloth straps between her fingers, instructing, "Like this."

"Like this," Emily repeated and followed the directions while remaining cautious and never letting Harold slip from her sight.

When the clack of stone striking stone shot across the camp, Emily jumped. She eased herself up with a shaky breath, seeing it was just a flint stone and striker, a small fire coming to life. A moment later, the fire blazed. Emily sank back onto her heels, gazing into the flames which looked soft in the hovering fog, a colorful orange glow around it. Richard worked a tent alongside the leader. It was for them, the side of it patched a half dozen times, looking like a sloppily made quilt. Next to it, they piled old tree branches and timber to burn through the night.

Emily sighed, feeling lightheaded, the remainder of the day slipping into evening in a blink. Richard settled next to her, bracing the back of his head. The cut above his eye was drying to a scaly brown. In the fire's light, the bruising on his face was hidden, but the swell had an ugly shine, the skin bulging.

"They're not what I expected," she said, speaking lightly, nursing his wounds. As she wiped away some dirt and the dried blood, Emily tried to remember what they were doing before the attack. Playing. They'd been playing and—her hand stopped—they were just playing. They were connecting. She jerked her hand away, Richard noticing.

He saw the look on her face and glanced over his shoulder. Returning his gaze to hers, he asked, "Emily? What is it?"

"Nothing," she said and took to staring into the group. There was a child gathering wood. Twelve or so, he had hair like Peter's and eyes like Sammi. Emily couldn't help but think it was her boy. It wasn't, though, and she absently said, "Sometimes, I think I see my son everywhere."

"I'm so sorry that happened," Richard told her, taking the cloth and wetting it some more. He returned the favor, cleaning her face. The sweet smell of the burning wood and the crackle and pops set a mood that made her sleepy. She closed her eyes, thinking of her son, Richard saying, "I didn't know."

"Food!" someone shouted. Unlike the commune, the Outsiders didn't fear being heard.

"Loud enough," Richard joked, clearly thinking the same.

They helped each other up as one of the Outsiders poked their head between them to say, "We eat around the fire."

The sun was setting. Not that Emily could see it. Not that they'd seen it since she was a child, save for the few days when End of Gray Skies had worked. The sands were dimming, and the fog had grown darker, nearly black. With the absence of light, the air was colder, and she found herself nearing the fire.

In the fire's light, the pocket of fog was thin enough to let her see nearly everyone. The leader of the Outsiders sat cross-legged, a large collection of food in front of him. To his left, women and children sat—hungry stares fixed on the food. A smaller fire had been built and set ablaze to their left, and it was there that Emily saw Harold.

He was sitting alone. But this wasn't a children's table like they'd had at family gatherings before the clouds fell. Harold was sitting alone because he wasn't invited to sit with the Outsiders yet. Deep in her heart, she felt sorry for him. It was brief and then gone in a blink like the embers burning into the night sky. Never could she forget who he was and what happened to Sammi.

"Please," the leader motioned across the fire. There, between the women and the men, Emily sat with Richard. They were close enough to the fire that she could feel the burn on her skin. Ash and hot embers spat from a hissing log, the smoke catching her eyes and watering them. She nodded to the leader—a thankful gesture for inviting them to eat. Richard did the same, a low growl rumbling from his stomach.

The leader made up a large plate, passing the food over to one of the women who placed it in front of them. Wild vegetables and chunks of meat. While the meat was raw, it looked fresh. Long thin slats of wood stood upright in the sand. The woman plucked the stick, showing it to Emily and Richard, and then speared a piece of meat on the end.

"For the fire, like this," she said, dangling it over the flames. Within moments, the smell of cooking meat was answered with a hunger pang. For the next hour, there was little said. They ate and smiled at one another, enjoying the hot meal and a warm fire.

"What were you doing out here?" the leader asked, throwing scraps of his food to some wild dogs. Emily hadn't noticed them before and wondered if they'd been there all along.

The dogs snarled and nipped at each other, fighting for the food. The leader slapped his hands together and made a low guttural sound. The dogs stopped, took the scraps and ran beyond the fire's light. The act was impressive. In the commune, dogs were difficult to tame, let alone keep as pets.

"We don't see many dogs in our commune," Richard said, making small talk. "It's good to see them around."

"Well, you might say that we grow our own food," the leader said with a chuckle. He grabbed a nearby pup, bringing it onto his lap while making a wet, smacking sound with his lips.

"What?" Emily's mouth fell open while staring at the food on her plate. "I was eating—"

"I'm kidding!" he interrupted, the chuckling turning into a laugh. He glanced around, the others joining. "They're our hunting dogs. Rabbit, squirrel, an occasional cat. Whatever is left." The pup panted joyfully while the leader dug his fingers into his scruff, petting him. His face turned serious, and he repeated, "What are you two doing outside your commune?"

"We're going to the machine," Emily began to say. Her throat was suddenly dry, voice breaking. She reached for the water, drinking it fast to cool the burn in her throat.

"And to find my son to bring him home," Richard finished for her.

"Executives?" the leader asked, wagging his finger between them. "Either of you?"

Emily looked over at Richard, surprised by the question. "No, but how do you know about our executives?" Richard stirred, ready to speak, perhaps to share that his wife had been an executive. Cautious, Emily carefully placed her hand on his arm, adding pressure to her fingers in the gentlest squeeze, an inconspicuous hint to keep that information quiet—for now, anyway.

"I couldn't be sure. Mostly I only know the rounder ones to be the executives from your commune," Geoffrey added. He moved his arms in a wide circle, the group laughing, "You know, the fat ones."

Emily flushed, heat on her chest and neck, seeing an image of what Peter had become in his last years of life. She pulled her arms around her front as if it was her size she was hiding from the group. Nobody seemed to notice, though, and she asked, "You've seen them?"

The leader picked at his teeth and made sucking sounds. Brow raised, he said, "Your executives, the fat ones. They travel to and from the machine with your morticians. Sometimes, they carry things. Sometimes, they don't." He held up a finger, long and skinny, the middle knuckle swollen. "We saw a mortician alone once, spoke with him. That's how we came to know what he called himself. He wasn't going to the machine, not that last day. Instead, he took to the ocean like a fish."

The fire snapped, a spark spiraling upward, dancing on the heat until it disappeared into the fog. Emily waved her hand, throwing air over her skin. The fire was too hot, too much for her.

"He went into the ocean? What else did he tell you?" Richard asked. When he noticed Emily fanning herself, he handed her his water. "Are you okay?"

"I'll be fine. Just a little warm," she answered, lying and realizing that she might not be fine. The flash of heat spread all over her body, and she fanned her face, adding, "The fire is getting to me."

"On that day, your mortician said that he was done. That he was done working for them," the leader began. "He told us a story about blood and how in his job he would pass a body to the farming floor. And with every one of them, he was to save some of their blood and transport it to the machine."

"Blood?" she asked, her voice trilling unintentionally. The leader's face was lost in a blur and Emily felt herself sway like the flames above a burning log. She blinked away the soft image and focused on what the leader was saying. "Transporting?"

"Your mortician gave us his last one." From his hand, the leader produced a small glass vial, the tube perched between the tips of his fingers. The fire's reflection bounced from the round glass, a dark mass inside the tube. The leader passed the blood to one of the women, who then gently placed it in front of Emily.

"Look at the lettering," Richard directed, turning the vial over. "It's the same as the index card."

"Why would the mortician collect blood from their dead?" Emily lifted the vial. The liquid a deep magenta, the edges of it brighter red as she held it against the fire. "What happened next?"

"Your mortician gave us a wave and walked out there," the leader answered, pointing toward the sounds coming from the ocean.

"He didn't return?" Richard asked, sounding grave.

"It was the last we saw of him," the leader said. "But he did tell us one more thing. He said that the dead only live a year, and then they bring *us* back."

"Bring us back?" Richard asked with a look of shock, disgust even. "You mean they live a year, and the machine brings them back?"

"Like an expiration," the leader explained. "As if they were a perishable at the market."

Emily felt how Richard looked. "How can the dead be brought back?" The lightheadedness made her blink rapidly. The leader shrugged and shook his head. He was only repeating what was told to him. "Is that why he went into the ocean?"

"That's right," Geoffrey said. "The mortician told us that he never wanted to come back again. He wanted it to be over."

Another wave of heat swam up Emily's back and sweat beaded on her face. Her insides felt hot, and, for a moment, she thought the flames had somehow jumped inside her lungs, burning her throat and mouth. She drank and listened, trying to understand what it was that the leader was telling them.

The fire's smoke shifted with a short breeze and closed around her and Richard like the fog. She was certain that the air had become hotter, baking her insides, coursing up her spine and through her veins. She tried to catch her breath but felt as if she would suffocate breathing in the heat.

"What does any of that mean?" she heard Richard ask.

"And we've seen a girl who looks like you," the leader added, his focus on her. "The one with the red hair."

"Sammi?" Emily asked, voice soft like a whisper. "She's my sister."

"That's impossible," Richard said, tension rising.

But their words faded in a chorus of ringing bells, chimes thumping in Emily's head like a million heartbeats. The fire was fading, too, slowly vanishing from her sight until it disappeared. Emily realized what was happening, she was falling backward and was going to pass out.

TWENTY-ONE

Her legs felt weak and the faint urge to cry made her lips tremble. Isla stepped back, uncertain about what Phil Stark was telling her. But didn't she know? Reanimate. She'd given herself that clue again and again. For fifteen years, beginning the days after Nolan died. After she had died and been brought back.

"Tell me more about your plans," she said, hungry to hear what they were. Phil's shoulders slumped forward, and at once, Isla sensed his hesitation. But not quite a hesitation. Annoyance, maybe, for having to explain what he meant. She glanced at the lab journals wondering if they'd had this conversation already. How many times? "My memory. It's like Swiss cheese sometimes."

"The gaps," he commented, tapping the side of his head, a distantly crazed look in his eyes. She eased away slightly, the look of him concerning her a bit. Had he been like that at the mall? She didn't think so. *A copy of a copy?* she questioned, thinking whatever technology this was, it wasn't perfect. *The government? If so, then why?* "I started this—all of this—and I'm going to end it."

"You were the architect?" Isla blurted, recalling some of

what had happened at the mall. In the fifteen years since, her thoughts had been of Nolan and his death, the way he died. But those moments had grown less important. Until now. "When my fiancé was killed, those men beat you. They said it was because you'd been responsible for all the machines."

A nod, brow rising. "They were supposed to save the world," he said, patting his chest. He made a fist and thumped it then, hard enough to frighten her. "I thought I'd be a hero. You know, honored for such an achievement."

"Instead, you've become like the man in the lighthouse. Am I right?"

Phil gushed with laughter, a smile brimming. "I like that. I'm the lighthouse keeper." He turned serious then, motioning to the lab journals. "One for each year you were brought back."

"Why a year?" she asked, stomach turning at the idea that, somewhere in this machine, there were previous versions of herself.

"I'll tell you, but please understand that I had nothing to do with it," he said, nodding. He kept nodding until she reciprocated. "I only came to understand who was behind it, and why, after the clouds fell."

"I'll try," she said and tried to clear her mind.

He held up a finger, saying, "It's one year. Not a day more. That was a part of the original design. It's insurance, you might say. With the exception of a few like you and me, those brought back aren't given the chance to be aware. They're locked, the lights keeping them as simpletons. Zombies to follow directions."

"Zombies," she repeated and looked at the lights. "That's kind of cruel."

A shrug. "It's what I call them." He rapped his knuckle against the side of his head as he told her this. "As they near the one-year mark, they grow immune to the lights and become aware, returning to their former selves."

"The aging. I've seen some of them age overnight."

He jabbed the air, pointing at the lights. "It's built in, like a circuit breaker. The lights trigger the process near the end." Phil dipped his head, adding, "You've gone through it. We all have."

She grabbed her chest, certain he was wrong. "I would've remembered."

"Impossible. By that point, the wiring in your brain prevents long-term memories from forming."

The gaps, she thought, shuddering. "What, then what happens to us?"

"You don't want to know about that," Phil answered, a look of disgust fixed on his face.

"The annual cycle. The cloning. Who is behind it?"

"Not us," he answered, shaking his head harshly. "I didn't understand any of it until I..." His voice faded and his expression went blank as his eyes drifted past her.

"When you what?"

"When I killed myself," he said abruptly, his focus returning. "Once the initial reactions had leveled out, I couldn't leave this place. I was locked in here. It was a death sentence, really. Watching my daughters visit, watching others I knew to be dead suddenly appear here, minds empty like their faces. They were turned into zombies. The guilt of it all, I couldn't take it anymore."

"And then the machine brought you back," she added, continuing his explanation. "It brought you back and now you only have one year like the rest of us."

"I've been working out a way to stop the machines ever since," Phil added, nodding, his expression bearing shame as he regarded the lights.

"If you're the original architect, why can't you shut it down?"

He leaned forward, eyes fixing again on the lights, saying,

"It was never supposed to be shut down. Not until they were ready to come here."

"They?" she asked, growing concerned, the crazed look in his eyes returning.

"I kept clues too. Like you did with your lab journals. That's how I figured out what happened." Her gaze followed his hands as he motioned upward, pointing above them. "*They* gave us the technology to build the machines, telling us it would save our planet. But that wasn't at all what it was for."

"What was the technology for?" Isla asked, thinking of the endless mineral analysis. "What exactly have I been helping with?"

"The machines. They were never for us. They were built for them, for their arrival." Phil grimaced as he spoke—a look of suffering in his expression. "It won't be long now before they come. Which is why I have to destroy the machine. Destroy all of them before it's too late."

Confusion eclipsed her fright. Were these the frantic words of a lunatic, or a sincere warning from a fellow scientist? "Phil, just what do you mean 'for them'?" He eyed the ceiling again, indicating they were from above. Catching on, she reeled back. "Oh, come on! You can't be serious?"

"As serious as you were dead," he replied without pause, the look of him as scary as his words.

She shook her head in stunned disbelief. "Phil, please tell me you don't believe what you're saying."

"Believe me!" His hands were on her in a flash, fingers gently clasping her face, a pleading look in his glassy eyes. "I wish more than anything in *our* world that it wasn't true. I wish that I'd never been persuaded. But it *is* real and if you think about all that you've seen, you'll know it too."

"Aliens. Our planet?" She couldn't break their stare, his lower lip trembling while he carefully touched where her chemo was. She was free of the cancer now, of the death sentence that had been a certainty. There was nothing in this world, in *their* world, that could save her. For one moment, she allowed herself to be completely open-minded and to believe the man. "Phil? Why our planet?"

"They want it for themselves. It's like baking a cake in an oven. You've been mining the ingredients, feeding it into the mix, and the machines have been pumping the batter out for fifteen years. They're transforming our planet."

"Transforming? What?" she muttered, legs giving out. She braced herself, understanding. She caught the edge of the lab table and plopped into her seat. Her heart pounded in her chest, soured with knowing what she'd been a part of.

Crying silently and mourning her contributions, Phil Stark went on and on, explaining the sciences of transformation and how they'd all been betrayed. She became lost in the drone of his voice, the words circling around her like a great storm, spinning out of control until she was dizzy. She cried harder, slapping her hands against her face, mumbling, "The machines were meant to save us. They were meant to rescue us from our past."

"Five machines... mining into the *Earth* until they all converge and become one! Don't you see? They are all connected!" Phil continued, voice rising into a yell. She peered up, his head rocking as if preaching to a congregation. By now, she wasn't even sure Phil knew she was there. What had the years done to him since the mall? "And when that happens, when the machines finally converge on that single point deep in the middle of our planet... we'll have lost our home *forever*. FOREVER! And I hate to break it to you, boys and girls, if we don't act fast, if we don't do something now, we're gonna fly right past that point, and we won't be able to turn back. We'll miss the exit ramp, with no way to turn around! Oh, it's coming. Oh, it's HAPPENING!"

"ENOUGH!" Isla screamed at him, unable to listen to his

ramblings anymore. Phil stopped abruptly, his jaw sagging. "Tell me what to do. I want to help end this!"

Phil seemed to step out of his preacher's pose, advancing toward her slowly and lowering himself until he was closer. He wiped the tears from her cheeks, saying, "Thank you." She looked deep into his face and thought how impossibly exhausted he was. "That's all I wanted to hear."

TWENTY-TWO

When the first hand groped her, Sammi thought it had to be a figment of her imagination. That she'd walked too close to the others, brushing against one of them. But their hand? It was touching her belly, fingers clutching absently. And it stayed there a little long too, didn't it? *It's my imagination. That's all.* But when the second and third pair of hands came, it was more obvious, a sense of danger exploding in her head with a fight-or-flight response triggering her legs.

"Declan!" Sammi clenched her jaw and covered her middle. Her heart shot into her throat as terror twisted through her. The horrors he'd spoken of were real, there was more to this machine than what she could see.

"Stay close, and hold onto this," he returned, leading them into a maze of bodies. He wrapped an arm around her waist, his grip secured on the tether strap. She held her end tight, fingers straining. He spoke over the growing shuffle, saying, "I'll protect you."

"Who'll protect you?" she replied. He didn't hear her, though, the crowd becoming heavier and more congested, swarming like bees in a hive. They closed around them, another pair of hands on her. They wrenched her shoulder this time, spinning her in the other direction. "Declan!" she screamed, the tether strap straining.

This can't be, she thought wildly. How many times had she traveled the corridors before and never touched someone? A hundred? A thousand? The lights stayed dimly lit, blinking a message for the passing eyes. All but her. Sammi tugged on the tether strap until Declan turned. His expression was tired with worry.

"We have to keep going," he told her, demanding.

"I'm trying to keep up," she mouthed. "Slow down—"

Sammi's words were cut off by a commotion, more bodies came between them, attempting to separate her from Declan. The top of his head stayed in view, his arms raised like he was bobbing in a sea, drowning. People came at them from every direction, compressing, squeezing. There were hands on her back and legs and breasts and arms, the swarm moving her farther and farther away, leading her down a separate corridor.

"Sammi!" Declan screamed for her.

"Declan! They have me!" Low groans filled her ears, their mouths sagging, the swarm speaking in an oddly uniform chorus. She tightened her hold of the tether strap and pulled. From the other end of it, the bodies were jerked clear of her sight, flesh slapping, grunts and wheezing followed tumbling bodies. Declan emerged, swinging his arms and legs to fight their attackers.

"Hold onto me!" he yelled, grabbing her hand. Sweat stood out on his face, bangs pasted to his damp forehead. His eyes were filled with alarm. "Hold on and don't let go!"

"My baby!" she screamed, realizing the horror of what was happening. *It's why the machine let Declan inside. It let him be with me. It needs this.* A jolting pain shot through her like electricity, erupting behind her eyes, a hint of the messages spilling into her brain like boiling water. She turned away, unable to finish. "Declan, they want our baby!"

"I got you!" Declan replied, his grab harsh, painful even. Sammi struggled to follow, tripping over a body, hurdling another, a hand squeezing the inside of her thigh. She cried a painful yip, batting and kicking at a woman. The chorus became deafening, an impossibly incessant clamor that she was certain would destroy the fragile clockwork inside her ears.

With one hand on the tether, he swung the other crazily like a madman. Over and over, his fist connected with faces and shoulders and anything else in his way. One man's nose exploded and sprayed blood and snot over them. Another woman's eye swelled instantly, yet she kept coming, the lights demanding it of her. Declan hit them again and again, clearing a path. He elbowed an older man and kicked at another woman, the path closing fast as if they were being swallowed by a forest of flesh-eating vines.

Why do they want my baby? That question kept her moving, a motherly instinct taking over. *Hold onto him! Hold on!* An elbow caught her side, the jab a painful thief that stole her breath. Sammi doubled over, the strain on the tether pulling Declan off balance. She stumbled getting back to her feet. Her heart seized when something warm ran between her legs. The sudden touch of it was wet and it made her stop dead. *Oh, please let that be pee. Please!*

"Sammi, look!" Declan yelled. Hope came in the form of a small keyhole. It was just a glimpse of light at first, a ribbon of it growing, jutting from an open door. Sammi saw something unlikely then and guessed that she had to be imagining it. She saw a man standing at the door, waving, his face like the one she'd seen in her dreams. They were dreams of Emily and her mom and dad, before the clouds fell, before the mall.

"This way!" she heard the man say.

"Dad?!" *I must be losing my mind,* she thought.

The man yelled louder, "Over here. It's safe."

The machine heard the man, too, and turned on him. The lights blared and the bodies swarmed on the man, his face covered by fingers clawing at his eyes and nose and mouth. He was tall and strong and shooed them off like flies. And what she saw next had to be a mistake. The man laughed as he fought the swarm. He laughed, swinging his arms, punching, and kicking until the opening was clear. The stranger seemed to enjoy himself as he opened a woman's head and broke a man's arm.

The distraction was all they needed, and Declan hurried them down the corridor toward the open door. When they were next to him, Sammi searched the man's familiar face, his neck and cheeks scratched raw, the skin pink and raised. When his eyes met hers, the laughter he'd enjoyed stopped. He did a double-take, shaking his head in disbelief.

They looked into the room, which she recognized to be one of the labs. It had long tables and glassware across the surfaces with large cabinets and shelves filled with equipment. But unlike other labs, at the farthest side of the room there was a large metal door with a single round window that looked like an eye. *A camera?* she thought, believing it was watching them.

"Sir, thank you—" Declan began, holding the tether strap. But Sammi couldn't hear him. She moved closer to the stranger who wasn't a stranger at all. In his face, she saw Emily's eyes. Her nose was there too. Her trance was broken, Declan asking, "Sammi?"

"Dad?" she asked.

"Quick, hurry," was all the man said as they slipped past him. He shut the door, closing it on a set of fingers, slamming it, the bones crunching. "You'll be safe in here."

Her thoughts returned to the jab at her side—the one that doubled her over, and the rush of something warm between her legs. She hesitated, afraid of knowing the truth. Sweat teemed across every part of her, and she glanced down at her legs, holding her breath. She expected to find blood but didn't. Eyes closed, she breathed a deep sigh, tears cutting the sweaty grime on her cheeks. It had become oddly quiet, Sammi dried her face and searched the room to see where they were. The stranger stood nearby, staring with disbelief stuck on his face. When she returned the look, he asked, "Emily?"

She shook her head, correcting him, "Sammi."

He rapped the side of his head hard enough to make a hollow thump, "Of course! Fifteen years. My God!"

Declan jumped in front of her when the man tried to approach. "Whoa!"

"It's okay," she assured him. Declan turned, brow furrowed. "Declan, this is... he's my dad."

"Your father? Father of Emily and Sammi Stark?" Declan said, asking, repeating himself. She didn't know how he'd react, her father's name synonymous with the disaster that befell their world. Opinions had split over time, but hers never wavered. She'd always followed what Emily told her. That their father was the one who'd tried to save the world. Not destroy it. She'd never asked Declan what he thought, but from the change in mannerisms and look on his face, she could see it was bad. "Save the world from climate change? That's what the machines were supposed to do?"

Her father blinked rapidly, ignoring it, saying, "Phil Stark." He stuck his hand out, adding, "I can't say I'd heard that one about oil. I guess in fifteen years, all kinds of rumors sprang up about me."

"A few, yeah," Declan answered, taking his hand cautiously. "But you did save us back there. That counts for something."

"How?" Sammi asked, daring to move closer, his face almost the same as when she'd seen him last. It was the beach, the day of the gray rainbows. Only, he'd been beaten terribly that day, his lip busted, his eyes swelled. Today, he looked like he had before the clouds fell. When she reached to touch him, he flinched slightly but then allowed it. "You should look older, but you haven't changed."

"They brought me back," he said, sounding guilty. He dipped his head like it was a confession. "I didn't mean for any of this. You have to know that. Both of you."

Declan motioned to the center of the lab. A younger woman sat alone, quietly perched on a chair. Her hand had been bloodied and bandaged. She waved to Sammi, putting on an odd grin as if she recognized her. Sammi shifted uncomfortably, squeezing Declan's hand. "Isla?"

"You remember me," the woman said with surprise. She approached, arms stretched, a tearful smile on her face. "You're so grown up."

"I think I remember you. Emily, my sister, she told me stories," Sammi said, images of the mall returning. The food court and the horses at the carousel. She saw what happened to the woman's fiancé, too, adding, "There was a man with you. He wore a uniform?"

"Nolan. My fiancé. He should be remembered," Isla said solemnly and hugged her. Pulling back, she asked, "How? How are you here?"

"That doesn't matter," Declan blurted, interrupting. "We're escaping from this place."

"Good," Phil replied. "You'll have to."

"Why?" Sammi searched the room, alarm rising. "What's going to happen?"

"We're going to shut the machines down."

TWENTY-THREE

The sound of a wave crashing came to her like a yawn—slow at first, easing, and then all at once. Emily regarded it, stirring, believing it had to be a dream, the big waves from before having been whittled smaller years earlier. Her eyes sprang open to find darkness, thoughts racing while passing in and out of confusion. She gripped a handful of sand, the ocean breakers lapping gently. *The Outsiders. I'm with Richard.* His warm body was next to her, rising and falling in the throes of a deep sleep. Emily recalled the dinner around the fire and the sudden feeling of exhaustion taking over.

I'm in the tent, she remembered, looking around, the canvas glistening wet. *I'm in the tent with Richard.*

Andie. The classroom, she thought, blinking away the last of a dream, a distant wonder stirring: would she ever teach again?

It was a dinner with the Outsiders, she told herself, the ocean lapping steadily like a lullaby, the tide higher. Richard's soft snores encouraged her to sleep more, but she couldn't. Emily decided that she'd slept enough. *Are we alone?*

Propping herself onto an elbow, she had to drop back at once and brace the front of her head. It pounded heavily, a throb knocking from inside her skull, trying to escape. Turning onto her side, arresting a spin, she remembered the dinner. "Shit. I passed out," she mumbled. "Sammi? He'd said something about seeing Sammi?"

The smell of fire pulled her attention, and she turned to see if anyone was outside, curious who else was awake. Beyond other tents, the faint glow of red and orange flickered, the leader of the group and a woman huddled nearby, stirring the embers. Some flew upward, dimming moments later, the sight like the fireflies she'd chased when she was a child. The fog was light, the camp in a large pocket.

Thirst touched her throat like the sand between her toes, dry and scratchy. Emily decided to chance a visit at the fire. Richard rolled onto his side, leaving behind the cold where he'd been lying against her. Without any thought, and as if by instinct, Emily rubbed his back, affection growing for the man.

Emily tried to shake the sleep out of her clothes and hair, but in the fire's dim light, she didn't much care how she might look. And as she had hoped, it was the leader sitting near the burning logs, his legs and arms crossed in a tidy bundle. He sat, fixed like a statue guarding his small group. Meditating perhaps, or perhaps this was how he slept? When he heard movement, his eyes popped open and found her through the flames. He tilted his square jaw, motioning to the seat next to him. A chill raced over her, the air cold, the heat inviting.

"Morning," she said, voice cracking as her breath fogged in the early dawn. "I apologize, passing out like that." The fire popped, shooting an ember in front of her. The red glow stayed bright for a moment, but then disappeared in a puff of smoke.

"You're fine now?" he asked. She nodded with some certainty and then motioned to the water beside him. He passed the bag. Emily gulped a mouthful, wetting the dryness clinging in her throat. "Easy. You don't want to get sick." She regarded the warning and sipped some more.

"Thank you," Emily said, returning the water. The leader waved it off, telling her to keep it. "Appreciate it."

"Your man? He's awake," the leader asked, poking the fire, embers racing to their death. Emily liked the sound of his question. *Your man.* "I need to tell you what's been planned. What we are going to do."

Richard sat next to them, rubbing the sleep from his eyes. Emily found herself shifting to close the distance between them and offer him the water. "Here."

"What I wouldn't do for a cup of hot coffee," he commented groggily.

"We come across it every once in a while," the leader said. "Old markets with a few overlooked supplies." He leaned forward, adding, "The vacuum-sealed packets. That's the trick. They're the only ones worth taking."

"My mouth is watering just thinking about it," Richard said, and made small, lip-smacking sounds.

"I'll see what we can do. We may have some." The leader snapped his fingers, a boy around twelve approaching, the leader whispering to him.

As they spoke, Emily found Richard looking at her. He offered a lazy smile, the fire spitting another ember, a log hissing. The fog was lighter, the sun rising and showing her the rest of the group, some sleeping around the fire, some in their tents. "Are you feeling better?" Richard asked. When she nodded, he continued, "Good. Had me worried."

"Tell me what you know," Emily said abruptly. "I remember some of what you said about our mortician and my sister, Sammi." Touching her hair, holding it up. "Like mine."

"Yes. The red hair," the leader answered. "We saw her and two other women come out of the machine. There was a young man on the beach, Declan they called him. They took him inside."

"Declan?" Richard asked. "That's my son?"

"Sammi is dead," Emily said, hurt, thinking the leader was playing a game.

"Dead?" Geoffrey asked. His focus shifted to Richard, asking, "Your boy? Dead too?"

"God no!" Richard said loud enough to stir the slumber from a few around them. "Jesus—" he stopped then, his mouth hanging open. "You said two others. They knew my boy?"

"The girl, the girl with the red hair called her Hadley—"

Shock reigned on Richard's face, the fire dancing in his wet eyes.

"Sir, with all due respect, the people you are talking about are dead." Emily heard the emotion in her voice and wanted to be stronger. Nervously tucking hair behind her ear, she added, "I participated in Sammi's cleaning. I watched the mortician pass her to the farming floor where..." She couldn't finish, and impatiently dried her tears.

"The morticians. The machine and the vial," the leader answered. "One of the morticians told us how the machine brings people back—people from your commune, to work and to run the machine."

It was what he was trying to tell them before she passed out. The leader held the vial in the fire's light, the blood inside having come from someone in the commune. Peter perhaps? "It's why you've had to stay away. Like you said last night."

"But why?" Richard asked. "None of this even sounds possible. The machines are just machines built to save the oceans or something."

"Are they?" the leader asked, sarcasm edging his voice. "Before your mortician stepped into the ocean, he showed us something. He showed us the truth."

"Did it have to do with my sister?" Emily asked, thoughts rising about what was said before she passed out. The fire had been too much when the leader was explaining that they'd seen a woman with red hair like hers. Emily combed fingers through her hair, asking, "The woman who looked like me. Did the mortician say anything about her?"

"It's the blood. He'd brought your sister's blood to the machine," he said, eyes leveling with hers. When she nodded, he continued, "We didn't understand what it meant until we saw you, and proof of what they're doing inside the machine. You understand?"

She nodded, trying to find her voice. But her heart had swelled like a balloon and was lodged in her throat. "I... I understand. What else did the mortician tell you?"

"Come," he urged, waving them closer to see.

Emily braced herself while the leader extended his hand and smoothed the sands. He began to draw figures, the fire's light shimmering gold while he drew a large circle and punched five divots around it. A single line was added next, connecting the divots to a single point at the center.

"That's the Earth," Emily began, studying the drawing. She pointed at the divots, recalling some of what her father had shared. "And these, they're the machines. Five oceans. Five machines."

"That's right," he returned.

Before he continued, Emily pointed to where the lines intersected, asking, "That intersection at the center. What is it?"

"You know about the five machines," he said, nodding. "But you don't know what these lines are?"

"What are they?" she asked impatiently, feeling anxious.

"The mortician said the machines are mining. They're mining deep into our Earth, converting the minerals into this fog," he told them, touching the low-hanging clouds.

"Mining?" Richard asked. Emily sensed the disappointment and anger. She felt it too. Just what were the machines? What were they really? "They were supposed to save the environment."

"The mortician said it was a lie," the leader countered. "What they're actually doing is *changing* the environment, transforming it."

"That can't be." Emily shook her head, stunned. If this was the truth, did her father know all along? Did he know what would happen, that people would die? Richard grimaced, red-faced. How much was lost? The world they knew, the families! Stomach flipping with a nauseating ache, she asked, "But why would we do this to our own—"

"Nobody ever said anything about *we*," the leader interrupted her, his eyes gazing upward. "Changing the Earth wasn't intended for us. It was never for us."

Richard followed the leader's gaze, a deep frown forming. "What!? Are you trying to tell us aliens planned all this?"

"Aliens?" Emily reared back, the idea of it too far-fetched to contemplate. Hot saliva filled her mouth with a threat. But what if they did see Sammi? What if? Still, aliens? Emily looked at the leader direct, insisting, "That can't be what you meant!"

"That's exactly what I'm saying," the leader replied, leaning back. "The mortician said that they're coming soon, just as soon as the change had been completed."

"Whoa, I'm sorry but!" Richard began, moving to leave. "That's quite the story and all, but—"

"Richard, wait," Emily pleaded, pulling on his arm, urging him to return. "What if it's true? Think of all that's happened the last fifteen years."

The leader held up the vial of blood, adding, "Think of how it's possible they're bringing people back."

"Well... there was that sheep they cloned. Dolly, its name was," Richard began, his words fading. "How can you prove it?"

Geoffrey dragged his fingers across the drawing, cutting into the gold light before sitting up to uncover a bundle placed front of him. "It isn't a matter of proving anything," he answered. His voice remained steady, almost unemotional. "We've seen enough to believe it, which is why we're going to end it."

Emily recognized what he had immediately. It was an explosive, bricks of it, a dirty white color that reminded her of putty. It had a distinct smell like old cars and oil-stained garage driveways. She didn't find herself questioning the validity of what the leader learned from the mortician. Instead, Emily asked, "Is it enough?"

The leader broke character for just a moment, a broad smile appearing, a shine glimmering from his teeth. "This is just a sample. We've got more than enough for a significant explosion. We only need to figure out where to use it that'd best cripple the machine for good."

"And then what?" Richard asked, brushing sand at the explosive. He hung a thumb over his shoulder. "That's just one of five."

"The convergence," Emily answered for the leader. "We stop the mining, and they'll never reach the intersection."

"That's when we go after the remaining machines."

Doubt found Emily with a shuddering thought. "What if we're wrong, though, and it makes things worse?"

The leader of the group looked at Richard and then to her, the fire's light showing a crazed and excited look on his face. "Then we'll finish this whole sorry mess! Once and for all!" He belted a raucous laugh that made her jump. A seriousness came over him then and he covered the explosive, rubbing it as if soothing a baby back to sleep. "If we do it right, taking down one should take down all of the machines. They'll fail systematically and you will finally see the End of Gray Skies."

TWENTY-FOUR

Phil followed his daughter and the young man she called Declan. And every time Sammi turned or spun around to face him, Phil saw his wife, her mother. There were other times when he saw Emily, the resemblance to her older sister uncanny. If not for the years separating them, they could have been twins. And all the while he wondered how much Sammi remembered from that day. Did she remember what happened to her mother? Or to him?

"How did you know to help us?" Declan asked. "I mean, you're not like the others. How could you know we weren't like them either?"

"I can read the lights," Phil answered, pointing up. He rolled his hand around, middle finger sticking up, gesturing to the lights.

Sammi stood at the door, facing it. "Dad? What if they come in?"

"We should be okay in here," Isla answered, busily working at the computer terminal. "I put an override in the computer to secure the room."

"We're safe," Phil added, drawn to be closer to his daughter, disbelief gaining, having thought he'd never see her in person again. When he moved nearer, caution fixed in her expression and he sensed fear.

"What are you doing?" she asked, stepping away, arms folded defensively.

"I just can't believe you're actually here," he told her, putting on a smile, but it felt awkward. He made a joke next, closing his eyes, wriggling and playfully saying, "They liked to cuddle! They crawled on me with their funny-looking feet and their funny-looking tails!" He was laughing and opened his eyes to see Sammi staring at him, her face drawn with deep concern.

"Phil, she doesn't remember that," Isla said, trying to sound supportive.

"At the mall?" Sammi commented, voice thin, a grin appearing. "You were joking about the rats in the service tunnels."

Phil's heart lifted, hopeful. "You do remember."

"Pieces," she told him, letting down her guard. "Just pieces of it."

"You've grown up so much." Phil dared another step, his hand out. Sammi surprised him when she took it. "I've missed too many years. For you and your sister."

"She's a teacher now," Sammi told him. Phil closed his eyes and listened to the sweetness in her voice.

"A teacher." It stung his heart to hear. But it was a good feeling. "That's wonderful."

"Dad, can you help us get home?" she asked, the moment ending abruptly.

A thump. The noise bouncing off the walls. It was the door, the only way in or out. "Zombies are persistent, aren't they," Phil told them with a snort. As if on cue, Sammi let go of his hand, retreating toward the blood vault with Declan. A louder thump. *An elbow*, he thought. *Or maybe they used their forehead this time.* There are times when concern is only a vague thing, a passing thing. Then other times, it is steeped with terror and rooted through every fiber of your being. It's dread, and it filled him. He faced his daughter. "Sammi? They certainly want you. Both of you?"

His daughter glanced at Declan who'd moved to put his arm around her and cover her front. His heart skipped, familiar with what he was seeing. He'd made the same gesture himself. Twice in his life. Before he could ask, Sammi answered, "It's our baby."

"Sir, that must be it. Right?" Declan asked, his voice filled with worry. "Why, though?"

"It's the DNA," Phil said, shutting his eyes. "To add it to their technology." A crash at the door jarred them, erasing the discussion as noises grew beyond the door. He stole a quick glance at the lights, intrigued by the machine's tenacity. "Fucking zombies."

"Zom— what?" Declan asked, confused and concerned.

"When they follow those—not aware that is—I call them zombies—" he answered, grabbing a table, dragging it. He waved his hand, Declan joining, "—start bracing the door."

"We can't let them have the baby," Isla said, jumping up and putting herself between the door and Sammi.

"I think I might understand what's happening," Phil exclaimed, breathing fast, the lab tables impossibly heavy. Another crash, stopping Phil and Declan while he studied the door, searching for any signs of the metal buckling.

"Why would a machine need my baby?" Sammi screamed.

"Phil! We're close, aren't we?" Isla asked him. "Closer than you thought."

Phil nodded, sweat teeming. "The mining! It's almost complete."

"What the hell does that mean?" Declan shouted, piling chairs onto the table.

Phil answered, speaking rapidly while counting in his head. "They want to begin the next phase."

"What phase?" Sammi asked. "What do you mean?"

"More!" he shouted, grabbing a desk. The door was giving, metal bending, the force shearing it. Years of isolation meant Phil suddenly felt the urge to laugh. He imagined the zombie bodies piling up behind the door. A dozen? A hundred? One after the other, pressing against the metal, bones breaking, flesh ripping, the ones at the bottom suffocating in the madness to break through the door. He controlled himself, clearing his expression. "We're running out of time."

"Please," Declan yelled at him with a mix of fright and fury. "Phil! Tell us what to do!"

Phil understood the need. He understood the need to mix the alien technology with their own. First, it was just the technology used to build the machines. Only nobody knew they were aliens. Not at the time when they were convincing him and the others that it was the only way to save the planet.

Regret blew through him like a hot flame and zapped the strength from his core. He glanced at Isla and Declan and then at his daughter. But there wasn't anything he could do about the past. Not now. He could do something about their future. The aliens were almost done with the first phase, the mining. The next phase was much more than cloning a massive workforce.

"They need the young man's DNA to start a new population. They're in need of offspring DNA, half clone, a hybrid to initiate the next step," he said, speaking aloud, working through the problem. When he looked over, Declan shook his head, mouthing, "Not me." Phil froze with shock, his focus locked on his daughter. After a moment, he finally said, "Sammi, that would mean you're a clone?"

"I was... I am," she stammered, ashamed, eyes filling. "Dad, I died."

"That means the machine brought you back," Isla said, nodding to Phil. She turned to Declan, saying, "This was about you and now it's about the baby. I didn't think it was possible."

Death. His daughter had died. Phil wanted, no needed, to know more, know everything. A slam jolted him, the zombies piling higher, stronger. Now wasn't the time, though. "Sammi, you are here now, and alive. Can you hear the lights?"

She shook her head, covering her unborn child. Looking at her belly, she answered, "Not since."

"Good," he said, relieved. "Then you won't turn."

"Turn!" Declan said in a near yell. "Like my mom and sister!?"

"They were here too?" Isla said, the look on her face telling Phil she was working the problem too, piecing the puzzle together. They both looked to Declan, and he realized the machine had to have planned all of it. Somehow, it had drawn the young man here to initiate the next phase.

"Why?" he asked, the worry on his face returning. "What about them? Is that going to happen to Sammi?"

"It won't," Phil assured him. He flashed a smile but, given the circumstances, realized it made him look mad, crazy even. "She'll live the remainder of her life as long as she can't hear the lights."

"The lights trigger the programming," Isla added, shouting over the flood of noise. With each heavy strike, dust shimmered in the light.

"Thank God!" Declan said, holding Sammi.

"It *is* your baby the machine wants," Phil told them, setting another chair, the blockade reaching the ceiling. "You were right to suspect that, and it won't stop until it has it."

A crash came against the lab door, Sammi and Declan rearing back, flinching. It made them all flinch, Phil included. "Declan!" Sammi cried, the top of the door breaking. "I'm afraid!"

Declan took her hand. "I'm afraid too," Declan told her and gently brushed her cheek.

Phil stopped mid-step, noticing. "You looked like Emily just then. Exactly like her," he said, eyes growing. Another crash, his gaze darting to find safety.

"The zombies are here for my baby!" Sammi cried, the crazed noises drowning her voice. "Declan!"

"Help us," Declan pleaded. "Help your daughter!"

"Yes, I can get you out of here," Phil said, leaving the barricade. He cradled Sammi's face, drying the tears on her cheeks, and then gripped Declan's shoulder. "But you two will never be safe. Not until we destroy this fucking thing."

"We'll use the vents," Isla yelled. "This way." She led them to the ventilation system, ducking beneath a lab table and jerking the grate over the opening. The cover disappeared in a single move, metal clamoring. Isla backed away, pointing at the black void. "In there!"

"It'll take you to safety," Phil said, wiping his brow, attention jarred by the zombies. "Sammi, you go first, ahead of Declan."

Hesitant, his daughter knelt at the opening, eyeing the dark hole. Phil pressed, urging her forward. The ruckus outside spurred her on and she entered, the sheet metal making a *wub-wub* sound as she was swallowed by the blackness. "Declan, come on." Her voice bounced from the ventilation shaft. Declan crawled in, stopping to turn around.

"I'm coming back," he told them. "Once Sammi is out of here and safe, I'm coming back inside to help you finish this."

"Okay then," Phil answered, admiring the young man's commitment. His thoughts turned to the young man Emily had found after the clouds fell. Phil struggled with the recall, his Swiss-cheese brain teasing. *Was it Pete?* It seemed to him that with each year that passed, there were more holes to avoid. *It's the cloning. Has to be.* But he knew better. He knew the science was accurate. The problem was in his mind which had become a playground of psychosis.

The door to the lab crashed into the room, floor shaking, a

flurry of activity erupting. Arms and legs spidered in every direction, flooding the lab and swallowing any light from the corridor. Isla quickly ducked beneath one of the lab tables, covering her head with trembling arms.

She'll be safe there, Phil assured himself. *They don't want her.*

"RUN!" he screamed urgently, throat grating as he tried to be heard over the zombies. His mouth went dry, the swarm toppling tables, shattering glass and stomping on everything in its path. Phil shrieked with an excited laugh, the monotony of day-to-day inside the machine gone with the suddenness of the machine's pursuit—a true cat and mouse chase.

Laughter soon ceased. It was his daughter that was the mouse, and she was carrying his grandchild. Phil didn't have to look at the lights to know which of the alarms were being signaled. By now, he could sense it, he could feel it in his bones. A wall of flesh climbed from floor to ceiling, his eyelids peeled open to stare at the horror mounting in front of him. They were like rabid dogs, biting and scratching, breaking bones and tearing hair to get to his baby girl. And they were going to tear him limb from limb when they reached him.

TWENTY-FIVE

Moving faster, the sheet metal banged hard against her palms and elbows and knees. It was the raucous and mayhem behind them, the echo of it terrifying. She peered over her shoulder, seeing Declan's figure, shadows breaking the light from the lab. There were things about her father Sammi remembered. Like the fast talking and his whispering at times, lips moving while speaking to himself. He still did that. He did it a lot. And it was enough to make her uncomfortable. She saw concern in Declan's eyes too. More than a few times while following him around the lab, the noises in the corridor gaining.

And his behavior? The way he seemed to laugh at the zombies, daring them when they broke into the lab, his hair disheveled, coveralls dirty, waving his arms and pointing at the lights, speaking faster than she could keep up. In a way, he reminded her of the feral cats from the old theater: ragged and scruffy, with an untidy wildness in his eyes that warranted caution. As crazy as he might seem, he did know a lot of what the machine was and why it wanted them. That's why she believed he'd help them. She just couldn't shake the feeling of being a little afraid of him too.

"Right behind you," Declan whispered, putting a finger to his lip. She nodded, moving fast, brushing her knees and elbows against the steel. Stray lights jutted ahead, seeping through the sides of the vent. It was enough to give her an idea of what was ahead. Sammi glanced back once more, expecting to find her father behind them, but he'd disappeared back into the lab.

"Dad," she mouthed, hearing chaos erupt in the lab, screams and hollering, an avalanche of destruction filling her ears. And amidst it all, she heard her father screaming at the zombies. "Goodbye ya fuggers. I'll see ya on the flip side."

"What's he doing?" Declan asked, reaching her. "Sammi, I don't think he's right."

"He's my father," Sammi answered sharply. "He's protecting us."

"Let's get this party started," Phil hollered from the shadows. A steady *wub-wub* followed, her father catching up to them.

"Dad!" It was relief, that he was safely with them.

She hoped Declan would feel the same, but he only looked behind her father, asking, "What about Isla?"

"They don't want her," her father answered, flattening his hair and shaking the dirt from his hand. "She'll be fine as long as she doesn't get in their way."

"And you know where to go?" Declan asked.

"I should, I'd think."

Phil crawled around them, Declan asking, "Then you've been in here before?"

"Better, I designed this place," her father answered, taking the spot at the front. His answer came with a snarky chuckle. "But yes, I've spent a lot of time crawling around this maze."

"As long as you can get us out of here," Sammi said, her hand on Declan's. The lab's destruction continued, the swarm tearing the place apart looking for her. "Dad, lead the way."

"You're sure about your friend?" Declan asked, turning to face the lab.

"The zombie fuggers won't even see her," Phil answered. "She's invisible to them."

There was comfort in hearing Isla would be fine. Yet her chest was tight and her mouth terribly dry. Morning sickness? It was the first thing to come to her. Sammi tried to find spit, her head throbbing while she slowly rubbed her middle. A soft thump returned, tapping the palm of her hand, their baby telling her to move.

"I will," she answered, the rate of its growth unbelievable. It was all unbelievable, but then again it was as real as she was. "I will, my baby."

Minutes felt like hours as Sammi followed her father, Declan behind her while Phil volleyed directions while they navigated the maze. Her hands and knees ached from the shuffle, the sheet metal smooth but riddled with sharp fasteners that pinched when struck.

The zombie destruction, that's what Phil called it, faded to a low roar, and eventually turned distant before suddenly ending altogether. They stopped when the silence reached them, her father rambling on and on about what the zombies were all about, the few who'd become aware like she was.

Sammi had them stop twice more, knees and hands bruising. As Declan helped, her father never stopped, his words sometimes sounding wild. Explaining when the machines were built and how they had been lied to, deceived by what he kept calling *aliens*. Sammi decided that there had to be some truth to what her father said. But, a lot of it sounded like the made-up horror stories. It was this last thought that made her feel sorry for her father. It made her wonder and try and recall if he was like this before or if his time in the machine made him this way.

"You'll take care of that baby," her father stated, interrupting her thoughts. "It truly is a miracle, Sammi. I hope you two know that. A true miracle."

"It is a miracle," she agreed. As if the baby had heard his words, Sammi felt a bump inside her. Her heart swelled. "All of this is a miracle."

Declan had gone ahead but was slowing. From what she could tell, they were safe. They were also buried somewhere deep inside the machine. Declan turned to face them, and in the dim light, Sammi could see the weariness, the exhaustion.

"You're sure about the year?" he asked her father, brow furrowed. "I saw what happened to my mother and sister and what the machine—" Declan's lips thinned and his chin shook.

"Declan," she began to say. "You can't think that way. I'd never let it happen."

"But what if you don't have a choice?" he said. "Did my mom have a choice? My sister?"

"Like I said about the lights," Phil began, sitting up with his back pressed against the sheet metal. With his height, his head was low, neck bent at an angle. "As long as Sammi can't hear them anymore. Plus, once you get outside, you and your baby will be safe."

"They won't come after her?" Declan asked with a guarded look. Her father's face blanked a moment as if the idea had never crossed his mind. Declan continued, "How can you know it will be safe?"

"The lights," Phil answered. Eyeing the nearby wall. "Without them, there's no instructions to follow."

"See, we'll be safe," Sammi said, thinking her father sounded oddly sensible. He even sounded calm and not at all hyper. *It's a window,* she thought, feeling thankful. *It's a window to who he used to be.*

"I think I've learned everything there is to learn about the machine's cycle." Phil wrapped his fingers around his neck, stretching. "Including what happens before and after."

"What is it that actually happens?" Sammi asked, having heard some of it already.

"When the machine brings us back—its workforce, the labor to run this place—you follow the lights. And it isn't something you choose to do."

Sammi nodded, recalling how she had to listen to them. "It was like breathing. I didn't have a say about it."

"Exactly," Phil snapped with a teacher's excitement. "That's the programming integrated into the DNA and the cloning process." He held a finger in the air, dipping his chin. "But, I think it's only a shadow of *their* DNA, just enough to make the lights work. It's not perfect. I noticed that there are gaps. That's how some of us become aware."

"And it only lasts a year, which is what happened to my mother and sister?" Declan added. "The instructions, that's what drives them to that awful place?" His eyes looked wounded.

"Almost," Phil said. His tone reminding Sammi of Emily during one of her lectures. "That place you mentioned, it's the *soul* of this machine. By that I mean, its most vulnerable point."

"I don't get it," Sammi said, glancing at Declan, who looked like he shared her confusion.

"What I mean, it's to feed the machine," Phil added impatiently. He cocked his head, fixing his look on Declan, adding, "I'm sorry for what you saw. For what it's worth, they weren't there when it happened."

Declan touched the side of his head. "The arm, it zapped the people gray before they fell from the conveyor."

Phil stretched his arms, touching the walls of the air shaft, and softly added, "The machine consumes what it produces. It's the ultimate recycler."

"Why the year?" Sammi asked, concern for what could happen to her driving the question.

"That alien DNA I mentioned, the part that makes the lights speak. It doesn't have resilience, the human immune system killing it like it was a common cold. It's not an overnight thing, but by the time a year is up, sometimes sooner, the person will wake to complete awareness. They won't be able to hear the lights at all after that."

"I woke up early," Sammi commented, feeling more confused. A thumb. It might have been a fist or the heel of the baby's foot. She covered her belly, asking, "Because of the baby?"

"Maybe the additional DNA diluted the alien's?" Declan offered, shaking his head. "It's all so confusing."

Phil looked at them, his excitement becoming a penitent stare, "Yes. Yes, I think that was the risk the machine took in allowing you two... well, you know, to get pregnant. Only, it backfired."

"Sure did," Declan said, his voice rising. "By leaving the machine, Sammi and the baby will be safe."

Without another word, Declan gave Sammi a quick squeeze, kissing her. He reached into his coveralls and pulled out the index card. He gave it a long hard look, pushing his fingers over the numbers.

"What's that you have?" Phil asked. Sammi knew he'd want to see it. There were numbers, five rows of them, the card like a puzzle. Her father held out his hand, snapping his fingers. "Please."

Declan handed over the card. "It was my mother's, and I brought it, hoping to find out what happened to our End of Gray Skies." His voice trembled slightly. "But now I understand how much more is going on. Will this help you stop the machines?"

"End of Gray Skies?" Phil questioned.

"It was supposed to happen, the day I died." Sammi went to lift the coveralls and show the scar. She stopped, though. "Every five years, there's an attempt to shut the machines down."

"An attempt?" her father scoffed. He frowned and shook his head. "Someone at your place is playing games."

"The executives," Declan said under his breath. He pinched the index card, staring hard at it. "I saw it, though? The fog lifted. The sun came out."

"That's a maintenance window. That's all." Phil snapped his fingers again, eager to see the card. "Every five years or so the machines pause to measure and adjust. Once the boring is realigned, they proceed."

"Five years?" Declan said, a flush rising from beneath his collar. "The executives! They planned around it. For what? Morale!" He was screaming, voice carrying in waves through the air shafts.

"Shh!" Phil said, lunging and covering Declan's mouth. He pressed hard enough to turn his hand white, saying, "Shh, they'll hear you."

"Dad!" Sammi cried, jerking on her father's arm. Declan's mouth and nose were covered, his eyes bulging. "Dad, please!"

"Shit, sorry," Phil said, shaking himself free, falling back. "I... I didn't mean it."

"It's okay, I guess." Declan held out the index card. "The executives were lying to us the whole time. For all I know, this is bullshit too."

Phil took the index card and counted out the numbers. "This one, the third one down. It's familiar," he told them. "Maybe something to do with *this* machine. If I'm right, the other numbers, they'd have something to do with the remaining machines."

"So you can use them?" Sammi asked, feeling hopeful.

He shook his head, half nodding. "I don't know yet. Isla's

helping with it," Phil answered, the look on his face questioning.

"I told you that I'm coming back to help," Declan reminded Phil as he turned to push ahead. "When Sammi is safe, you'll let me back in?"

"Don't worry," Phil nodded, his eyes sparking as if a fresh stock of ideas had suddenly come to him. "I won't forget."

When they moved on, Sammi listened to the quiet shuffling, their passing from one air shaft to the next, then through another and so on until she thought they were going in circles. Her father talked to himself most of the time, planning an attack by using the computer terminal. He'd mentioned enlisting Isla's help too, that he couldn't do it alone. And on occasion, his constant drone was eclipsed by instructions to turn left or right. And finally, Sammi saw the familiar gray daylight that she'd known most of her life.

Home, she thought and pressed her feet into the black sands. They were outside, and while she was tempted to look back at the machine, she decided against it. After all, there was nothing for her there. She took Declan's hand, everything suddenly seeming terrifically quiet and peaceful as if the world had stopped. In a way, she thought the moment seemed quite ironic—the world hadn't stopped, hers was just beginning.

TWENTY-SIX

The cautions and concerns that weighed on her had disappeared. Not just the fear of what lay beyond the fog, but that sense of them being hunted was gone completely. It was security. Walking with the Outsiders had brought that, and for the first time, Emily felt relaxed. Still, there were the other worries, the ones hinging on unanswered questions. She thought of Peter, and the torn-up index card. There was the mortician, too, and whatever the executives knew about the machines. Whatever it was, it had led to Peter's death. Just what was it that compelled him to jump and end his life so tragically?

Emily stayed close to Richard, with Geoffrey the leader of the Outsiders within sight of them. She could see from his gait he was feeling freer too, walking a little looser, more relaxed. The tightness around his eyes, and that endless furrow had gone some. Not completely, but enough to ease the rigidness of his posture. There was security in the company of the Outsiders and their leader. That is, with one huge exception, their single bad apple—Harold trudging nearby.

The fog was favorable today, thin enough to show most of

the group. Emily kept her ears tuned to the ocean, its shallow waves lapping gently, an occasional fish jumping. A circle of men stayed tight around the group, their backs turned and their weapons at the ready to face anything that might lurch out of the fog. They were trained and substantial in size, leaving her to think nobody would be crazy enough to tempt them.

Women and children stayed at the center, protected in a bubble of safety. She thought of James, *Boo*, and for a moment imagined him with her, his face turned up to hers, grinning. She clapped her eyelids shut and squeezed the memory from sight. *You were my treasure.* And like Boo, the Outsiders kept their treasure at the center of the pack—the children. One of them ran ahead, dancing and kicking at the sand, two of them joining playfully. The sudden spout of chaos and fun was doused quickly by a stern grunt, the leader turning with hard, fearful eyes set. While there was security in numbers, silence was the best safeguard.

Tugging on Richard's arm, Emily led him toward the water's edge. There was safety there with the ocean guarding them from one side, the group from the other. There was the added bonus of cooling her feet in the water. Emily yanked her shoes off and eagerly tied the laces in a knot, slinging them over her shoulder before dipping into the light surf. Relief was instant, the water cold, a chill racing up inside her, goosebumps springing across her arms and front. She saw Richard notice and then turn away politely. She didn't mind that he looked and found it was getting easier to admit she sensed something more growing between them.

"It's cold," she told him, lifting her foot to wiggle her toes at him. "Wanna try?"

"I might," he said, lowering himself far enough to scoop the water and wash the sand from his hands. The sea lapped against the shore with a soft clap, the tide low, telling her they were near the middle of the day; six hours or so had passed since talking about what the machines were.

Richard surprised her then, his hand extended, fingers glistening wet in the gray daylight. Her heart swelled nervously, and she took hold. She saw the loose sand and realized his hand was offered to help her step over it. When his grip loosened to let go, Emily took a chance and squeezed affectionately. She found his eyes then, hoping he'd hold on a little longer. He returned the smile but let go, disappointment coming to her.

"Thank you," she told him, speaking fast, focus falling to the beach. It hurt and was a little embarrassing. Emily needed to mask the feelings, thinking it was too soon for him, too soon after his wife and daughter's passing. "I didn't see that."

"You don't want a twisted ankle out here," he commented, gaze lifting toward the fog walling around them.

"Look at that," she said, the moment forgotten. The sight was like a living memory, the mall and the way the fog would roll against the glass. The group was slowing, and she grabbed for Richard's hand whether he wanted it or not. "Hold up."

"Whoa," the leader grunted. It was a heavy cloud, the leader grunting again, signaling a stop. The heavy gray mist advanced silently, folding over them like a blanket. Before the men at the edges of the group disappeared completely, they closed in, tightening the circle around them. Emily squeezed Richard's hand before he disappeared too. He did more than squeeze a reply, though. He was next to her, arm in arm. This was the most dangerous fog, completely blinding. The leader grunted twice more, feet shuffling rapidly, sand kicked with the commotion.

"I'm scared," she mumbled, her legs trembling. While she'd always considered herself one of the strongest in their commune, it was this type of fog that frightened her most. This was what it was like when the clouds first fell, when it killed the most, including her mother.

"I'm here," Richard assured her, his voice near her ear.

"Thank—" she began to say, chest tight. When she turned toward him, the fog rushed between them. Richard disappeared in an instant, his touch the only way for her to know he was still there. "Thank you."

A hot breath touched the back of her neck, startling her. Emily jumped, spinning around. "Was that you?"

"Huh?" Richard asked, the direction of his voice telling her it wasn't, that it couldn't have been him. When she didn't reply, he asked, "You okay?"

"Yeah. I think." Emily brushed her shoulder, rubbing the back of her neck to be sure. "Just my nerves playing games."

Another hot breath. It touched her shoulder this time. A shriek rang out, ripping across her throat. The leader grunted twice, demanding silence. Emily pulled on Richard's arm, his muscles tensing. "What is it?" he asked.

"I don't know." They were blind in the fog, but Emily heard someone approaching, the sound of their gait telling her it was the leader. His grunt came within a few hands, just enough for her to see the outline of his tall figure. "I'm so sorry."

"With silence, we survive," he instructed, his tone like a reprimand, the same kind she'd used to scold children in her classroom. Skin flushed, the sting of nervous sweat pinching the pits of her arms, she nodded fervently. "Silence is survival."

A wheezy sniggering drifted from behind them—it was short and brief, and it was all she needed to hear to know it was Harold Belker. At once, she was back in their classroom, Harold taunting the other kids and laughing. He'd spent more than ten years in her classroom; there was no mistaking that sound. He was mean. *No, that's too nice.* Harold was evil and he'd killed her sister. Violence was survival, too, and if not for the leader's presence, Emily thought she'd rip the tongue from Harold's head and pluck the eyeballs out with a sharp stick, using them to plug his earholes. Her sister's killer would live. But he'd live blind, deaf and in silence. She wiped the back of her neck and shoulder again, disgusted by the idea of his breath on her.

"My apologies," she told the leader when he saw her shifting irritably. "I got startled."

Harold's laughter rose, the leader grunting and shoving past her. Water splashed; his step heavy.

"I'm sorry," Harold cried out. "Just a joke—" His apology was cut off by a whoosh and thwack, a stern beating following. Try as she might, Emily could never feel sorry for Harold, even if the punishment was swift and made her cringe.

"Ahead," the leader said abruptly, a commotion coming from in front of them. It was the call of a wild animal, a trot thumping in the wet sand. The leader brushed past her again, the smell of body odor following. His footsteps stopped and he repeated the wild animal's call. It was returned immediately. He turned and grunted at the group, feet shuffling, bodies migrating toward the center, the safety of the pack's bubble growing. Emily did the same, holding onto Richard's arm, following the others until the pack had knitted together into a tight bundle. Silence descended in the group while the wild animal calls continued.

"I think it's scouts," Richard whispered. "Two, maybe three, walking ahead to signal danger."

"Danger?" she mouthed, the bodies tightening around them, the heat suffocating like a heavy blanket. Sweat beaded on her head, and the lightheadedness from the evening's fire returned. She took to a knee and leaned on Richard, hoping he wouldn't mind.

"What is it?" she heard the leader ask. "What did you find?"

"The machine," a winded voice spat, choking to catch some air. "Ahead—a few hundred yards—the machine, and people. Two or three, I think. They just appeared outside of it."

Yards, Emily thought, having gotten used to the use of hands as a measure. The Outsiders had continued to use feet and yards. What mattered, though, was finally reaching their destination. They were near the machine.

"Emily, we're almost there," Richard said. He helped her stand, his arm around her middle, his face relieved. And for the first time since seeking out the machine, Emily felt the same.

<h1 style="text-align:center">TWENTY-SEVEN</h1>

"It's safer out here," Sammi mumbled, Declan thinking she was talking to herself. He glanced at her, her lips moving as she mumbled more, the words lost. She looked like her father in the outside light, but without the crazed eyes and stammering.

"Damn right it's safer," he answered, dabbing the end of his sleeve next to his eye where one of the zombies had scratched him and left a lump. When he moved, the sting of a hundred bumps and bruises and cuts sang out across his body. Other than with Harold, he'd never been in a fight in his life. Certainly, nothing like this either. He dared a deeper breath and waited, feeling for an injury that was down inside him, threatening. None came, though, and he eyed the fog as it grew thick and closed around them. "Home?"

"For sure. I'm ready," she answered, handing him the end of the tether strap. He'd almost forgotten about it after they reached the lab. But Sammi hadn't and that meant something. She grabbed his hand next, aggressively enough for him to feel it and wince. Brow raised, the look on her face turned apologetic. With her other hand covering her middle, she tugged on his arm, wanting to leave this place. She didn't look back at the machine. Not once. Not like he did.

She's free, he thought, keeping the words to himself. A much-needed relief came over him, a thought that she wouldn't be able to leave having sat at the back of his mind. When she tugged his arm harder, he saw that Sammi had truly disconnected from the machine. He touched her belly, joining her hand, thinking, *We're free*.

"Did you hear that?" she asked. Sammi stared ahead, eyes wide and afraid. "Declan—"

"Shh," he interrupted, his mouth hanging open, frozen in place. He locked eyes with her and gently pressed his finger against his lips. When he cupped his ear, the sound of skittering sands reached it. There was no wind, it was someone approaching, shuffling, their gait fast. He held up three fingers, hearing them from his right to left, surrounding them. The hairs on his neck stood and his eyelids peeled wide. He sensed they were being hunted, the horror of it consuming. Instinct took over, and he dropped to his knees, taking Sammi with him. She leaned heavily against his body as he wrapped his arm around her nervously.

From out of the fog, the first of them showed. There were arms and legs, a head and torso, the outline of a body which he thought looked like a ghost. More of them followed, spreading from the ocean to the farthest dune, making it impossible to go anywhere except back to the machine. They stopped, a line of them within a hundred hands, their arms down, shoulders back, fixed upright like prison bars.

"I'm scared," Sammi whimpered. He pulled her closer, the moisture of her warm breath on his neck. His mind went to the zombies. They must have believed they'd escaped the machine and followed them outside to capture them. But the clothes. Even in the gray light, the clothes were like the ones he remembered, only patched and sewn and then patched again. There was the odor too. The zombies didn't smell, it had been absent inside the machine.

Outsiders, Declan feared and braced for an attack, shutting his eyes, draping his other arm over Sammi's head. She began to cry softly, his comfort doing little to soften what was coming. "I love you, Sammi—"

"Declan?" a woman's voice shouted. "Declan. Is that really you?"

"Emily?" he asked, peering out, disbelief telling him it had to be a lie. Emily's narrow face seemed to swallow the world, coming into view, staring at him. His heart filled with shock when he saw her wide grin and a fresh tear falling onto her cheek. She leaned in and peppered his face with kisses but stopped abruptly and dropped to her knees.

"Declan?" Emily asked, motioning to Sammi. Declan removed his arm and revealed Sammi's long red hair. A gasp escaped from Emily as she covered her mouth. Sammi raised her chin from the safety of Declan's cover, opening her eyes to greet them. Horror and doubt struck his old teacher, and Emily shook her head, rearing back until the fog stole the features of her face. "That's not possible!"

"Hi, Emily," Sammi said, sounding cautious. Declan caught Emily before she fell over. He held her in place while she continued shaking her head, slow and orderly like she was reading from a book. Sammi dipped her face toward her older sister, adding, "Emily, it's... it's me."

Emily glanced over her shoulder at the others who were joining them. "They said you'd been seen, but I didn't believe it."

"The machine—" Sammi began to say.

"Dad!?" Emily asked, interrupting. She didn't wait for an answer, the space between the siblings collapsing. Emily took her sister into her arms, crying, "I don't care how. I don't."

"Dad. He's alive, Emmy," Sammi said, taking Declan's hand. "He said he's going to help us."

"Declan, son!" he heard his father's voice. Declan was lost for words, the sight of his father a shock. More than that, he looked different, the man kneeling next to Emily looked younger. He even looked healthier and not at all the sickly sight that had become the norm.

"How?" Declan asked, frowning, confused by the sight. His father patted his shoulder, firm and strong. There was no hint of his father's hands shaking or mouth and chin trembling. And the smell? Declan searched for it but found nothing that said his father had been drinking. More than anything, it was the life in his father's eyes that convinced him something terrific had happened. "You're here."

"We came for you," his father said. "We came to save you."

"It's good to see you," Declan said, tearing up, his father's hands on his face, searching the bruises. "And you too, Ms. Stark."

"Oh please. Emily," she exclaimed. "Just Emily."

"Yes, ma'am," he answered. She made a face, but his attention swung to the others with them. The three or four he'd heard coming had multiplied, their presence all around them. "There's so many of you."

"Hi, Mr. Chambers," Sammi told his father, sounding cautious. "It's good to see you again."

"Declan," his father said, slack-jawed, focus narrowed. "How... how can this be possible?"

"So it's true," a voice blurted from the fog. Declan covered Sammi, instincts taking over. "What the mortician spoke of. It was the truth."

"Who are you?" A tall man stepped out of the fog and knelt alongside them, and carefully pinched Sammi's hair. Declan shooed the man's hand away, but relaxed some when Emily and his father shook their heads. The tall man's long face showed no expression, but his eyes wandered back and forth, consuming every detail. Annoyed by the silence, Declan repeated, "I said, who are you?"

"Declan, this is the leader of the group that's been helping us," his father answered.

"You know us as the Outsiders," the tall man said, voice deep and smooth like the kind Declan had heard on the radio before the clouds fell.

"Outsiders?" At once, he shrank back with Sammi.

The tall man shook his head. "These are my people. You're safe with us."

Declan uncovered Sammi, the fog revealing more of his people, rows and rows of them forming a circle. They were in a pocket, and for the first time, Declan could see how many had traveled with his father and Emily. Men and women and children—families—just like the ones he left in their commune. The younger children squatted in the sand, picking at it while watching them, curiosity filling their faces. They weren't at all like the Outsiders that had been portrayed to him—the monsters he'd grown up learning to fear. Declan helped Sammi to stand with him.

"That's not fucking possible!" someone shouted. Declan reared up and balled his fists. The voice was as distinct to him as the first time he'd heard it. "She's dead. She can't be here!"

"Harold!" Declan exclaimed, clenching when Harold appeared from the fog, leaping forward like a predator hunting. Only, Harold didn't have the eyes of a hunter today. Declan cocked his head and forgot everybody around him. "Harold, I'm going to end you."

But before he could say another word, Sammi was gone from his side, her hands raised, fists at the ready. He followed, thinking how appropriate it would be if they killed Harold together. When he took a step, his father's arms were around him, holding him back.

"But Dad, he's a murderer!" Declan screamed while Sammi threw her arms like clubs, striking Harold in the face. It was flesh on flesh, Harold defenseless, horror-stricken like he'd seen a ghost. And in a way, he had, the dead returning to take their vengeance. Satisfaction touched Declan's heart when Sammi landed the third or fourth solid punch. The anger fueling his muscles drained out of him, this was Sammi's fight to have. Not his.

"Get her off me!" Harold cowered, covering his head as he tucked into a ball and fell. Sammi screamed and kicked, punching her murderer.

"You monster!" Sammi screamed, arms slowing when she began to cry. "I had a life and you stole it from me!"

"Let me go, Dad," Declan pleaded, wriggling loose. His father held firm, surprising Declan with his strength. "She's going to have a baby, let me go to her." His words carried a far greater strength than anything physical, and his father let go instantly.

"Declan!" his father answered, surprise stealing much of his voice.

"Oh, my," Emily said, standing to take his father's hand. Declan ignored their reactions and went to Sammi. She fell into his arms, sobbing.

"It seems that much of what your mortician spoke of is the truth," the leader repeated. "The machine does bring people back."

As Sammi cried into Declan's shoulder, there was uncertainty and fear on Emily's face, his father's too.

"Why?" Declan began, glancing at Harold whose gaze was fixed on the ghost from his past. Disgusted, Declan pressed, "Why is he here?"

"They're reforming him," Emily answered. "Can you believe that?"

"You can't reform an evil like that," Sammi spat sharply. "He doesn't deserve help. Not from anyone."

Harold grunted and swiped at the blood and spittle dripping off his chin. He got to his knees and then to his feet, groaning. The smile was next, and their old classmate snorted a piggy laugh as if nothing had happened. Immediately, the leader snuffed out the sound with the back of his hand. Harold's head whipped back, the rest of him following. Declan sighed, rage partially appeased. It wasn't enough, though. It would never be enough.

"We believe in reform," the leader added. "We believe in purpose, and that everyone is here to fulfill one."

"Sammi's right," Emily argued. "You can't reform him."

"Enough!" the leader demanded, weariness erasing the stony look. He raised a hand, demanding, "Not another word of this."

"Declan, tell us about the machine," his father asked and then motioned to Sammi. "Tell us how any of this is even possible."

"They used us, Dad," Declan answered, selecting his words carefully. How much should he tell them? "The machine... the *machines*, they were never meant to help us. They used us. They've used all of us."

"You know the truth then?" the leader questioned.

"We do," Declan answered. "Dad, Mom and Hadley, they were there too."

"What?" His father stabbed a look over his shoulder in the direction of the machine, shoulders slumped. "Are you saying they're alive?"

"Not anymore," Sammi answered for him. "But they were there. For a little while."

"Why then?" his father cried. "What's the purpose of any of it?"

"The people inside, they're a workforce," Declan explained.

"Dad called them zombies," Sammi added. "That's what they're like too. Zombies."

"What about the morticians?" the leader asked. "The executives that have gone to it?"

"All lies. The morticians bring the blood from our commune. And the executives, they tell the lies, including the End of Gray Skies, which was never going to happen." Declan faced the leader, asking, "How did you know?"

"Zombies? Your mom and sister?" Richard asked, disgust and hope filling his face, darting in and out of the fog, searching. "Are they with you?"

"No, Mr. Chambers. I'm sorry. It was too late," Sammi answered, the words stuck in her throat.

"No!" his father snapped, face cramped. "You're here. Why aren't they!"

Seeing his father get emotional brought fresh tears to his eyes. Declan had to tell him the truth. "When they were brought back, it only lasted a year. That's all they get, unless they leave the machine, like Sammi did."

"Then they can come back? Again?" his father asked, hope in his voice.

"Dad!" Declan nearly shouted. He shook his head, the hope on his father's face dulling until it was gone. "Dad, I'm going back inside. I'm working with Phil Stark and a woman named Isla. They're like Sammi. They're aware. We're going to shut the machines down. All of them."

His father crossed the short distance between them and took Declan's shoulders. When his father found the words he wanted to say, he asked, "But they might have come back, and you'll look for them. Right?" There was a look in his father's eyes that broke his heart. "You'll find them, and you'll bring them out of the machine!"

"No, Dad—" Declan began, frustration turning to anger.

"We can use this," Harold interrupted. He had left the

group and returned carrying a package. He circled cautiously around Sammi to stand next to the tall man. "I helped build it."

"What is it?" Declan asked, directing the question to the leader.

"When we learned the truth from your mortician, we decided to blow up the machine. To end gray skies."

Harold snickered, gaze turning maniacal while he mimed an explosion. Declan didn't find the humor, though, but was intrigued by the idea of a bomb.

"If you can show me how to work it, then I know exactly where to place it," Declan told the leader.

"You have a place?" Geoffrey asked. Sand shuffling, footsteps ascending, the leader moved around Harold and the package, Declan followed.

"I do. It's the machine's soul," Declan answered. "If we put it there, a bomb might do more than just cripple it. It could destroy it."

"But if the machine can bring your mother and sister back..." Declan's father argued. Anguish riddled his father's words. His father was right to ask, and it made Declan pause and regard the idea. What if he could bring them back?

"I can't answer for you or your commune," the leader told them. He held up a long finger and traced it along the package. "However, do what you will inside the machine. Our plans move forward."

"And I'm going to deliver it. I'm going to sit the thing right outside," Harold added proudly, pulling the cover away from the package. "I found the pieces to build it, so I get to set it off."

Declan's heart dipped when the light struck a bundle of electronics wrapped around light brown bricks with the letters 'C4' printed on them. It was the wiring, and the other parts Declan knew. He'd known them for years. Sammi had too, and when the recognition hit her, she clapped a hand over her mouth. Harold turned over one of the rusted cylinders, exposing a patch of metal with markings from Andie, their electronic classmate. And below it, Declan saw the large graying button he had pressed so many times before.

"Where did you get this?" Declan demanded. "Why Andie?"

"The electronics, we could use them with the recovered explosives," the leader said, pausing long enough to measure the reluctance. "Good people died to get the explosive. This must happen."

"Where did you find explosive?" Declan's father asked, frown narrowing.

"Amazing what can be found in a world left behind," the leader answered.

"But why Andie?" Declan demanded; the question directed at Harold. "You could have used electronics from an old stereo or television."

"We used whatever we could find, including Andie," Harold added. Declan knew the truth, though. Harold hated Andie. He hated anything to do with the class and commune. Harold ran his hand over the front of Andie, admiring the hodgepodge work. "Just need to turn it on and BOOM—it'll detonate!"

"It's Andie," Sammi cried, gently touching its front like it had a heart. And in a way it did have a heart.

Harold jabbed the large button. Andie jolted awake with a sudden sputter and shake, the unexpected commotion sending everyone back in a fleeting step. The rounded end of Andie's head turned as it voiced a familiar greeting, "Hi, everybod-dy!"

"It's not armed yet." Harold laughed raucously and showed a wiring harness. "Wow, are you guys dumb?"

"Yeah, dumb or something," Declan returned, wanting to slap the stupidity out of Harold. When their eyes locked, Harold's sneer vanished, his head dipping while he continued to work and shut Andie off.

"I can't believe you did that!" Emily scolded. She wasn't referring to the joke, Harold's scaring everyone. This was Andie. "You... you stole Andie from our classroom!"

"We took what was needed," the leader countered. There was no emotion. No remorse or empathy.

"Doesn't change the fact that you stole it," Emily continued, shaking with anger. "Who does that?"

"Recalculating." Andie's voice warbled with a hiss and pop.

"Shut up," Harold yelled, thumping Andie's head. "Thought I turned it off."

"Are you sure you know what you're doing?" the leader asked.

A long pause, Harold stared at Andie and the C4, an awkward smile appearing. "I guess we'll find out."

"Maybe it's not so wise to hit it like that," Declan's father commented.

"Stupid thing can't hurt us!" Harold replied, annoyed. "Can't do anything until we detonate." He lifted a small box that had been fashioned from other parts. At the center, Declan recognized it as being made from some of Andie's old parts.

"The switch on that box, the explosive is tied to Andie's projector?" Declan said, asking.

"Hi, Emily, is it time for our lesson, today?" Andie's voice chimed with the same robotic inflections programmed to entertain children.

"Turn it off!" Emily cried, emotion breaking in her voice. "Please!"

"Like this," Declan said, pressing the gray button, jostling it, the button temperamental.

"Uh ohhhhh," Andie announced, voice fading. "Is the lesson over, time to say goodbye?"

TWENTY-EIGHT

"Ms. Sammi, could you share what happened to you?" the leader addressed her, the use of Ms. feeling awkward. She held back the smile by thinking of those final moments in the theater. It was easy to do with Harold only a few feet from her, the rage inside stirring like something toxic, her body needing to expel it. The leader cleared his throat, catching her attention. "I'm sure it'd be difficult, but would you tell us?"

Sammi shrugged shyly, nervousness sweeping away the gnawing contempt for Harold. Instead, she was twelve again and standing in front of Emily's classroom. From somewhere deep she recalled Harold's stinging taunts, urging some of the classroom to sing: *Sammi Sunshine Sammi Sunshine Sammi Sunshine.*

"It's okay," Declan said, his hand gently rubbing her back. "We're safe."

"Are we?" she asked and glared at Harold. He was watching her with eyes slitted like a predator.

"He won't be a bother," the leader added. "Never again."

Slowly closing her eyes, the memories came forward like a rising tide. Sammi squeezed Emily's hand and stepped into the descriptions of all that she could recall. She began with where her new life started, her death. She also told them about the ruins of the theater and Declan crying and the warm light touching her skin and how, in those final minutes, she really did feel like Sammi Sunshine. There was a void afterward. *A big nothing, a blank spot*, was how she put it. And then in the next memory, she was inside the machine and thinking that she had gone to a better place.

"A better place?" someone asked.

"It's the technology," she explained. Pinching her shirt, she added, "The rooms are clean and new like my clothes. There's food too, like the way it was before the clouds fell."

"Gosh, why leave?" another person asked. "It sounds wonderful."

Her smile faded and she shook her head, sternly answering, "It's a prison. You don't have control. The machine lets you think you do, but you don't. It makes you work all the time, no choices, nothing."

"A zombie," Declan commented.

Sammi nodded, saying, "That's what my dad called them. Zombies."

"Like in the movies?" a younger voice asked.

"Yeah, but without the flesh-eating part," Declan joked. A quiet laugh.

The leader leaned forward, scratching his chin. "How does the machine do that? I mean, control you?"

"There're these lights. To see them was like breathing," she told them. "There was never anything to question, because nobody knew what to question, just to follow."

"Then the year was over?" Declan's father asked, a sad look remaining on his face. He lowered his head, adding, "That's what happened to my family?"

"I'm sorry, Mr. Chambers." It was all Sammi could think to tell him.

Cool air rushed over her fingers where Emily had been holding them. "Sammi, how did you get away?"

"It's our baby," she answered, bracing her middle. "I lost the lights, rejected is a better word. It was like I was amputated, removed."

"It's a miracle really," Declan said, shifting to sit closer. "Sammi was finally able to see the machine for what it was."

"What happened to the index card?" Declan's father asked. "From the executive floor."

"I gave it to the others, they're aware like Sammi," Declan answered. "They said they'd know what to do with the numbers. I think between what they do and the bomb, it'll be the end of the machine. Forever."

"Maybe you can you use this one too?" Emily asked, handing Declan a small pouch. He turned it over, staring at the fragments of coveralls sewn together, and loosened the cinch to show the pieces of an index card. Emily's voice broke as she added, "It's from Peter."

"From the executive floor, it's like the one my mom had," Declan said. He closed the pouch and tucked it away, asking, "The mortician? You said he was involved?"

"The morticians, more than one of them," Emily answered. She shook her head, "And we've no idea how long either. But they were bringing blood to the machine."

"That explains the reanimation," Sammi acknowledged. "It's how my blood got there."

"My wife and daughter, theirs too," Declan's father added. "Does anyone know how long the morticians and executives have been working with the machines?"

"Since the beginning," Declan answered, his chin quivering. Sammi tried to comfort him but felt the anger coming off him like heat. "They've been involved since the first day."

Declan went on to explain more of what her father told them, but Sammi got distracted when Harold moved. He'd taken a seat closer, and began rocking from side to side, his gaze meeting her eyes from time to time. Harold was teasing like he'd always done, anything to put her on edge.

"Reanimation," she heard the leader ask. "These people who are brought back. They're just substitutes. Or is it really them?"

"Am I a substitute?" Sammi blurted, suddenly offended by the question, the topic. When Declan and Emily tried to soothe the rising, she waved them off. "No, it's a fair question. Am I?"

"You're not—" Declan began to answer. He swallowed dryly, choking on the truth.

"Go ahead, finish," she insisted.

"When they first come back, like my mom and sister did, they're just a glimpse of who they were."

"A glimpse," the leader repeated.

"But when they wake up—that is, when they become aware —it's them again." Declan turned to face her, eyes glistening. "You are you, Sammi Stark. Understand."

"I understand," she mumbled and leaned back while Declan and the group continued.

Their voices went on and on, each drowning in a sea of chatter as her memories came to life. She could smell the salt and the musty damp air in the theater. She could hear the feral cat's crying mewl and the sudden sting from its scratch when she tried to free it from Harold's snare.

But who was the trap really for? Who was the one who'd been caught? Sammi felt the sting of tears realizing how she'd walked into his snare. She flinched when hearing the memory of the balcony's wood crack and splinter.

When the weightlessness took hold with that sense of falling, Sammi dug her hands into the cold sand, fingertips driving fast until they burned. She fought the impossible rise in her gut as air passed through her hair. When she hit the theater floor, the metal post stabbing through her, Sammi jolted hard, hands shaking.

"You okay?" Emily whispered. Sammi stared hard at Harold, seeing that he had moved again. Emily followed the scowl and took her arm. "I won't pretend to know what it must be like sitting across from him. But he can't hurt you now."

"I know," Sammi started to say.

"This one!" the leader announced in a booming voice, pulling her attention. "This one will go with you." The leader pointed to Harold, whose mouth dropped open.

"Uh-uh," Harold argued. "Outside. I was going to deliver it outside."

Declan's mouth curled, the sight of it giving Sammi something to smile at. "Harold, I guess you'll be with me," Declan said evenly, eyes leveled with the leader's.

"I'm not going in there!" Harold argued excitedly. "I'll blow the machine into a million pieces from outside."

"That's where you're wrong," Declan returned, the leader bracing Harold's shoulder, encouraging him to listen. "Like I said, I know exactly where to put the bomb."

"Fine," Harold said, peering up at the leader, fearing his insistence.

"You just need to show me how to detonate it." Declan's smile was gone, but he gave Sammi a reassuring look. "Harold, just don't slow me down."

"Take him," she heard herself say, seeing Andie's guts wired around the explosive. Emily could barely look, but in her gut, she felt that it was right, that he had to go. Declan whipped his head around, surprised. "He'll help. He'll carry Andie so you can lead the way."

"Then it's settled," the leader forcefully exclaimed. "And this is as far as we go. As far as we need to go."

Before Declan could say another word, Sammi wrapped her arms around him. "You promise to come back to me," she pleaded, placing his hand on her belly. "You promise to come back to the both of us."

Declan hesitated, saying nothing and leaving her pleas hanging, vulnerable. He shook his head, and she could see in his eyes that he couldn't make that promise. "I'm going to do what I can to make things safe for you," he told her. "To make things safe for the both of you."

She didn't have a reply but stared long and hard into his face while he wiped a tear from her cheek. He was going to go for them, for their family.

TWENTY-NINE

"Try to keep up," Declan shouted while Harold scurried like a rat across the sand. In the last ten minutes, the classmate he'd wished dead fell twice and nearly threw up while struggling to carry the bomb.

"Ya know, this fucking thing is heavy," Harold stammered. "And, by the way, *Dick-lan*, if you talk to me like that again, I'll give you a fucking thump!"

Without regard for a bomb that could turn them into fleshy bits of confetti, Declan spun around and shoved Harold with all his strength. Harold dropped back a step, barely, and snorted a piggy laugh. The smile flicked off like a lightbulb and he advanced, ready to return the push. Declan hit him, pain shooting into his hand like lightning. Shock weathered Harold's face and he fell, air rushing out of him in a single gust. Harold wheezed and gasped and tried to roll onto his side.

Declan jumped on him, taking advantage. He straddled him and held Harold down, the bomb sitting between them. Harold squirmed and swung, clipping Declan's eye, a pinch of blood dripping. The anger came up in a gush, uncontrollable, Declan swinging and connecting with Harold's jaw. Another jolt of fire and lightning flew into his arm, making him shout and reel back.

The punch sent blood and one of Harold's rotten yellow teeth onto the black sands where it skittered until coming to a rest. He spat and cried out a mess of garbled threats, but then quieted when the taste of blood registered. He froze as if uncertain what just happened. Declan saw him rethink the situation, his position and being defenseless. Other than the bomb, which was unarmed, Declan had the advantage. Harold seemed to concede, his jaw slack and his eyes filling.

"Listen, I'm going to say this once," Declan began. "The only reason you're not dead right now is because of that bomb you're carrying."

"You don't have the balls!" Harold shouted, spitting into his face, blood spattering. Declan flinched and wiped his face. Before Harold could move, he swung again. But at the last second, he pulled up to show mercy. He'd wanted to see Harold flinch, maybe even cry out a little, but Harold never moved, not even a blink; he'd been willing to take the punch.

Declan did something then that surprised even himself. He stood up and offered a hand, helping Harold back up to his feet. "I need you," he told him, hating the words, the sound of them. "I need your help."

"I know you do," Harold said, sneering as he continued forward, a hard and purposeful nudge jarring Declan. "You need me, the bomb and, of course, you'll need this." Harold held up the detonator, and then tucked it away in a pocket that was fashioned to the front of his coveralls.

"The machine is right over there," Declan said, wishing he'd landed that last punch. "Let's get moving."

The VAC-Machine seemed to swell when they reached it, the fog thinning like it had before. The whites of Harold's eyes were enormous, the machine heaving as though taking a deep breath. To Declan, that's exactly what he thought the machine was doing. Breathing. But not for much longer.

When the machine's skin rippled, a groan sounding, Harold jumped backward, clumsily tripping. He caught himself against Declan, the weight of the force nearly taking him to his knees.

"Calm down!" Declan told him.

"Wha—what's it doing!?"

"It's okay, I've seen this before." A deafening roar shook the sands, his feet swallowed clear up to his ankles. When Harold turned to run, Declan clutched his collar, shouting, "Just wait!"

Harold trembled, and what Declan saw was a fright that made him feel sorry. The moment didn't last, silence following along with a perfectly square door appearing.

"That's us?" Harold asked, shaking.

"I think so," he answered, the door riding on a sliver of black, the air wavy. Declan searched for Phil and Isla, a faint image appearing at the entrance, peering around, and waving them inside. "It's them."

"Hey there," Harold said, glancing briefly before his gaze dropped to the ground. Phil Stark looked unprepared, unsure of what to say. Maybe he'd expected Declan to be alone. Or did he know who Harold was and what he'd done to Sammi? Declan couldn't tell, but decided to say nothing. After a second, Phil gave them a nod.

"Was Isla able to figure out the index card?" But Phil seemed distracted, searching past the two of them as if looking for someone in the fog. "Phil! The index card?"

"Yes, yes, Isla has it," Phil answered impatiently. "She's still working on it."

"We brought a bomb," Declan said, stopping at the opening. "I'm going to take it to the soul and detonate it."

"Sammi. Is she safe?" Phil asked, continuing to search the fog. "I was hoping to see her again."

"She's safe," Declan confirmed. "She's with Emily."

"Emily!" Phil slapped his hands against the machine's opening as if holding himself back. He shook his head vigorously, lips moving before saying anything. "Good! That's good! They're together."

"The bomb," Harold said, jutting Andie in front of Phil.

"A bomb, you say?" Phil asked enthusiastically, picking through the wiring, stopping when he reached the C4. His brow rose sharply, eyelids flitting. "No shit. That's a lot of explosive."

"That place I saw my mom and sister," Declan began, hesitating. "Where the machine consumed them. That's where we're going."

"Consumed?" Harold asked, a spark of disgust flashing on his face. "What do you mean? Like, it ate them?"

"Something like that," Phil answered, unfazed. He looked up from the bomb, adding, "The soul, it's perfect. Destroy it, and the machine won't be able to kick over again. If we connect with the other machines, we'll bring this whole thing to an end. Now, we need to hurry!"

"Andie," Declan said, raising his hands to take the bomb from Harold.

"No way," Harold declared, a look of disapproval in his face. He stepped back, shielding the bomb like it was found treasure. "I'm doing it!"

"Hurry, you must hurry," Phil repeated, louder. "Bring him along if you must!"

"I don't have a choice, do I?" Declan asked, a momentary disgust turning his stomach. Harold sneered, seeing that he was going to get his way.

"This way!" Declan demanded and entered the machine. He touched the outline of Sammi's locket, making sure it was in place. With it, the zombies would leave them alone—after all, Sammi and the baby were far from the machine, safe.

Harold won't be recognized, though, he thought and

stopped, Harold bumping into him. "What the fuck, *Dick-lan?*" Harold snapped.

"The door to our dwelling. It wouldn't open for me," he answered, holding onto Sammi's hair. There wasn't enough of it to share. "You won't be able to pass through the machine."

"Huh?" Harold asked, confused. "What are you talking about?"

"Wait, I think I got it." He pulled out the pouch given to them by Emily. In it, he found the torn index card with the dried blood, and wondered if it would work the same. "The executives have been here."

"So what?" Harold said.

"You'll need this," Declan said insistently, stuffing the pouch into the front pocket of Harold's coveralls, his hand brushing against the bomb's detonator. "Carry this and don't lose it. It's the only way they'll let you pass."

"Uh... who will let me pass?" Harold asked, hesitating at the door leading to the main hub. "Who you talking about?"

"The zombies," Phil sang, tolling his eyes. A laugh slipped from his lips as he bounced his brows up and down. "Welcome to the funhouse."

"Funhouse," Harold said, clutching the front of his coveralls like the pouch was some kind of talisman to ward off evil spirits. Declan faced the door and moved close enough for Sammi's hair to register. It opened with a sweeping whoosh, a thousand bodies parading back and forth. As he'd suspected, none of them cared to look in their direction. Before entering, he heard Harold whimper and mumble, "What is this place?"

THIRTY

Isla flipped the card over for the hundredth time, searching the number but not seeing anything. She stared hard until the fibers of the card came into focus. They bled across the blue lines, the red one at the top too. Phil handed it to her, saying it would help. *Help how?*

"And what are these numbers?" she asked, turning the card back over. The letters were dimpled, a few pressed deep enough to feel on the underside of the card. She traced the rows while trying to find a pattern.

It's not Fibonacci. Not square or cube. And definitely not a linear sequence. It wasn't often a puzzle left her baffled. She flipped the card on its side again, the corner snapping. "None of the numbers resemble anything I've seen in here."

Phil didn't answer her. He had that look in his eyes again. The one that told her he thought he had to fix what was broken. That meant her lab. A broken chair in hand, he'd praised that she was okay and had cursed what the zombies had done.

He glanced at her and then around, taking in the mess, righting a table, chunky glass skittering across the floor. The zombies had left nothing untouched: Anything not put away had been trampled, shoved, thrown until it was broken. She waved the card, catching his eye. But it was her lab journals that had his attention—tossed wildly and splayed open—looking like a pile of dead butterflies.

"I'm sorry about your lab," he told her and pulled a chair up, fixing the backrest before sitting next to her. "I'm sure we can salvage most of it. I mean, we're going to need the lab when this is over. There's so much to do."

"Need the lab?" she asked, brow pinched. She rolled her chair closer to him. She could feel the urgency on him, the sour smell of sweat too. She wet her lips, shining to the idea of an afterward. "Need my lab? For what?"

"Well—" he started to say, but stopped when he began cleaning up her journals. "Well for starters, a lot of those zombies are going to be waking up. They'll be people again. Like they were before."

"I don't follow," she said, intrigued but concerned with the scale. There were so many.

"They'll be aware. Like we are."

"That's right," she answered, glancing toward the blood vault behind him. She shook her head. "Phil, that's too much work if it's just the two of us."

"It is. That's why we'll figure it out." He pointed to the index card, adding, "First, we've got to understand what that means."

"Well, like I said," she said, presenting the card between them. "There's nothing that stands out. Nothing in common, anyway."

Phil asked, "What if they're the numbers to the other machines? You know, like access codes."

"Access codes?" she questioned, the idea having merit. Cautiously, she asked, "What makes you think that? They could be anything, like identifications to blood samples."

"It's the count," he told her, running his finger over the numbers. "We built five machines. There're five sets of numbers."

"One set per machine," Isla said, warming to the idea. She rolled her chair in front of a terminal. The keyboard's keys were cool to the touch, warming as she navigated to the machine's internal systems. She heard a positive *humph* from Phil when she accessed some of the engineering systems. She could tell he was impressed by the level of access. There'd been a lot of downtime between shifts. Couple that with being aware, and a lot got completed. "Here we go."

"I didn't realize you had this level of access," Phil commented, moving close enough she could hear his breathing. Screen after screen appeared. Some with engineering diagrams. Others filled top to bottom with source code.

"Yeah, I learned to get around," she said, scrolling through pages and pages until finding what she wanted. She turned to him briefly, eyes meeting, then leaned in as if confessing, "I used to be a bit of a computer hacker."

"Me too," he said, moving close enough to whisper. "But back then we were just called ourselves nerds."

"Nerds," she scoffed, focus returning. "I'll show you what this nerd can do."

And with a flick of her wrist, she highlighted a few of the passages, copying and pasting them into the empty fields staged on a second screen. Chair creaking, she saw Phil sitting back, mesmerized by the swiftness of her work. His approval encouraged her to tap harder and faster, search every nook and cranny of the system until something clicked. Minutes passed, her frustrations growing. Phil lifted the card, asking, "Maybe I was wrong?"

"I'm not ready to give up yet," she countered, another half dozen screens appearing. She'd traveled to the inner workings of the machine and bumped against the safeguards in place to prevent her from doing damage. Hesitating, fingers hovering, she was close like a surgeon near a patient's most vital organs. It was what the engineers considered the operations kernel—a central component to how the core systems functioned. "There it is," she yelled, clapping her hands.

"There's what?" Phil asked, eyelids opened wide. He smiled excitedly, shaking his head with a squint, "What is that? I might have embellished about my level of nerdom."

"The numbers. You were right. They're a key to gain access," she answered, voice fading while she considered what she could do. "I'm going to need a copy for safekeeping to make it easier to access again."

"Access which part?" he asked, lips moving as he read the screens. "I've never seen this part of the system. What part of it are you in?"

"I'm deep, way deep," she answered.

"What other machines can you access?"

"All of them," she answered, hopping up and down in her chair, carried by the enthusiasm of the accomplishment. "It'd be like I was sitting at a terminal in the other machines."

"No shit," Phil dropped one of the lab journals, his mouth hanging open. "That is impressive. What else can you do in there?"

"I don't know all the terminal commands yet but see this over here?" she asked and pointed at the screen. "That's the machine closest to this one. And this one over here? That's the machine farthest from us."

"Swiss-cheese brain," Phil said, bracing his head, cringing briefly. "It's coming back. I remember them."

"Check out the layouts. They're identical." She breathed fast and realized her heart was racing. Isla didn't slow down. Doing more was the answer. Exploring the other machines. She smacked the keyboard, entering commands that sent them flying through each machine, establishing a presence on them that allowed them to easily jump from one to the next with the tip of her finger. "Done! I've established sessions for each machine. And they're stable."

"Isla, what is it you said you do here?" he asked. He picked up one of her oldest journals, plunking it back down on the table. And while the keyboard tapping resumed, she saw him staring at her through the screen's reflection. "Whatever it is, you're obviously very good."

"I analyze the ore from the mining, and then recalculate the alignments," she finally answered, sounding nerdier than she wanted. It wasn't hard to sense that she was like him. A nerd, as he'd put it earlier. As if to confirm this, she quickly added, "And I'm the best at it. I'm always the best."

"It looks like you're the best at this too," he suggested, motioning to the screen. "I wouldn't have been able to pull this off, even with the access codes."

"Fifteen years. I had a lot of time to practice," she said jokingly. She smiled at him before turning back to the screen. "You would have gotten as far I did if you had the numbers too."

"Let's try accessing that machine," he said, pointing at the one closest. She liked that he didn't push her hand away, leaving it there until she was ready to continue working.

"Sure thing," she said. "Should be as simple as..." And as she touched the keyboard, a new view surfaced that resembled the rooms and corridors around them. It was the master floor plan for their level. Isla traced the outline of a corridor, guiding her finger to the same lab room they occupied. Her mouth went dry, curiosity building. "Let's see who is there."

"I want to shut it down," Phil said abruptly.

"We can't avoid the built-in failsafe..." she began and then paused, thinking, working the problem and its complications.

"Why?" he asked. "You said we have full access."

"The failsafe prevents a complete shutdown," she answered. "By the time we get to the last machine, it will have detected that the first machine is offline, tripping the workflow to put it back online—"

"Well, shit!" he yelled, standing. His face was red, and she hadn't even told him the bad news yet. Lips tight, he looked down, asking, "What?"

"That's only part of the problem."

He rolled his eyes and waved his hand, telling her to continue.

"Well..." She didn't have an answer and hated disappointing him. Isla entered the commands on the other machine, testing them, the terminal spitting up the word "Denied" over and over. She elevated the privileges, trying again, but like the first time, the terminal said no, denying the command to shut down. The amber colors began to blur as she moved in and out and up and down. Finally, she confirmed her suspicions. "Phil, we need someone in the other machines to do this. The access codes gave us the authentication which got the sessions."

His eyes grew wide with understanding, and he continued, finishing her thought. "But the authorization to enter the command must be done locally. It can't be executed remotely."

"Exactly," she answered. "Each machine command must execute at exactly the same time."

A deep sigh, Phil instructed, "Then let's knock on the door and see who's home."

Her focus swung back to the screen, commenting, "We'll start here, the other machine's lab at the same location. See it?"

"Yes," he told her. "I see it."

"Let's hope someone is there, and they're receptive to the plan."

"Can you talk to them?" he asked abruptly.

"That's the idea," she answered. Cracking her knuckles, wringing out the tension, she placed her fingers on the keys. She clicked on the lab room, a small terminal window opening. In the top-left corner, a cursor appeared, winking and waiting for her to type. "How about I start with something simple?"

"That sounds easy enough," Phil said. "Try hello?"

She nodded, typing H—E—L—L—O. She pressed enter and the cursor jumped to the next line. "It's sent."

They waited. And after a minute when there was nothing, her heart sank. Chair creaking, Phil was standing again, pacing while mumbling, "Without somebody to synchronize the commands, the machines will stay online."

"I'll try the next machine," Isla said, impatiently, and quickly accessed the next machine and navigated the floor plan, flying through the maze of rooms and corridors until landing on her lab. When the terminal window appeared, a cursor blinking, she typed:

H—E—L—L—O.

And again, they waited. But this time, someone typed a response.

Y—E—S?

"You've got someone," Phil yelled in her ear, patting her shoulder and planting a kiss on her cheek.

"It worked," Isla chirped, relief warming her while holding Phil, his embrace sudden and needed.

"Ask them their name," he said. "Go ahead."

"Right," she said. "We don't want to come off as rude." Isla happily typed in the question, the glow from the terminal feeling just a little brighter on her skin as she inched closer in fascination.

W—H—A—T I—S Y—O—U—R N—A—M— E?

There was a long pause. Long enough to make her think she'd lost the connection, the cursor blinking. But then the first letter of the reply flashed and her insides crumbled. She kicked, forcing the chair back from the screen. The response made perfect sense. Didn't it? After all, she was the best at what she did. She'd always been the best. So why wouldn't the machine take advantage of that? The machine was all about efficiency and that meant having one of her for each machine was the most efficient thing to do.

I—S—L—A.

THIRTY-ONE

"Try to keep up," Declan yelled, sweat beading on his face. He shot a look over his shoulder in time to see Harold throwing him the middle finger, a favorite gesture of Harold's since learning about it in the second grade. Declan grunted, the motion slowing Harold more while he secured the bomb. There was more in his classmate's face. More than annoyance and struggle. There was terror. Harold was overwhelmed by the alien world inside the machine. Declan dismissed it, telling himself not to care. He did, though, a small part of him understanding. "We've got to get through that door."

"Jesus," Harold shouted, a woman knocking into him. Through the shock and terror, Declan saw a humorous awe in Harold's eyes. "Did... did you fucking see that?"

"Harold!" he scolded. "Just keep up and follow me, don't look at anything."

"Who are all these people?" Harold asked, breathless, feet stomping. "And was that who I think it was? From our class—"

"Like I said, try not to look," Declan interrupted. "There's a lot here that doesn't make sense."

"Tell me!" Harold insisted, the fright turning to horror, chin quivering. He began to nod, asking, "It's like Sammi, they bring back the dead?"

Try as he might, Declan searched the bowels of his being to drum up a pinch of sympathy for the man he hated more than anything else in this world. "Yeah, something like that." Harold took a shuddering breath, and, for a moment, Declan thought Harold was going to bolt, drop the Andie-bomb and run. He didn't, though. Instead, he appeared level-headed and sincere. "Show me where to go."

"Good, get in front of me," Declan instructed, his gaze falling to the bomb, to Andie's dormant face. They picked up the pace, the bomb jostling but remaining secured. When they reached a set of double doors, he stopped them, his hand on Sammi's lock of hair. He nudged Harold forward, telling him, "The pouch from Emily, I mean Ms. Stark—I want to see if it'll work."

Harold only stared at him, perplexed. He shook his head, needing more. Declan patted his front, the lump in the coverall pocket still there. Harold nodded, and stepped closer like he was nearing the apex of a cliff. The doors slid into the walls, the tall panels retreating with a whoosh. Harold jumped, startled, a laugh slipping. He tested it again and again, jumping back and forth, forcing the doors to open and close.

"It works, Harold, let's keep going," Declan said, clutching the lock of Sammi's hair. The DNA? It had to be. Like Sammi's hair, Peter's blood gave them a pass. It meant that he must've been here. From the corner of his eye, the lights caught his attention, a message flickering to a group of zombies. But if Peter had been here, did the machine remember? Declan got the answer when the zombies turned to approach them. "Don't look now, but the cavalry is coming."

"Shit, what? This makes us visible?" Harold asked, holding up the pouch.

"Yeah, something like that," Declan answered, placing his hand over the pouch to cover it. "Put it away and don't lose it."

"Or what?"

"Or you'll get lost in here and there'll be no way to get out."

"Good to know," Harold muttered, the earlier humor doused.

"Stay close, the other side of this door gets a little crazy," he warned, peering into the main hub. "They'll leave you alone as long as you don't do anything stupid."

Declan nodded with a hard stare until Harold returned the nod, saying, "I won't. Nothing stupid." Three steps in and they had to stop, Harold was slack-jawed, gazing around at the enormity of the room. A second later, the first shove came, and Harold was bumped from behind hard enough to make him stumble off balance, the Andie-bomb sliding. Declan lurched back, grabbing hold of Harold's shoulders, holding him upright. Harold glanced wide-eyed at the bomb, saying, "Shit! Thanks. You know I armed it as soon as we entered the machine. That could have been bad."

"Bad! You should have let me know," Declan snapped. "It's best to stay out of their way."

"That's great, *Dick-lan!*" Harold spat, annoyed. "You should have said that back there."

"Well, now you know." Declan shrugged.

"Are they awake?" Harold asked. He didn't wait for Declan to answer and pointed at one of the zombies. "Shit, I know that guy." Before Declan could stop it, Harold's arm was out, his hand taking hold of a young man's arm. The man spun around, dismissing the attention, the gaze empty, the look making Harold let go like he'd just touched a plague victim. When he turned back, Declan saw the disgust register, Harold insisting they continue.

"Forget what you see here. It'll make it easier," Declan reminded him. "None of it matters, anyway. Just follow me."

"This can't be. None of it," Harold argued, trying to reason with what was impossible. "It is like Sammi. But that doesn't make it right. Does it, Declan?"

Declan pinched his lips, choosing to ignore Harold, choosing to search for the corridor where he had seen his mother and sister enter. *Five*, he counted. There were five larger corridors circling the machine's hub like spokes on a wheel.

"Old," he mumbled, recalling what he'd seen. The corridor they wanted had the old people, the ones aging, their expirations like a birthday. Only, it wasn't any birthday he'd imagine any of them wanted. What he saw next made him cringe, stomach flipping as the images spilled into his mind. It was the bones crunching too, the memory of the machine eating. "Zombies or not, they are people."

"What is? People?" Harold asked, listening, voice lacking concern. He was making small talk, a means of comforting himself while they traveled this alien machine.

"Give me a second," Declan answered sharply, studying the faces, searching for the wrinkles and the gray and the slowing stride. To the left, just behind them, he saw a corridor, the old and the dying. *Do they know what's waiting for them?* "In there."

Declan turned to take off, Harold yelling, "Wait up!"

"Hurry!" Declan shouted over his shoulder, reaching around and jerking on Harold's arm. "See it? That one!"

"What do you mean, that one?" Harold asked impatiently. "Where does it go?"

Declan ignored the questions and waded through lines of zombies, the crowds merging single file where they hurried up to wait. That's what this was. A place where they all hurried up to wait for something to happen. Deep in the recesses of thought where his humor still had a fighting chance, he wondered if that was what Hell was like. A place where you waited in line after line, never getting anywhere.

A zombie bumped him, jarring him from the senseless thoughts, Harold's clopping steps close behind. He turned into the corridor, the count of heads too many, the bodies clogging the pipe from one side to the other. It forced him to slow down. When he turned, Harold was two or three bodies away from him, the look on his face like that of a little lost boy.

A tether strap, he thought, wishing he'd tied one between them. When he turned again, Harold was walking aimlessly, the glow of white iridescent bright on his ruddy cheeks. If he hadn't been carrying the Andie-bomb, Declan knew he would have let the zombies take Harold and the machine keep him.

"Hold on! We're almost there," he told him, grabbing Harold's arm and leading him away from the hub. Iridescent coveralls filled the corridor for as far as he could see, the eyes blank—empty and unemotional—waiting to take their turn to die.

Look straight and concentrate, he told himself, passing the bodies. *It's a death march.*

"Whoa!" Harold stopped abruptly when they reached the end of the corridor, the faint murmur of mechanical chewing riding up the cavern walls.

"This is it," Declan told him. Harold shook his head, standing firm, mouth hanging open while he gazed into the cavern. Declan pointed down, adding, "It's the machine's soul."

"What's that sound?" Harold asked, his gaze following the conveyors around to the far walls, moisture glistening. His face cramped with a wince, a stench rising from the machine's dark gullet reaching them. "I don't know if I can—"

"You said you would do it!" Declan demanded. "You have to, Harold."

"But—" he stopped when the truth of what was going on inside became clear. The machine chewed and swallowed, over and over. "Jesus. God. This place—"

"Get a hold of yourself," Declan shouted. He couldn't be sure if Harold heard him, though.

"I wanna go back," Harold mumbled, inching forward, looking down at the steep drop-off. Declan followed, his stomach lurching into his throat. "Declan, I can't—"

"We're going," Declan said coldly, speaking into Harold's ear. "I don't give a fuck how afraid you are. Get moving."

Harold pointed at the countless others flowing into the cavern from the other corridors. His finger followed the conveyors' downward spiral, stopping when he reached the deadly fingertip stings, the bodies sliding to the jaws beneath. He shuddered, cheeks ballooning. Declan jumped out of the way, Harold's stomach emptying. When he righted himself, he wiped his mouth, asking, "Where do we go from here?"

"Down there," Declan answered, sounding grave. "All the way to the bottom is where we have to take Andie."

THIRTY-TWO

Isla didn't know whether to cry or vomit. The back of her throat grew slick with the threat of the latter. She swallowed, mouthing the count, "Five." There were five machines. And in one of them, there was a woman with the name Isla. She thought of the odds that anyone would have the same name. She knew better, though. She knew that it was the work of whoever was behind the machines, making certain the same level of coverage was in each of them.

Still, she felt a cry stirring, a scream of disgust rising. She held it back with a bite of her tongue. In the low hum of the machine, its vibration in her chair, she tasted the blood of life on her tongue. Was it life? Was it the kind she'd been born with? Two parents. A mother who'd nursed her and a father who'd cared for their home. Or were those just stolen memories from Isla, the first one with the cancer?

The question of who and what she was sparked in her head like a lightning storm while staring at the screen spelling out her name. Now wasn't a time for a debate, though. After all, what if she decided that a clone wasn't human? Then what? Did it mean she'd have to end her life to prove the point? Isla thumped the keyboard, and glared at Phil. If he hadn't saved her—that is, the original Isla—then none of this would have mattered.

"What's the matter?" he asked. She looked up at him. Glaring as he read the screen. She jabbed a finger at him with an accusatory look, eyes piercing, a low groan chased by coarse words. She saw understanding on his face, and he said, "It's what the machine does. The reanimation."

"I didn't expect it—" she began to say and thought back to one of the stolen memories. It was the last one from that day. Phil had picked the original Isla out of the surf and sands while the gray rainbows stabbed the skies and the fog spun in a winding storm that would have surely killed them both if he hadn't done something. She pawed at her arms and then clutched the space where the chemo port would have been. "It's not me, is it?"

"It *is* you. Just not the same you." His words tumbled from his lips, but Isla barely heard him.

She returned to the terminal screen, the debate in her brain quieting. If there was another Isla out there, and they'd both been cut from the same cloth, then she could help. This other Isla could help end this.

Phil felt sick to his stomach. Utterly gutted, the questions about his actions weighing heavy. He'd meant well in that moment on the beach. But it didn't mean anything to a person who'd wanted death more than life. What he didn't dare tell her was that if he'd known about the reanimation, he would never have brought her inside. She didn't need to know that. Not now.

"It doesn't matter much now, does it?" Isla muttered, returning to the screen.

"Isla, please understand, I just couldn't let you die out there."

"I wish you had." Her words were more to herself than to him and she shoved her hands over the keyboard, typing fast and harsh. She stopped a moment to turn her head. Without looking at him, she said, "I'd be with Nolan if you'd left me be."

"You don't really know—" he began but stopped himself. Who was he to say more. He didn't know her beliefs and the look she gave him was enough to shut his mouth. "Isla, I am sorry."

"I'd made my peace with death once," she pouted, sniffing. He nabbed a cloth from a nearby shelf, one of the few still intact, and handed it over. Eyes bloodshot and puffy, she peered up. "I guess I'll have to make peace with life too."

On the screen behind her, another Isla appeared in the second to last machine, typing to say hello. Phil had considered his specialty and what it meant to the machines, to the aliens running them. As the architect and engineer of something so complex, it made sense they'd clone him again and again, using the labor wherever it was needed. Isla's specialty wasn't lost on them either and, for that reason, she could very well have a presence in all of them. An idea struck him, and he put on his best *Isla, I have an idea* face.

She saw it and shrugged, "What?"

"With more of you, this could actually work in our favor."

A frown. "How so?"

"Who knows you better than you?" he nodded.

"There's more?" she said, pressing her fingers firmly to the screen. She jumped up, the chair spinning back until it clopped over in a roll. When he saw her heading to the door, Phil chanced taking hold of her before she could run away. In his arms, Isla's heartbeat was strong. It was life and he dried her tears and pleaded, "Isla, I need you."

"It's a lot to take in, knowing there are more of me." Her head fell to the side, her gaze dropping to the floor. "This isn't life."

"It's not what we'd expected," he told her, remembering how he'd felt that first time he learned of the truth. To be fair, he told her, "I don't know if it helps, but you're handling it much better than I did."

"I am?" she asked, and looked up, curious what he meant.

"Uh-huh." Not knowing what else he could do or say, he pleaded again. "Help me finish this."

Phil picked up her chair and placed it in front of the termi-nal, encouraging her to take a seat. She let out a shaky breath, holding his hand a moment longer before letting go. From her desk drawer, she pulled a cloth and began to clean the screen, removing the smudge.

"You hate fingerprints?" he asked, making small talk to add levity.

"I know, weird right," she said. "But I like a clean screen—can't work on it otherwise."

"I understand," he told her, feeling a little vindicated for some of his own idiosyncrasies. "Get comfortable, we've got some work to do."

"So now what?" Isla asked, her words sticking in her throat.

"They need you," he answered. On the screen, the other Isla was typing. "Let's finish what we started."

As she typed, she asked, "Your daughter, Sammi. And Declan. He was coming back."

"He's here and he brought help," he replied, wondering where in the machine Declan was now. "They're going to disable the machine."

Clearing her throat, she asked, "Disable it. You mean mechanically?"

"It will prevent this machine from ever being able to start again, eliminating the failsafe."

"But not the trigger, the other machines," she added, typing fast. Isla was remembering what they'd planned and started typing instructions.

"The failsafe? Disable it?" the other Isla typed a reply. It was followed by one question, *"Why?"*

"We need to tell her," Isla said without looking at him.

"You're right. We need to tell all of them if we're going to coordinate this."

"It's to shut the machines down," she answered, fingers blurring over the keyboard. "All of them."

The green on black cursor blinked without a response. Phil glanced at the lights, adding, "If Declan follows through with it, it'll be exactly the distraction we need to work with the others."

"You mean, to work with me *at* all the machines," she replied. In the screen's dim reflection, he saw her brow furrow. She looked up, asking, "How will we know if Declan was successful?"

"They've got a bomb." Isla stopped. Froze was a better way of putting it. Scaring her wasn't his intent, so he added, "I thought you should know about it."

"You think?" she said sarcastically. Glancing at him with a nod, "Yeah, thanks for letting me know."

"That's how we'll know if Declan is successful."

She leaned away cautiously. "I guess we will."

The cursor's blinking jumped with the other Isla typing, the words appearing, H—E—L—L—O W—H—O A—R—E Y—O—U?

"What do I tell her... *me*... the other Isla?"

"I'm not sure," Phil answered, having just seen this Isla's reaction to the truth. "Maybe it'd be best if we say nothing?"

"No. That won't do," Isla answered, surprising him. "I want them to know. All of them. If they *are* me, I mean, the same as me, then they'll want to end this too."

Isla leaned in, nearly touching the screen with her nose. She glanced at him through the reflection. He said nothing but shrugged and hoped she was right about how they would react. He took to his seat to help. Isla tapped furiously on the screen, reaching out to each machine, each Isla, and told them everything. Phil watched her work, mesmerized by the efficiency with which she was able to correlate the stories, momentum gathering across them. From one Isla, two of the others were working with each other, and then soon after that, there were three and then four, all with one objective, a coordinated system attack.

He felt something then. Something that had escaped him for a very long time. It was hope.

She's right, Phil thought. *They're going to follow what she tells them and we're going to shut this down.*

THIRTY-THREE

"Watch it!" Harold grunted, waving an arm. Declan got out of the way, but nudged Harold again who was peering over the edge, lower lip twitching. His mouth dropped open as if to scream, but no sound came out. When Harold turned back, he asked, "There?"

"That's right, we have to climb down there," Declan instructed, and raised a hand, eager to nudge some more.

"Quit it!" Harold shouted, fright and anger mixing on his face. The hard expression softened, and he peered over his shoulder, asking, "We can't just drop it in?"

"Uh-uh. We need to go far enough down there to clear the walls," Declan answered, taking a step closer. Harold retreated, the heels of his shoes near the edge. "It's the only way to make sure that Andie does the job."

"I don't want to be in this place," he stated flatly. Harold's color had disappeared, and for a moment, Declan was certain he would pass out and fall. "I don't think I can go down there."

"You will." Without warning, Declan punched Harold in the chest, the force pushing him a step. Harold shook awake from whatever trance he was in and glared at Declan, his eyes on fire. "Finally! There you are!"

"There you are?" Harold repeated and he lurched forward, fists high in the air. Declan held his place, expecting the punch but refusing to flinch. Harold swung, knuckles passing by Declan's jaw close enough to feel. Harold was in his face next, saying, "Don't fucking push it, *Dick-lan!*"

"Right," Declan muttered. Harold spun around and surprised him, jumping onto the metal landing, the clamor echoing from the chamber. Declan followed, the drop hurting his feet and legs. He shook it off and led them across the grated floor to the farthest edge. Daring a look, Declan focused on the point below them where the chewing and crunching was a constant and thought he might never be able to forget that sound.

"Where to now?" Harold asked, reaching the end of the walk. Leaning over the rail, he launched a wad of spit, the phlegmy mass falling fifty hands or more to where it splattered onto a woman's head. "Bullseye."

"Knock it off," Declan said, objecting. He pointed at the cavern's wall, the rock jutting and drippy. In the light, the jagged stones glistened like teeth. "There's only one way down. We've got to climb."

Had it been this humid before? Declan realized that the machinery was moving at a quicker pace. He faced the corridors and then the conveyors and noticed they were moving faster too. Not just faster, but there were more bodies packed on them. The whirring from the death arm sang in unison, delivering its touch a tap at a time. And like the jaws chewing beneath the arms, the sound had become rapid like someone panting—faster, one body after another. *The machine is eating more.*

"Watch this," Harold said, working up more spit. He took aim, Declan slapping him hard.

"Are you through?" he asked. Blood trickled from Harold's nose. Declan cleared his throat. "We've got one shot at this. Understand?"

"I warned you already, but I'll give you that one for free," Harold spat. "The next time, expect something in return."

"That's fine," Declan answered impatiently. His voice shook as he spoke. "I hate that I need you. But we're out of time."

As if to answer him, Harold worked another throaty rumble from deep in his chest and launched it over the rail. The second one followed the same path as the first, hitting an old man. And like the woman before, the zombie remained still, never moving. "Bingo," Harold said without the laughter. "Naked freak! Now you're limp and sappy too."

"Down there," Declan said, ignoring Harold's antics as he pointed to the next landing.

"That's right, *Dick-lan*... I hit limp 'n' sappy *down* there!" Harold continued to roar.

"Enough!" Declan yelled, and then tried to compose himself. "You first."

But when Harold took to the edge of the rail, wrapping his fingers around the round metal, he stopped. "Wait. That's too far of a jump," he confessed.

"The wall!" Declan said, frustration in his voice. "I said we'll climb."

"Climb?"

"I did it before," he told him, half lied. "Climb across the wall to the lower landing." Declan squeezed his hands, making fists, a painful ache reminding him of the last attempt.

"But—"

"What! Don't tell me that you're scared."

"The fuck I am!" Harold answered, words trailing while he searched for the bottom. "Already gave you a free pass earlier. Better stop pushing me."

He climbed across the wet stone, using the jutting rocks like ladder rungs. "Like that," Declan said, encouraging Sammi's murderer. Initially, he couldn't help but feel impressed by the effort. Harold had always been a better climber. If Declan wanted to be truthful, Harold had been better at almost everything since they were kids. "That's it. You got it."

"What is that?" Harold yelled. Declan searched out what Harold focused on and saw that it was the mechanical arm. Harold stopped climbing, the arm's long gray finger tapping the head of a naked woman. Color spiraled out of her and, a moment later, she slumped over, falling when the floor beneath her opened. The woman slid off the conveyor and disappeared, bones crunching.

"Holy shit!" Harold yelled, grinning from ear to ear. "Did you fucking see that?"

"Let's keep moving," Declan said glumly. He couldn't be certain what sickened him more, the machine's appetite or Harold morose reaction. Harold didn't move. Instead, he kept staring, two more bodies disposed. Declan reached above and nudged Harold's middle, poking just below a rib.

"Watch it!" Harold yelled, swinging his foot. The bottom of Harold's shoe grazed Declan's head, the scrape stinging. "I gave you a warning, didn't I? And the next one won't just scratch your pretty face."

The fresh cut opened and bled into his eyes, blinding him. Declan tore some of his coverall to bandage his head, a yell coming from the wall. From the corner of his eye, Harold misplaced a hand and slipped. Declan launched himself, pressing his middle against the railing, clutching it while grabbing Harold's arm. "Grab hold!"

"Help me," Harold pleaded. Declan strained, feeling the muscles rip in his arm.

"You'll need both arms. If I can reach the bottom rail, then I can pull myself up." Harold pawed at Declan's arm with both hands, climbing him like a rope. But his weight and strength were too much, and Declan felt his feet slipping from the grated floor. His stomach shot into his throat when his balance swung farther over the rail. Harold was going to pull him over.

"Stop, Harold, I'm falling over!" he screamed, and pinned one of his legs between the railing bars to brace himself. "I can't pull you up."

"I'll pull you down if you don't," Harold threatened, his voice breaking. "I'll pull us both down! Now give me your other arm!"

Declan hesitated, but then saw the detonator perching on the lip of Harold's pocket.

"It's time," Declan told him, and in that instant, he decided Harold's fate.

"What?" Harold asked, his bemused expression quickly turning into a plea.

Declan ignored Harold, and pinned his other leg behind the rail, securing himself to the landing. He leaned over, swinging his free arm, punching Andie's large gray button one last time.

"Hi everybody," Andie sang, the voice stirring childhood emotions.

"What are you doing?" Harold cried, voice shouting. "What do you think you're doing!"

"Fuck you, Harold!" Declan answered and plucked the detonator from Harold's pocket.

"No! No, you can't do that!"

"You killed Sammi!" he told him, fixing his eyes on Harold's piggy face. He stared into the evil that he had known most of his life. He looked for the promise of anything worthy to save but found nothing. "You killed her!"

"Please, Declan," Harold begged. "Oh please, it was an accident, I swear—"

But Declan never let him finish and loosened his grip just enough to feel the last of the evil slip from his fingers.

"Andie! Show projector!" Declan screamed the command, the bulbous orb rising out of Andie's head. He heard the faint echo of Andie's voice but couldn't make out the words over Harold's screams. And as the two fell, Andie's orb beamed an arrow of brilliant light that circled around and around, painting everything it touched in a beautiful array of white light.

When the projector was at its brightest, Declan wished his mechanical friend a final goodbye and then pressed the detonator. There was one other time in Declan's life that he had seen the sun. Today he saw it again in the form of an enormous ball of fire racing up from the machine's soul. It moved silently at first. A fiery mass of orange and red and white flame, roiling like the fog, consuming everything and everyone in the cavern.

The shockwave came first, causing bodies to tumble and fall mercilessly from the conveyors. Arms and legs spilled over the ledges, careening toward the volcano erupting below them. Declan held onto the platform—his head thrown back as the heat blasted upward next. In that moment, the air ignited and was like an oven, making it impossible to breathe. Declan pulled himself back to the landing, falling to his knees while securing himself to the grated floor. He dared a look below, but the brightness was too much. The cavern's black depths had suddenly become alive as a monstrous fire crawled up the walls, consuming everything. A blink. Declan had nothing but a single blink before he knew that he was going to turn to ash if he didn't get off the landing.

"Climb," he tried to yell, but his throat had scorched in the heated air. He blindly reached up, searching for the opening. His hands and feet found exactly where they needed to be as though some kind of magic helped push him out of harm's way. When he saddled the cavern's opening and crawled into the corridor, the flames exploded over his head. Its force threw the zombie parade onto their backs and shattered the lights on the walls. Declan covered his head, feeling the heat burn his hair and scalp. He shut his eyes, pressing as hard as he could against them, fearing that his eyeballs would melt. The heat was tremendous, and the air remained suffocatingly hot.

A sip, he told himself. *Just a sip or you'll pass out.* The air burned, and his throat instinctively closed. *I'm going to suffocate.*

A notion of dread swam through his head as a welcome rush of cool air blew over his face. He opened his mouth to breathe it in. The fire pulled on the air, sucking it in from all corners of the machine. He dared another sip, taking in just enough to stay alive.

Declan crawled along the floor as blackness crept into his eyes. But he pushed, gulping at the charred air. The flames dancing along the walls and ceiling, burning, and melting everything they touched. As he reached the machine's great hub, black smoke billowed upward, filling the enormous chamber and hiding the lights. When the fires finally crawled back into the cavern like a dragon to its lair, the air began to return.

Declan eased up onto his knees, choking and vomiting. Soon he knelt forward and was able to get to his feet. A rumble came from the cavern. *A second explosion?* he wondered and realized that the Andie-bomb may have set off another explosion. His only other thought was to run.

THIRTY-FOUR

It was fluttery excitement that filled her insides. It was like a tickle and then it wasn't. In a way, Isla had started to think this was a second chance. Before the clouds fell, there were no second chances. Except for the lucky. And she'd never been one of those types. She looked at Phil. Looked at him hard when he wasn't paying attention and wondered if maybe being brought back meant more than flesh and blood and bone. Reanimation was of the soul and mind, too, and it meant being whatever she wanted it to be.

Isla caught herself staring again and forced herself to spin the chair and get back to work. The screens were full, an open session to each machine, a dull ache remaining, the truth of how the machine had used her troubling. It was the question that wouldn't settle. The one she was sure her sisters were asking too. That's what she called them, her sisters. They weren't cousins or second cousins. They were her and she was them. But who was closest to the original Isla?

A touch. Gentle and warm. In the screen's reflection she saw Phil reading the conversations. Time was running out, and by now, her sisters were as aware of their predicament as she was.

It was the systems. A hundred or more splashed onto additional screens Phil had added. Her sisters were doing the same exact maneuvers as she, mirroring every move in near perfect synchronization, guaranteeing a unified system attack across all the machines.

"The programming is easy enough," she mumbled, talking to them, typing it into the chat at the same time. "Just a simple relay, tripping one component and then another. The trick is making sure it's in series so that only a few vital systems remain on."

"Like life support?" Phil questioned, standing to look around. The inside of the machines were completely cut off from the outside. It could be Mars or the moon. It didn't matter. Whatever was happening on Earth couldn't impact inside the machine. "Yeah, we'll need air and water and food. That or a lot of body bags."

"Let's avoid that, okay," she commented, fingers moving faster and faster as more commands were typed in and executed. And all the while, as she pressed the enter key, her gaze jumped to the lights on the wall like they were sleeping guards, unaware of what was happening.

"This'll be permanent?" Phil asked. "Forever?"

"That's the plan," Isla nodded, a smile slipping as she glanced in his direction. The idea of the machine not running anymore felt almost as strange to her as sharing company with another person. After being reanimated year after year, she decided she could do with the change. "Yes, it's forever, but only if we want it to be. Once we control the machine—the machines —we'll be able to turn any of the systems on and off at will."

"That one! I remember that one. Select it," Phil interrupted, voice sharp. Isla tripped an animated switch, her sisters doing the same, the coordination nearly in sync. A dial appeared, Phil motioning, "Rotate it twenty degrees clockwise and not a degree more."

"Clockwise," she repeated and looked for confirmation. When he nodded, she did as instructed, all the while watching the other sessions, making sure her sisters followed her lead. The dials turned the twenty degrees, each sister typing that it was complete and that they were ready. Isla knew it was time. "Done."

"That's good," Phil replied, his hands on his hips while reviewing each change. He stopped and looked up, lips moving silently before saying, "That's it, right?"

"We're all set," she answered, putting her hand in his. She searched for assurance from him about what they were about to do, knowing there was no turning back. His gaze was steady as she told him, "We're ready."

"I'm ready," he agreed and signaled to finish. Isla took a deep breath but then hesitated. Her finger hung in the air—an inch from changing their world forever. Phil cradled her hand and moved it forward, touching the keyboard. "We've come this far. It's time we finish it."

"Finish it," she repeated, her lungs emptying in a single breath. "God, please let this work."

She pressed the enter key. Not just pressed it. She gave it a good thump. She had a second chance in life, but with this change, she was ensuring the machine would never have another chance to steal their sun. One by one, her sisters followed, the newly programmed code executing in each session, its results flying up the screens. Isla tried to blink, but was frozen, staring while the processing completed the changes.

"Is it done?" Phil asked, the screen suddenly emptied.

"Hold on." Isla bounced the keyboard's spacebar and searched for an active cursor. Her sisters flicked on and off, their sessions disappearing and then coming back. "It's the delays.

The machines are relaying a lot of data around the world and it's not instant."

"You're talking about a propagation delay," Phil said, voice soft while the transactions bounced from screen to screen.

"That's right. I think it's almost done, though," she said, uncertainty hinging her words. The machine suddenly groaned and heaved like a mountain coughing volcanic ash. Isla raised her hands, unsure of what was happening. She turned to Phil, asking, "What was that?"

"I'm not sure—" he answered, stopping short when vibrations reverberated through the floor, the room shaking strong enough to topple chairs and lab equipment. Whatever the zombies had overlooked in their attack, the quaking took care of. Glass shattered, skittering across the floor like rain. "Maybe it was Declan, the bomb."

"The bomb!?" Isla yelled, her screens returning to normal. She searched each session, her sisters not saying a word about the same reaction. "Are we safe?"

"Yes," he answered unconvincingly. His hands eased over her shoulders with a gentle squeeze. "This machine will never run again."

"Well, given the way that felt, we'll be lucky if anything is salvageable."

"It might have been the mechanicals too, shutting them down abruptly," he answered, uncertainty in his voice. "Just in case, warn the others."

Hands shaking, she warned the others, typing into each session about what they might experience. The responses came immediately, reporting back how their machines slowed until stopping. "They didn't get the shudder."

"Then it had to be Declan," Phil exclaimed, a wicked smile appearing on his face. "They've reached the soul of the machine and destroyed it."

"Then there's no turning back," she said. A small reservation dying. She paused to consider what it was that they were going to do. After all, this had been home for the last fifteen years.

"That's right. No turning back," he repeated, putting his arm around her. She leaned against him and continued turning the dials and flipping the switches, making sure life support wasn't compromised.

The door to the lab opened, gusting a charring stink that filled the lab. It was the smell of burnt air and a smokey figure appeared. He entered, the door shutting behind him as he collapsed. A gasp slipped from her lips, smoke rising from Declan's body. His coverall was blackened, some of it still burning, embers falling around him. Phil leaped from his chair, patting him down until the hot glows were extinguished.

"It's done!" Declan yelled in a rasp, his breathing wheezy. He seemed oblivious to the fact that he was burning, a strangely satisfied smile appearing, his teeth glowing against his soot-covered face. "The soul! The machine's soul. I destroyed it!"

"Let's get you up," Phil said, urging Declan to stand.

"I'm okay," he said, struggling to his hands and knees. His hair was singed, curling and matting in spots with wispy smoke floating ethereally around his head. "Just need a minute."

"The bomb?" Isla asked, the stink of burnt flesh causing her to choke. It wasn't from Declan, though. It had been carried in from outside the lab. "How big was it?"

"Big," Declan answered, shaking, hands trembling. Beyond the smoldering odor, it was his face that was the most frightening. The whites of his eyes beamed like lights—surrounded by skin that had darkened and bubbled until it peeled back. *First and maybe second degree*, she wondered, hoping it wasn't worse. "Very big."

"What happened to your friend?" Isla asked. "Phil mentioned you brought someone to help."

"Killed in the explosion," Declan answered and then hesitated. "He took the bomb to the bottom. Did it work? Is the machine dead?"

"I'm sorry about your friend—" Phil began to say.

"He wasn't a friend," Declan interrupted. "He was responsible for Sammi's death. He wasn't anyone's friend. Did it work?"

"Sammi's death!" Phil yelled, reeling back. The suddenness startled her, Isla studying his face. There was anger and hurt as he demanded, "Why didn't you tell me?"

Declan wasn't fazed by the reaction, eyes wet, as he answered with a question, "Did it matter?"

"You killed him?" Phil asked, the rage tempered. Before Declan answered, Phil waved away the question, saying, "What's done is done."

"Did it work?" Declan repeated.

Phil shook his head, saying, "This machine won't function anymore, not for mining and recycling, anyway. We're breaking the failsafe restart cycle now. Isla?"

"Seems to have worked," she answered weakly, unable to break her stare. It was Declan's ears. She had never seen anything like them. One was nearly completely gone, burned away to just a lobe. The other had fared better—blackened like his face and split across the middle—fresh blood dripped from the wound. There was no fixing those injuries, not that she knew of. The machine perhaps? She motioned to the bleeding, "Declan, there's some water and a first-aid kit."

"Thank you," he wheezed and wavered suddenly, falling forward, his front striking the lab table. He shook himself and focused past her, staring at the terminal's screen. "You can see the other machines?"

"Not just see them. We can talk to them too," Phil answered. "We've made contact with each to shut down their core systems along with this one."

"Why not shut it all down?" Declan argued. "I mean, turn it off. Turn everything off, completely, once and for all."

"We can't," she explained. While that had been an initial thought, she considered what would happen next. How many people would be awakened? How many would die without help? "Without the lights, they'll become aware like us, like Sammi."

"They'll need help transitioning," Phil said, opening a first-aid kit. He unwrapped a square patch of gauze and pressed it to Declan's ear, a low grunt following. "We can keep life support going near indefinitely so they can continue living here."

"Life condominiums," Isla said, trying to joke. Brow raised, Phil laughed lightheartedly, but Declan didn't crack a smile.

"Will the clouds lift?" Declan asked, eyes half-lidded while he washed some of the soot from his face.

"It'll be the End of Gray Skies. Yes, they'll lift," she said, her reply registering on his face.

"When?" Declan blurted, suddenly rigid and alert like a live wire.

"Now," she answered, and, without hesitation, Isla punched in the last of the codes, confirming the plan with her sisters. "I hit this key, and we'll end the machines' hold on our world."

"Do it, Isla," Phil yelled, a crazed look returning like she'd seen when he appeared in the lab. It was both frightening and contagious, her finger poised over the enter key. "Do it!"

For a long moment, nothing changed, and they traded looks with disappointment building. The lights glowed, the insides orange and red like Declan's burnt clothing. They grew brighter, a siren erupting, both building loud enough to suffocate their senses. It was the machine fighting back, the aliens initiating a second failsafe, the components she and her sisters shut down suddenly flicking on and off in a state of flux.

Declan screamed and grabbed at his head, the raucous alarms coming from everywhere. Isla did the same, crying out, her voice disappearing in the noise. She dug her fingertips deep into her ears and felt her insides begin to vibrate uncontrollably.

"The mall," she screamed, remembering the same, understanding what had happened in the days before Nolan's death. Phil read her lips, nodding, recognizing it too. The room tipped to one side, and the lights on the wall shattered in a silent glassy rainfall. Her equipment was next—the remaining test tubes and beakers cracked in a blink, disintegrating into a crumpled pile.

Something warm and wet kissed her cheek, turning cold almost at once. Another kiss touched her other cheek, the warmth sickening, her hands covered in blood. *The blood vault,* she wondered, and pushed herself up, holding onto the lab tables. She made her way to the round window and lifted onto her toes to peer inside. The articulating arms had stopped moving. She screamed at the top of her lungs, "It's working!"

It was the finale; the machine was attempting to restart but couldn't. It couldn't do anything without the other machines. In a way, this was the machine's death wail. It was dying. Blood bubbled and oozed from the thousands of vials, seeping through the cracked glass, puddling beneath the shelves. Her heart sank when images of Nolan's smile faded from her mind. A distant thought had come to pass, one where Nolan came back like the others, like her.

The vibrations and sound proved too much, and any hope of using the machine's computers to resurrect her lost love disappeared into a bloody puddle. As if confirming this last thought, the round window splintered and exploded, spitting shards of glass in a tantrum. Isla tumbled backward, falling into Phil's outstretched arms. He had followed her, catching her before she struck the floor. When she turned to thank him, she stopped. In his expression, she saw a kind of relief that she had known once a long time ago. It was the relief that ended her pain, and opened her eyes to a world she could never have known existed.

"You're free," she mouthed, hoping he understood. She cried for him then and felt the stabbing pain of her run into the caustic rains when she thought death was the only answer. "You're free, Phil." And when she found his eyes, she saw the years of turmoil begin to melt. She rose as high as she could onto the tips of her toes and kissed the tears away from his face before placing her lips on his. His chest tightened and then became loose as sobs riddled his breathing.

"It's finally over," he managed to whisper past the ringing in her ear. "I can feel it."

When the sound ended, they stood in the quiet, searching the lab to take measure of the remains. They waited. Isla scoured the walls, tentative and nervous like a guilty child hoping that her parents didn't see what she'd done. Once she spied the lights on the wall, trying to catch an accusatory glance. To her relief, the lights were gone, their insides blackened and empty, dimmed for the first time since this all started. And if she was right, they were turned off forever.

THIRTY-FIVE

The excitement kept the pain away. But when the lights went out forever, and the blood vault ceased to function, Declan felt the burns come alive. He wanted to scream, had to scream, but held it in. It was in his lungs too, the burn that made them feel like they were still on fire. And maybe they were. Maybe the cells and tissues making up his insides were still smoldering. He opened his mouth, half expecting to see smoke rise like he was a chimney. It didn't, though. Not that it mattered. The machine had scorched his soul—a retaliation for him having destroyed it.

Sammi and the baby will be safe. With this last thought, he dismissed his injuries and carefully peeled his hands away from his ears and realized that one of them was gone. Blood crept through the sooty stains on his arms and hands, and he began to wonder how bad his face looked. Carefully, he touched his cheeks and then his mouth. With the injuries there was a new fright. Would he ever look the same?

Isla and Phil stood by the blood vault, hugging, and crying together, finding one another in the success of their system attack. *I need Sammi.* It was just about all he could think of, and he touched the locket, the hair singed but thankfully intact. The skin on the back of his hand was a bubbly mess and he realized that he'd guarded Sammi's locket when the explosion chased him thought the corridor.

The need to be with Sammi grew more urgent and replaced all others. He glanced at the shattered lights, and his heart swelled at the thought of being a father, knowing that his chosen was back and safe—forever. The machine had tried to take away their world, and in stopping it, they had brought her back to him. He watched Isla and Phil, grateful for what they had done. *How can I ever repay them?*

"Come back with me," Declan blurted, breaking the silence.

"It sounds funny, now," Isla answered, ignoring what Declan asked. She motioned to the ventilation system, the vents near the ceiling and floor. Phil and Declan followed her gaze. "The air exchange is on, but something is missing."

"It's the mining," Phil exclaimed, nodding aggressively. He lifted one foot and then the other. "I don't feel the vibrations. It is truly shut down."

"We blew that up," Declan added. Wiping the charred soot on his hands. "That thing will never work again."

"What about the rest of them?" Phil asked, making his way back to the screens. "Any signs of the other machines looping back to reset?"

Declan picked up a chair and placed it at the table for Isla to sit. Every part of him had become stiff with injuries, the suddenness causing a scream. He dropped the chair and went to his knees. "Sorry."

"Not at all. Let me," Phil said, offering another chair for him to sit down. "We need to get those burns looked at. There's supplies you can take with you."

"You're not coming?" Declan asked. "And you?"

"I may," Isla answered, shaking her head. "But not yet."

"Why?" Declan asked like it was an affront to all that was good. "Why would you stay?"

"I know you won't understand this, but my place is here now," she announced, glancing at Declan and then back to Phil. She motioned to the screens, the texts filling them. "We have a responsibility to everyone who is waking up. Someone needs to help them."

"The zombies?" Declan asked and looked at Sammi's father. His voice rose with disgust. "Fuck it. I say leave them."

"It doesn't work like that," Phil told him and shook his head. "They didn't choose this. Nobody did."

Isla wove an arm through Phil's, joining them and adding, "They're going to become aware. Like us. Like Sammi." She glanced up at the dead lights, adding, "It's probably already happening."

"I get it," he said, feeling bad for his choice of words. The task was daunting, and he asked, "How... where do you even start?"

"With them," Isla said, turning back, tapping the keyboard, a fresh session opening. The panel filled with characters streaming across it, windows popping to the foreground that Declan tried to read but couldn't. Isla traced the text messages with her fingers, reading each of them, her lips moving silently from message to message and window to window. "It's my sisters. They're not just me, but they're thinking exactly like me too."

Phil's eyelids flashed wide. "They've started?"

Isla smiled, the corner of her mouth rising, tears filling her eyes. "Can you believe it! It's like they read my mind."

"In a way, they did," Phil told her.

"Amazing," she said and continued tracing the text messages. A laugh slipped, which she was quick to catch, pressing her fingers to her lips. "They're all talking to one another too. That didn't take long."

"They really are like sisters," Phil added and rubbed her back. Isla's expression slowly changed, a frown replacing her smile. She swallowed dryly, cringing, her lips disappearing in a thin line. "What? What is it?"

"Phil, there's someone with them," she answered.

"Which one?" Phil asked, concern rising.

"All of them."

An ache shot into his heart, Declan asking, "We're not going to lose the End of Gray Skies, are we?"

"Who is there?" Phil asks calmly. Declan could sense the fear as Isla tried to answer Phil's question.

"It's... it's you."

Phil sat back, his body becoming rigid. He straightened himself and brushed his hands over his front, clearing away nothing. "Me?"

"Uh-huh," she answered. "It's like what we did was repeated in every machine."

"I suppose that would make sense," he explained and continued to primp his coveralls as if readying to meet them. "The machines needed me, having been the lead architect. Why not?"

"He's helping them like you helped me," Isla quickly added.

"Good! That's good," Phil said. "We're all the same, which means the thinking and decisions were the same too."

"Come with me," Declan interrupted, repeating what he'd asked them. "Come back to the commune."

"No," they said in unison, exchanging a brief look with sympathy and honor on their faces. It was a cursory glance, and he could see it was with little consideration for his offer. They'd already made up their minds to stay, and nothing he said or did would convince them to leave.

"I'm grateful to you for what you've done here today," Phil began, choking up and swiping at his cheek. "I'll come to see Emily and Sammi, though. It'll be soon. But first we have to work this, finish it."

"Are you sure?" Declan asked, knowing the disappointment Emily and Sammi would feel.

"Declan, you take care of yourself and take care of my daughter and grandbaby."

"I will," Declan nodded, pulling Sammi's father into his arms. "I promise."

"Take care of that," Phil added, motioning to the burns. "Don't want you to get sick after all this."

Declan turned and exited the lab room, never to return, but in his heart, he knew he'd see Isla and Phil again, soon. Maybe a picnic on the beach with Emily and Sammi and their child— Phil if their baby was a boy, and Isla if their baby was a girl.

THIRTY-SIX

The machine was different. The corridors were filled with confused stares—chins pitched up, searching the empty lights on the walls. The outside of the machine looked different too. The skin was no longer an animation of color; it had dulled like the skin of an apple past its time. To Declan, the machine looked dead. *But there is life inside*, he reminded himself. *A lot of life.*

The first touch of sunlight came as a shock. It needled the burns and warmed the part of him that had gone unscathed. From the break in the sky, the sun peered through, winking as it returned slowly, taking back what was lost. To the far left and right, breaks of blue sky rippled between the gray and white, expanding and moving as if dancing to a silent tune.

A sudden breeze stirred from somewhere deep offshore, tipping the edge of a breaking wave and sending the briny smell to flow past Declan. A second and third wave rose, the swells rising higher than he'd ever seen or felt before. It was the waves of yesterday, the ones that had lay dormant, the sun waking them. The wind was mounting too, ridding the land of the fog's acrid stink, sending it away for good.

He shuddered in the cool breeze, the burns playing a fickle game of pain and chills. He dug his foot into sand, stepping forward, covering his eyes against a glare that had been more alien to him than of this earth. In the distance, the air shimmered above the beach, the heat already returning, the sands finally warming again. And past the shaky images, Declan saw the small party that he had left behind. In it, he saw Emily and Sammi waiting.

Sammi waved first and pointed at the sky, dancing in the playful light. He waved back to her and quickly pushed his hands down when he saw the Outsiders coming forward. It was a reaction, a learned response. But there was no danger here. They'd helped, after all, and he waved with both arms, suddenly aware that he was crying.

The leader waved, throwing his fists into the air in a quick snap, screaming joyfully, rejoicing in the victory. Declan searched the faces to see if anyone was looking for Harold. They weren't. Nobody was going to miss him, but, in a way, Harold had helped make this happen and that could never be forgotten.

A shrill sound rolled across the beach. It was Sammi and Emily, whooping and hollering and pointing toward the ocean. It was a change and he felt it come across his skin like a hug. Declan searched where they were pointing, the waves foaming white, tipping and spraying, the first rainbows appearing. They were full of color and were the first he'd seen for fifteen years.

The burns eased some in a cozy breeze, the sea spray beading on his head and face. Declan dropped to his knees, fixing to watch the End of Gray Skies. The rainbows became more brilliant, reaching down and touching the ocean where they turned into the perfect union of color—bands of red and yellow and pink and green, the remaining hues a blur behind his teary eyes.

His heart sat in his throat, and he tried to reach out and

touch the impossible sight. Within moments, the sunshine spawned smaller rainbows in the ocean spray. They floated all around him, the warm moisture lifting them into the sky. When his finger touched the color, he pulled back, uncertain of what to expect. His finger passed through, spurring a laugh. Sammi was closer, kicking the surf playfully, her beauty shining in the sunlight in a way that he'd only seen once before. But today that beauty wouldn't be eclipsed by death. Instead, it was a testament to their new life. Emily and his father were close behind her, but Declan couldn't hold on and fell backward, the air leaping from his lungs.

"Sammi," he mouthed, his voice gone.

"Declan!" she yelled, dropping next to him, assessing the injuries. Red hair flew around him as she carefully peppered his face with kisses. "Oh God! Look at you!"

"Isn't it wonderful?" he answered. Emily and his father were there next, eyes fixed with dread and worry. But Declan shrugged it off, his appearance insignificant compared to what was happening all around them. He didn't want them missing any of it and insisted they look. In a raspy breath, he told them, "It's over. We ended it."

"It is," Sammi returned. A soft and delicious wind rushed up the coast, sending her long hair into the air. "It really is."

"Smell that?" his father asked.

"So fresh," Emily answered.

And over the breaking waves, Declan could see forever. Finally, he could see the giant surf far from their shores and hear it roar and feel it rumble like giants playing a game of fast-tag. The ocean was larger than anything he could have imagined—a vast sea of blue reflecting the open sky. Tears washed the stain of the fire, and for a long time he could say nothing. Instead, he held Sammi, thankful to have her back.

"Amazing, look over there," his father said. From the far edge of the black sands, the grounds began to turn and change color in the new light. They may have always been like that, but with the strong sunlight, the brown they'd known was nearly gone. "Just amazing."

"Is it supposed to happen like that?" Sammi asked with a touch of concern. She laughed giddily, adding, "I love it."

"After all the years of waiting, I suspect things will look very different now," Emily answered, excitement breaking in her voice. "It's our world and it's waking up."

More of the ground came to life, showing colors they hadn't seen in what felt like forever. It wouldn't be long before the first plants bloomed and climbed and swallowed years of decay. Declan imagined a few small plants at first, sprouting and opening into flowers. In time, the flower petals would be enormous, fitting in the palm of his hand. And as the blooms unfurled, the flowers would turn to face the sun, reunited like long-lost lovers.

"Look over there," Declan told them, raising his voice over the pain. They turned to face their commune. The distant buildings jutted up from the ground, crooked and decaying, covered in patches of black resin. To Declan, they looked like a mouthful of jagged and rotten teeth, but they were home, and his heart ached to be there.

"I think it needs a little paint," Emily laughed.

"I think it needs a lot of paint," Declan's father added.

"It's home," Sammi said, her voice shaky. She took hold of Declan's arm and joked, "I get to pick the color."

EPILOGUE

They were witness to the birth of lands once thought to have been barren, the touch of sunlight making them fertile again. And with the sunlight, the Earth's great lungs blew, the winds climbed high and traveled the long distance from the west to the east. With them, they carried the seasons, the snow and the cold of winter returning. The birth of spring showers with razor-sharp lightning and the crack of rumbling thunder. The dry summers with hot breezes and trilling insects. And autumn colors with festival harvests. The sea had found its voice, too, tall waves biting, the black sands retreating, and even the tides brought sea grass that had been thought lost forever.

Without the lights to drive the alien programming, Sammi never heard the call of the machine's soul—the recycler. She went on to live a life with Declan as had been their hope from the beginning. It was two. Twins. There hadn't been just one child, but two that they raised after the End of Gray Skies. But unlike their parents, the twins never knew a world without the sun. They never experienced the dread or felt the dangers of walking in a world forever captured in a heavy fog. They played outside, untethered, and ran freely with the warm touch of the sun. They even ran hand in hand with their grandfather, who visited often from the machine, staying longer and longer each time.

Emily loved again, taking a chance with her heart, reaching out and asking Richard for his hand. Declan's father had found his second love, but never forgot the pain of losing his first. He and Emily went on to work at the school, only now they added something new to the curriculum: an afternoon recess held outdoors.

The executive floor was no more. With the machines shut down, the executives disappeared, having run away with the burden of guilt weighing on their shoulders. Some were found dead on the beaches—sand-fleas cleaning the scourge of the earth. And those executives who had tried to make a difference, like Declan's mother, found a new calling as a new leadership formed. Small governing bodies worked together to keep the commune running, and the families fed. A democracy was born, borrowing from their history to help forge their future.

Sammi and Emily often traveled to the machine and visited with their father and Isla. Phil and Isla stayed together and created a new commune for all who had become aware. Declan became an ambassador of sorts, visiting more than any other, bringing back new technologies to better the commune and encourage its recovery.

In his walks to the machine, Declan often found himself staring up, his hand clapped against his brow, shielding his eyes from the glare. He looked for the star that Phil spoke of, the one he'd long suspected wasn't a star at all but an alien ship. When he saw a shine, a wink in the black canvas of night, he wondered if they were still watching, and if they would return. But at some point, the tenth year or so, he decided to stop searching for what was not there.

With the End of Gray Skies, the world eased out of a fifteen-year sleep, stretching blues and greens and reds all over the globe. The Earth sprang to life, and before anyone realized what was happening, trees grew, and flowers bloomed, and even the wet mossy coverings were replaced by wisps of tall green grass.

The first bird was spotted many years later. A white gull with mottled patches of brown covering its breast. Perched on the beach, on stilted yellow legs, the bird drummed up bits of food from the surf. Other than the few in the mall and later, in their building, the birds were thought to have been gone forever, but soon more returned, making their homes in the fresh green of the trees. To Declan, they were like the rainbows—small, feathered miracles, flying and singing, a living splash of color in the air.

The moment spurred a thought that was filled with sentiment and emotion. Somewhere in the feelings, he suddenly saw letters and words and sentences coming together. Without giving it further consideration, he reached for his pocket where there would have been a writing stone and some old parchment, an idea of telling this story coming to life much like their world was doing now. When he found the pocket empty, he decided to hold onto the storytelling for later, and to do what he'd once vowed he'd never do again. Declan was going to write.

He followed the feathered wonders flitting from branch to branch. Home was new again and he touched the scars around his face, the wounds healed like their world. They'd only just started to rebuild, but already, so much had been accomplished. There was a lot left to do, and without the machines, they were finally free to do anything they wanted.

A LETTER FROM B.R. SPANGLER

Dear Reader,

I want to say a huge thank you for choosing to read *When the Dawn Breaks* If you did enjoy it, and want to keep up to date with all my latest releases, just sign up at the following link. Your email address will never be shared and you can unsubscribe at any time.

www.bookouture.com/br-spangler

I hope you loved *When the Dawn Breaks* and if you did I would be very grateful if you could write a review. I'd love to hear what you think, and it makes such a difference helping new readers to discover one of my books for the first time.

I love hearing from my readers – you can get in touch through social media or my website.

Thanks,

B.R. Spangler

KEEP IN TOUCH WITH B.R. SPANGLER

www.brspangler.com

facebook.com/authorbrianspangler
x.com/BR_Spangler
instagram.com/brspangler

PUBLISHING TEAM

Turning a manuscript into a book requires the efforts of many people. The publishing team at Bookouture would like to acknowledge everyone who contributed to this publication.

Audio
Alba Proko
Sinead O'Connor
Melissa Tran

Commercial
Lauren Morrissette
Hannah Richmond
Imogen Allport

Cover design
Damonza.com

Data and analysis
Mark Alder
Mohamed Bussuri

Editorial
Jen Shannon
Nadia Michael

Copyeditor
Rhian McKay

Proofreader
Catherine Lenderi

Marketing
Alex Crow
Melanie Price
Occy Carr
Cíara Rosney
Martyna Młynarska

Operations and distribution
Marina Valles
Stephanie Straub

Production
Hannah Snetsinger
Mandy Kullar
Jen Shannon
Ria Clare

Publicity
Kim Nash
Noelle Holten
Jess Readett
Sarah Hardy

Rights and contracts
Peta Nightingale
Richard King
Saidah Graham

www.ingramcontent.com/pod-product-compliance
Lightning Source LLC
Chambersburg PA
CBHW061802190726

48289CB00007B/2033